DEATH IN THE GREAT DISMAL

DEATH IN THE
GREAT DISMAL

Eleanor Kuhns

This first world edition published 2020
in Great Britain and the USA by
SEVERN HOUSE PUBLISHERS LTD of
Eardley House, 4 Uxbridge Street, London W8 7SY.
Trade paperback edition first published
in Great Britain and the USA 2021 by
SEVERN HOUSE PUBLISHERS LTD.

British Library Cataloguing in Publication Data
A CIP catalogue record for this title is available from the British Library.

ISBN-13: 978-0-7278-9023-8 (cased)
ISBN-13: 978-1-78029-722-4 (trade paper)
ISBN-13: 978-1-4483-0443-1 (e-book)

This is a work of fiction. Names, characters, places and incidents are
either the product of the author's imagination or are used fictitiously.
Except where actual historical events and characters are being described
for the storyline of this novel, all situations in this publication are
fictitious and any resemblance to actual persons, living or dead, business
establishments, events or locales is purely coincidental.

All Severn House titles are printed on acid-free paper.

Severn House Publishers support the Forest Stewardship Council™ [FSC™],
the leading international forest certification organisation.
All our titles that are printed on FSC certified paper carry the FSC logo.

MIX
Paper from
responsible sources
FSC
www.fsc.org   FSC® C013056

Typeset by Palimpsest Bo
Falkirk, Stirlingshire, Sco
Printed and bound in Grea
TJ International, Padstow,

PROLOGUE

'You want me to do what?' Rees asked, staring at the man next to him. He had not recognized Tobias at first. When taken by the slave catchers, Tobias had been a young man. He was still a young man in Rees's opinion, but he no longer looked it. Now gray threaded his hair, grooves scored his forehead and his eyes were haunted. He looked as though he'd experienced the worst of what man had to offer. Rees felt a burst of sympathy.

'I want you to accompany me to Virginia,' Tobias repeated. 'To the great swamp.'

'That will take five days at best,' Rees said, sitting back in the creaky porch chair. 'Maybe as long as a week. Maybe even longer.' With the coming of winter, the days were growing shorter.

'Please,' Tobias rushed on. 'Ruth is pregnant and wouldn't come north with me. She was afraid. And it was difficult, so difficult, even with the help of the Quakers. I don't dare go south to fetch her without help.'

'But you made it back home,' Rees objected. 'Won't the Quakers help you again? I don't understand why you need me.'

'I don't think they run the railroad south,' Tobias said with a faint smile. 'Besides . . .' His eyes drifted away from Rees to the yard and the barn behind it. It was late September and the hills behind the farm were a mosaic of gold, orange and red interspersed with the rich dark green of the firs.

'Besides?' Rees prompted. Tobias was keeping something back; Rees knew it.

'Besides, it is even more dangerous now.' Tobias's gaze returned to Rees. 'A man named Gabriel Prosser led a slave revolt. Planned it, anyway. Right around Richmond. Everybody real tense. They're planning to hang him in October. I need a white man beside me. Ruth trusts you. You were kids together here. You're the only one I know who will travel.' He swallowed, his expression beseeching.

'How did you find me?' Rees asked, instead of acknow-ledging Tobias's request. He was tempted, no denying that. Most of the harvest was in and he'd finished his final weaving commission. After a summer spent working on the farm, he felt restless and was ready to do something different.

'I went to Dugard first. It was your son that told me where you were. He said you gave him your farm.'

'Yes. We moved to this farm.'

'Will you help me?' Tobias asked, leaning forward. Rees looked at the eagerness on the dark face peering into his. Rees hesitated. He should say no, he knew he should.

'Maybe,' he said instead. What would Lydia say? His journey would leave her alone on the farm with the children for several weeks; he couldn't see her agreeing to that.

'I think you should go,' Lydia said, stepping through the front door.

'Really?' he asked in surprise.

She nodded. 'I know the signs; you're getting restless.' She paused but Rees did not speak. Since the circus had come to town in the spring and he'd been attracted to the beautiful rope dancer, the relationship between him and his wife had been strained. She was edgy with him. Sometimes he caught her staring at him and lately she'd become prone to crying fits, for no reason he could see. 'But, if you go,' she continued, 'I want to accompany you.'

'What?' Rees jumped to his feet and the chair crashed to the floor behind him.

'I'd like you to join us,' Tobias said eagerly, turning to face her. 'Ruth will join us readily if there's another woman.' Then, catching sight of Rees's expression, he added, 'If possible.'

'It's too dangerous,' Rees objected.

'Predictable,' Lydia muttered.

'It'll be easier to travel through the South if everyone thinks you are just a man and wife with your slaves,' Tobias said, grimacing. Rees leaned forward to clap the other man's shoulder in commiseration, but before he touched him Tobias flinched away. The involuntary cringe made Rees himself jerk back. What had happened to Tobias in Virginia?

'It would be a long trip for my horse,' Rees said. 'Especially pulling my wagon.'

'We could take the cart,' Lydia suggested.

'You couldn't get them through the swamp anyway,' Tobias said. 'Unless . . .' He paused a moment, thinking. 'You could leave them at a livery in Norfolk.'

'Hmm,' Rees grunted. He didn't like the thought of leaving his horse and wagon anywhere. 'We're finishing up the harvest. Even if I wanted to help you, this isn't a good time.' He made that one final objection.

Tobias turned to look at the fields. The corn and wheat were cut to stubble, but pumpkins spotted the fields with orange, and buckwheat, the second planting, waved in the breeze. 'You wouldn't be gone long,' he pleaded, his eyes reddening as though he might weep. 'Plenty of time to finish this.' He waved his hand at the fields.

Rees, who could not abide tears, especially in another man, held up his hand. 'All right, I'll think about it.' Of course he couldn't go. It was a long distance and even if they hurried, they might not return until mid-October or later. By then Maine could see snow.

'Please,' Tobias repeated, sensing Rees's longing and pressing his advantage. 'Most of your crops are in and you got help bringing in the last of them.'

Since that was true, Rees did not argue. The Shakers had made good on their promise to assist him, and some Brothers were even now in the fields. Besides the Shakers, Rees had hired a few of the landless men who wandered the roads looking for work. 'If I were to accompany you,' he said, 'and that's a big "if", Lydia Rees must remain here.'

'If you go, I go,' she said. Rees shook his head, but she ignored him. Turning to Tobias, she said with a smile, 'I know Ruth well. Let my husband and I confer. Come back tomorrow for our answer.'

His face lighting up with hope, Tobias rose to his feet. 'Tomorrow then.'

As Tobias jumped off the wooden deck and began crossing the yard, Rees said to Lydia, 'You know this isn't possible.'

'If you leave without me, I will follow. You know I will,' she said.

Rees frowned at her. Always watching him, that was his wife. He felt a combination of shame and irritation that she still did not trust him. 'Lydia,' he began. But she interrupted him.

'We need to talk about last spring and what happened,' she said. 'Here, at the farm, we are too busy and always distracted.'

'It will be a long and grueling journey,' Rees warned, hoping to discourage her.

'You know some of the Shakers are traveling south to check on their Georgia and Florida communities,' Lydia said. 'We can follow them in the cart. And Annie and Jerusha can watch the children.'

ONE

Rees felt a trickle of sweat roll down his back. Although it was now early October, the heat and humidity in Virginia slammed down like a hammer. He wasn't used to this heat, especially at this time of the year. In Maine the weather was already cooling, and the air was as crisp and tart as a fresh apple. Here every breath was thick with the cloying scents of a hundred different plants.

Rees looked back over his shoulder at Lydia. They'd been walking over three hours, but she seemed to be bearing up well. As Tobias had suggested, they'd left horse and cart in Norfolk. The Shakers had brought them the rest of the way, dropping them off within walking distance of the swamp. Now that they were off the road – and preparing to hike through the swamp – Lydia had taken shelter behind a bush and changed into her boy's clothing. Once belonging to Rees's eldest son, the shirt, vest and breeches were worn, almost tattered, but thoroughly disguising. She'd put her auburn hair up under a hat as Rees stowed her dress in the satchel he carried over his shoulder. Rees also had changed – from his better breeches, shirt and jacket to old and worn breeches and shirt.

Now Tobias waited for them several paces ahead. Rees hoped the other man knew where he was going. As far as Rees could tell, there was no discernible path through the tall pines and the thick undergrowth below. Although they'd passed fields of tobacco and cotton, Tobias had been careful to stay within the bands of trees.

'We're going to cross a road,' Tobias said now. 'Be real careful there.'

Rees did not think the drops of perspiration on Tobias's brow came from the heat; he was nervous. No, he was scared. Rees began looking around, waiting for some large animal to jump out at them. But except for birdsong and the faint whisper of the wind through the trees within the patch of woods, it was silent.

Tobias paused at the edge of the dirt road and peered through the thorny greenbrier vines. Seeing nothing, he cautiously circled the brambles. Pausing within the undergrowth, he looked up and down the road once again. Seeing nothing, he burst out of the shelter and started across the road. But a white dust cloud at the top of the hill heralded the arrival of something – or someone. Two riders came over the hill. When they saw Tobias they increased their speed, galloping straight at him. He tried to reach the other side of the road, running for all he was worth, but the horses easily caught up. The riders reached him as he plunged into the underbrush on the other side.

'Stop runnin', boy.'

'Massa,' Tobias shouted.

Taking the musket off his back and pulling his powder horn and shot bag from his satchel, Rees turned to Lydia. 'Stay here,' he said before leaving the shelter of the trees in his turn and racing across the road.

As the white riders dismounted and went after Tobias, Rees followed the sound of voices into the underbrush.

The two white riders had Tobias in their grasp. 'What're you doin' out here alone?' the tallest of the men asked in his slow drawl. He wore a buttercup yellow coat, despite the heat, and a white waistcoat. Tall black boots, now dusty from the road, went almost to the knees of his newly fashionable trousers.

'Nuthin'.' Tobias sounded different, his speech losing the crisp Maine consonants. His posture had gone from upright to a kind of servile crouch. The young, shorter man, dressed more casually but wearing a top hat, shook Tobias threateningly.

'Where'd you get those boots?'

'Hey,' Rees said loudly.

'Go about your business,' the tall rider told Rees.

'He's mine,' Rees said, trying to mimic the other man's leisurely dialect.

Both men examined Rees, their gazes fixing on his musket. 'Out huntin'?' The speaker turned to look at Tobias. 'He looks like a strong young buck. I'll give you fifty dollars for him.'

'Not for sale,' Rees said curtly. He thought for a moment

that these men would not listen to him but after a brief pause the two men brushed past him and returned to the road. Rees followed them, making sure their horses galloped away. Then he pushed his way back to Tobias.

'You all right?' he asked. Tobias nodded although he had collapsed to the ground. Perspiration glistened on his skin and big damp moons darkened his shirt under his armpits.

'You took a big risk,' he told Rees in a shaky voice. 'Just because you're white doesn't mean you're safe. They could have figured you for an abolitionist and whipped you just as hard as they would me.'

'I'm going to get Lydia,' Rees said. He was trembling so hard he wasn't sure he could hold his musket. Instead of sprinting across this dusty lane, he walked on legs that shook uncontrollably. Lydia came out to meet him, taking his arm.

'Esther was right,' Lydia said. Rees nodded.

Sister Esther, an escaped slave who'd made her way north to the Shakers, had scolded them when they left. 'You've no business going south,' she'd said. 'You're totally unprepared. I hope and pray you don't get Lydia killed on this mad adventure.'

'We're committed now,' Rees said.

Tobias had recovered enough to stand up. 'It's not far now,' he said in a shaky voice as Rees and Lydia reached him.

'What happened?' Lydia asked.

Tobias and Rees traded glances and wordlessly agreed to say nothing. 'We don't have time now,' Rees said. 'I'll tell you later.' He was still trembling and Tobias was clenching and unclenching his hands, whether from fright or anger Rees couldn't tell.

Tobias started off, setting such a punishing pace that neither Rees nor Lydia could keep up. He began to worry that they would lose their guide; the thickness of the trees, the brambles and other plants meant that Tobias disappeared within a few yards.

The third time that Tobias waited for them he said tersely, 'We need to get out of sight while it's daylight. Hurry.'

'We're going as fast as we can,' Rees said, turning to look at his wife. Both of them were panting and her cheeks were scarlet. 'We've been walking for hours.' And he was hungry.

None of them had eaten since breakfast that morning and it was now several hours past noon. Tobias grunted.

'We're not that far from the lane,' he said, turning and disappearing once again in the greenery.

It wasn't just that he was fast. He snaked his way through the underbrush without making a sound or breaking any branches. Rees, taller and probably two stone heavier, couldn't do that. Even his steps were noisy, crunching over the leaf litter on the ground with crackling thumps.

Tobias led them toward a large downed tree. Rees couldn't understand why – until the other man lifted a board artfully covered with branches and leaves, revealing a hole underneath. 'This way,' he said, squirming through the opening. Rees struggled to press his huskier body through, discovering that the small cavity opened up to a much larger hollow. A rough ceiling had been formed above their heads and tree roots poked through the dirt that made up the walls. Stone steps led down into the gloom. Ducking his head against the low ceiling, Tobias descended into the darkness underneath.

Lydia followed him and then Rees, bending almost double.

A cave had been dug deep into the soil. It smelled powerfully of damp and dirt. Dimly lit by oil lamps, the den was occupied by several people in ragged clothing. A family, Rees thought, since he saw a number of children. They fled to the comfort of their mothers' skirts when they saw the big white man enter their home. But, to his surprise, they didn't cry.

The men all rose from their stools, their shoulders tensed. Although weaponless and barefoot, they were ready to fight to protect their friends and families. Rees's heart began to race and he stood straighter, fists clenched. He was taller and heavier than anyone else here, but he knew he could not battle four or five men at once. There was no room for fighting in this den either.

'He's helping me get Ruthie,' Tobias said as he collapsed to the ground. Both Rees and Lydia looked at him and she went to his side.

'Are you all right?' she asked. He nodded, blowing out little puffs of breath. 'You must love Ruthie very much.'

'I do,' he whispered, turning his head aside.

There's more to this story, Rees thought.

'What happened?' one of the men asked Tobias, although his eyes never left Rees.

'Two . . .' Tobias cut his eyes to Rees. 'Two white men tried to take me. 'Lucky for me, my friend Rees here jumped in.'

Some of the tension left the room. Rees relaxed a little. He had never thought of his white skin before. But now, in a room full of black people, with he and Lydia the only whites, he experienced a sharp realization of how it felt to be an object of suspicion and fear because of that skin. He didn't like it and turned a glance of surprised sympathy upon Tobias.

'We be eating soon.' One of the women stepped into the center of the cave. 'Join us.'

Rees opened his mouth to accept. He was very hungry after his day hiking through the woods. But Lydia spoke first. 'Are you sure you have enough?'

The woman, who carried herself with an air of authority, looked at Lydia – and her boy's clothing – with interest. 'Yes, chile. We do. Swamp food.' She paused and when she spoke again it was to Tobias. 'You plannin' to leave at nightfall?'

'Yes. We're heading for the Great Dismal.'

'Mos' people head the other way out of that swamp,' she said with a chuckle.

'Ruthie's there,' Tobias said.

'Oh honey,' said the woman, 'she could've been recaptured by now.' The words 'or worse' hung unsaid in the air.

'I have to try,' Tobias said stubbornly. The woman offered him a pitying smile but said nothing further.

When night fell, people began to move outside. The women pulled away the branches and other debris disguising the fire pit and set up a cooking fire. The scanty smoke drifted lightly across the ground as they made a corn porridge and roasted game meat over the fire.

'It's turtle,' Tobias told Rees in a low voice.

The steady whine of mosquitoes and the sound of slapping punctuated the quiet conversations. Frogs croaked nearby, filling the air with sound. Lydia reached into the satchel for a small stone crock. 'What's that?' Rees asked.

'Esther gave it to me. Something to keep the mosquitoes

away.' She tugged at the lid but it was so tightly closed she couldn't budge it. Rees took the crock and with some effort twisted the lid off. A fresh minty scent flooded Rees's senses. When he inhaled deeply, he caught other fragrances: lemon and something else that was sharp and astringent, and underneath it all the sweetness of honey.

'What is it?'

'Herbs. Pennyroyal I think. Lemon. Maybe sage. All pounded into a salve with beeswax and oil.' Lydia spread some on her face. 'She promised me it would keep away the mosquitoes.'

Rees hesitated. The paste smelled feminine. But he could already feel stings on his hands and neck. After a few seconds, he took the pot from her and liberally smeared the mixture on his skin.

'Eat up,' Tobias said, handing first Rees and then Lydia wooden bowls filled with the yellow mash. 'No hot food tomorrow, or any food most likely.'

Lydia looked at the bowl. 'Spoons?' Tobias, smiling, shook his head. So Lydia and Rees imitated the others and dipped their fingers into the hot cereal. Rees decided he had to eat it quickly. Not only was it still quite warm but it was not tasty. He did not think it even included salt.

As soon as they finished eating, the men began to drift away, vanishing into the forest. The family went next, a young man guiding them.

'Headin' north,' Tobias said when Rees wondered aloud where everyone was going. 'Everyone but Auntie Mama. She lives here. Keeps this space for travelers.' He put down his wooden bowl. 'And we got to get going too. We still got a long way.'

TWO

Morning found them at the edge of the Great Dismal Swamp. Rees, who had spent a restless night slapping at mosquitoes – despite the salve that was meant to keep the insects at bay – awoke groggy and irritable. Although

Tobias had not pushed them as hard during the night, he had still set a rapid pace. All of them were hungry, but far worse than the hunger was the physical discomfort. The insect bites maddened them with their itching, and the scratches from the branches and brambles they had pushed through in the dark stung and bled.

As the first light of dawn poked its fingers into the swamp, Rees looked around. They had bedded down in a stand of loblolly and long-leaf pine trees. Pine needles carpeted the ground. Not far away, at the end of the piney growth, was an alien landscape. Trees reached to the sky. Rees recognized oak, maple and hickory but what were those trees with the skinny narrow leaves? Underbrush; thick thorny greenbrier vines and a variety of bushes, made a solid green wall underneath. Tobias found an opening in the thicket and gestured to Rees and Lydia.

'Walk exactly where I walk,' he said. 'Mostly we'll be on dry ground. Mostly. Not always. And watch for snakes. Lots of copperheads and cottonmouths here.'

They stepped inside. Although he expected the swamp to be silent, the air reverberated with the sound of insects, a high-pitched rattling whine. He looked up but could not see the source of the drone. Thick greenery and tall trees occluded the sky. Despite the bright sun and the blue sky above, the light within the swamp was dim. Glittering black water snaked across the ground in every direction. Vast trees with swollen roots like the thighs of some enormous giant sprang from the wet. Now Rees knew why Tobias had advised not taking his horse and wagon; there would be no way to get them through the tangled underbrush and mud.

He wished he had worn stout boots instead of shoes.

'Is it safe to travel in daylight?' Lydia asked Tobias, looking around her in concern. 'Safe from slave takers, I mean.' Like Rees, the blotchy marks of many mosquito bites marred the skin of her face and neck. She'd rolled her long sleeves down to cover her arms and hands and pulled her stockings up to her breeches.

'Usually.' Tobias bit his lip. 'They come here sometimes with their dogs hunting the escaped slaves. We'll have to be careful. And real quiet. But the swamp is too dangerous after dark. Besides snakes, bobcats and bears hunt here. Alligators too, so I've heard.' As Rees gulped, Tobias nodded. 'If we're lucky and don't meet any of them, we'd be as likely to fall in the water and drown as anything.'

Rees looked around once again, understanding why people called this dark place dismal, and shivered despite the steamy warmth. He wished his desire to help Tobias hadn't overridden his sense. Most of all he wished they hadn't come. Lydia slipped her hand into his and he squeezed it comfortingly even though he was scared too.

Tobias handed around the stale bricks of day-old cornbread. Rees took a bite of the hard dry bread. 'Water?' he asked.

The other man gestured to the black water. 'It's drinkable,' he said. 'Don't worry; it doesn't taste bad.' Rees stared at the black pools surrounding him. A faint green scum drifted across the surface and ripples betrayed something moving underneath. He did not think it was fish. He shook his head. 'Let's go,' Tobias said as he turned and started forward. A plop as some animal jumped into the water sounded nearby. Lydia jumped. Rees exchanged a glance with her, and they ran to catch up with Tobias.

The ground below their feet was black and moist and it shuddered a little with each step. It was disconcerting and more than once Rees found himself jerking to one side or the other to keep his balance.

They walked deeper into the Great Dismal until it seemed that this was all the world, and nothing else existed outside its borders. The dense vegetation, the water and the thick peaty earth muffled the sound of their footsteps. Still the insects' loud buzz whined overhead.

Rees had put Lydia in the middle, between him and Tobias, and he looked around frequently – just in case a slave taker was behind him. After a few hours of walking he saw she was beginning to flag. 'We need to rest,' he said, and then repeated it more loudly. Tobias slowed and then stopped and turned.

'All right,' he said. He took a small bag from under his shirt and handed around the remaining chunks of stale corn pone. 'That's the last of it,' he said.

It was, Rees thought, even harder and less edible than it had been before. Lydia sat down on the ground to eat hers. Rees looked around for a tree stump or something and spotted a dead fall a little way off. He had to tiptoe through a pool of black water to get to it. Just before he reached it, his left leg sank into the ground up to his ankle, then to his calf. 'Help!' he cried. He could feel his leg sinking even further.

'I told you not to go off the path,' Tobias said, hurrying to Rees's side. Bending over, he grasped Rees's knee and tugged. With a horrible sucking sound, as though the maw of an animal was only reluctantly surrendering its prey, Rees's leg came out. Tobias pulled him back to the drier ground.

Thin brown mud coated Rees's leg from knee to foot. Trembling, he just sat where Tobias had left him, despite the uncomfortable sensation of damp soaking through the seat of his breeches.

But Tobias couldn't settle. He paced restlessly around and around. 'Not far now,' he said, cracking his knuckles.

Why is he so nervous? Rees wondered. The swamp? Slave takers? Lydia turned and exchanged a glance with her husband. She looked worried; Tobias's anxiety did not inspire confidence. 'How much longer do you think?' Rees asked aloud, staring around uneasily.

'I hope to reach the village by nightfall,' Tobias replied. Rees and Lydia exchanged a second look. They were already tired. When they started walking once again Rees took Lydia's arm.

Although trees covered the sky and the sun was only occasionally visible, the temperature rose steadily. It was so hot and humid that the air felt solid. Both Rees and Lydia began gasping for breath.

'I've never perspired so much in my life,' Rees muttered.

'You ever come south before?' Tobias asked. Rees shook his head.

'No point. I weave for the farm wives who've been spinning all winter. Here, in the South, there are already weavers.'

'The slaves,' Tobias said, his tone flattening. 'Every plantation has at least one weaver. And the owners rent out their slaves to the little farmers so even they don't need a traveling weaver.'

'It's not right to own another person,' Lydia said. A former Shaker, she was a firm abolitionist. Tobias glanced at her.

'Better not say that to a white person down here,' he said. 'You'll get whipped or worse.'

Lydia nodded, her lips tightening. Rees heard her mutter, 'It's not right.' Tobias was too far ahead to hear her.

It was late in the afternoon when they reached an even lower-lying area filled with water. Cattails grew thickly around it. 'Rest,' Tobias said. He picked one and stripped off the outer covering. He handed pieces to both Rees and Lydia and when they stared at it in bewilderment, he bit off a chunk, chewed and swallowed.

'It's edible,' he said.

Rees took a cautious bite. It tasted bland but was not unpleasant.

'We'll make one last push,' Tobias said, gesturing at the black liquid stretching away from them. Rees peered at it. He couldn't see through the black tint and that made him nervous. How deep was it? Small trunks, barely more than bumps, lined the shores and trees with swollen bulges grew out of the water, their leaves fluttering against the sky.

'What is that tree?' Lydia asked.

'Cypress,' Tobias answered.

'Why is the water so dark?' Rees put his hand in it and stirred, watching the dark tint fade as the water came up in his palm.

'Don't.' Tobias reached out as if to grab Rees's arm but hesitated. 'Let me check for gators first.' Rees snatched his hand out so fast drops flew everywhere. Tobias picked up a long branch and stretched it into the water. He thrashed it around until the water foamed up. When he pulled the stick from the pond, he stared at the water carefully. 'All right,' he said. 'We go through it.'

'There's no other way?' Lydia asked, her voice rising to a shaky falsetto. Tobias shook his head. 'How deep is it?'

'Mmm. Up to your knees maybe.' He turned and added, staring at both Rees and Lydia intently, 'Follow me exactly. Understood?'

Rees gulped. When he spoke he tried to sound normal.

'Yes.' He looked at Lydia and tried to sound reassuring. 'I'll walk right behind you.' He realized he'd failed to appear unafraid when both Lydia and Tobias gazed at him in concern.

'You'll be fine,' Tobias said. 'Just follow me exactly.'

'I'll carry the satchel above the water,' Rees promised Lydia.

She managed a brief nod but said, 'That's not what I am worried about.'

Tobias stepped into the water and began walking forward. Rees put his hand on Lydia's shoulder and squeezed. Lydia swallowed and tentatively put her foot into the pond. Rees followed closely, putting his left hand under Lydia's armpit to keep her stable. With his right hand, he lifted the satchel to his chest to keep it and its contents dry.

Despite the warmth of the water, it hit with a shock. Clouds of silt spiraled upward and drifted through the black water in a brownish film. The footing was fluid and unstable and so slippery that every step had to be taken with care. Rees stumbled, losing his grip on Lydia as he fought for his balance. She stopped and he could hear her sharp exhalation. Regaining his equilibrium, he stepped forward and grasped her shoulder once again.

Tobias was moving quickly. His eagerness to reach the opposite bank – and obvious nervousness about remaining in this water any longer than he had to – filled Rees with dread. He began pushing Lydia forward.

They were halfway across when something slid around Rees's lower legs. Uttering a scream, he jumped, lost his balance and fell backward. 'What?' Lydia cried, turning. 'What?'

'I don't know. Something touched me.' Rees gasped in a big breath, tasting mud and dirty water.

'Hurry,' Tobias shouted from the bank. 'Hurry.' He pointed at a brown snake lying coiled upon the water.

Lydia began plowing ahead, using her hands at her sides like scoops to help. Shuddering, Rees hurried after her. Why had he agreed to do this? And with his wife, too. Guilt stabbed him, sharp as a knife.

Although the journey felt as though it had lasted an hour, it was probably no more than a few minutes. Rees felt as though he'd be trapped in this filthy water forever when, finally, the ground beneath their feet began to rise. The water dropped to Lydia's knees, to her ankles and finally all three of them stood on the dry ground under a stand of loblolly pines. Rees took off his shoes and shook them. The leather, like his clothing, was soaked through. His linen shirt, his breeches and his vest were stained brown everywhere the water had touched.

He glanced at Lydia, sitting beside him on the muddy ground. Dirt streaked one sunburned cheek. 'Sorry,' he whispered.

'I wanted to come,' she said, without looking at him. 'You tried to warn me.'

'I didn't know it would be like this.'

When he'd told her it would be dangerous, he'd thought of bad food, bad roads, bad weather. Not the casual threat directed at Tobias that, at best, could have cost him his freedom. Or this alien landscape with its treacherous ground and swarms of insects and the snakes and alligators hiding in its black waters.

Would she have argued so hard to come if she had known what they would experience on this journey? More to the point, would she have wanted to accompany him if she had trusted him? Nothing had happened with the rope dancer: that was the truth. But Rees had desired her, and she had responded with warmth. They'd enjoyed a friendship that might have become something more. Now he was many months removed from that time he could admit Lydia had been right to worry. He did not want to believe he would have left his wife and family behind, but he had to admit he had been so enthralled it was possible.

Lydia was so frightened for the future of her marriage she'd felt she had to watch over him. To do that she had to leave her children behind. She would never have been willing to abandon them otherwise.

He looked at the snake still floating on the water and shuddered. What would happen to their children if he and his wife died here? They would be orphaned because of his selfishness.

Lydia suddenly leaned over and touched his hand. 'Don't feel so guilty,' she whispered. 'I insisted on coming. You could not have prevented me.'

But it was his fault she'd insisted.

'Only a few hours of daylight left,' Tobias said, breaking into Rees's thoughts. 'We'd better hurry.'

Rees glanced at the sky. From what he could see, it was still a clear intense blue. 'We've got a few hours still,' he said.

'It gets dark early under the trees,' Tobias said. 'Besides, most of the animals come out as soon as it starts getting dark. Especially snakes.' He pointed to a ripple in the water. Rees peered at the V-shaped ripple. 'Cottonmouth,' Tobias said. 'They swim under the water.'

'Snakes,' Lydia said weakly. 'Are they poisonous?'

'Cottonmouth sure are.'

Rees thought of the thing slithering past his legs in the water and gulped.

'It might not have been a snake. That touched you, I mean,' Tobias said, correctly interpreting Rees's reaction. 'There are other creatures here.' Rees did not think he wanted to know what they were. When Tobias turned and started up the slight slope, Rees helped Lydia to her feet and they scrambled after him as fast as they could.

THREE

The ground continued to dry out as they passed through the pines. Although the soil remained damp it no longer bounced underfoot. But, as Tobias had warned, the light began fading beneath the trees. 'Not far now,' he said, puffing a little as he trotted up the slope. Neither Rees nor Lydia replied. The effort to keep up with Tobias left them breathless. Tobias was not moving in a straight line but sliding through the thick vegetation in a serpentine path. Rees, terrified that he would lose sight of the other man, kept pushing Lydia ahead of him.

Tobias's path straightened out. Rees saw his pale-blue shirt at the end of a long fairly straight tunnel, roofed by interlaced branches. The dim light shone upon them with a greenish cast and their feet crunched over the dead leaves on the forest floor. The loud crackling was shocking after the quiet steps on the peaty ground. When they reached Tobias on the other side he said, 'Now we wait.'

'Wait for what?' Rees asked as Lydia pulled the pot of salve from Rees's satchel. She smeared more of the insect repellent on her face and neck and handed it to Rees. Although he thought he smelled the faint fragrance of burning wood, that odor was overpowered by the penetrating minty scent of the salve.

'I hope we don't use it all before we leave, and have to travel back through this swamp,' Lydia murmured.

'Here they come,' Tobias said.

'Who . . .?' Rees began as three men materialized out of the trees.

Of differing shades, from very dark to white, the men were barefoot and clad in rags. One had almost no shirt at all. And all three were armed. One carried a scythe with a long handle but the other two brandished guns. One was such an old musket Rees doubted it would fire – although he didn't plan to test his guess. They stared menacingly at Rees and Lydia.

'What'd you done?' The darkest of the men shouted at Tobias. His white teeth shone against his dark skin. His top two front teeth were separated by a large gap.

'I come for Ruthie, Scipio,' Tobias replied, rolling his shoulders forward. 'He's helping me.' He gestured at Rees. Although the other two men stared at the white intruder, Scipio never removed his gaze from Tobias.

'Ruth don't want to go with you,' he said, laughing mockingly. 'There're other men . . .' Tobias lunged forward, fists up. As Rees grabbed him, the man with the lightest skin clutched Scipio's arm. He was a handsome fellow with large hazel eyes, light brown hair and fair skin lightly tanned. Rees would have thought him white but for his hair, as curly as a sheep's.

'All right, Neptune,' Scipio said, stepping back. 'All right.' Tobias strained forward as though he would follow.

'Don't,' Rees said in a low voice. Tobias breathed hard for a few seconds before he visibly forced himself to relax. Rees cautiously took away his hand.

'I want to talk to Jackman,' he said.

'You risked all of us,' said the third of the men. 'No white man knows this.' He gestured behind him. 'Until now.' This man was older than the other two and he held his scythe with easy comfort.

'Let me talk to Jackman,' Tobias repeated. None of the black men moved. 'You know me, Neptune, Toney,' Tobias added pleadingly.

The three guards exchanged a silent message. 'Take 'em to Jackman,' Scipio said. 'But first . . .' He gestured to Rees and the gun he carried.

Neptune moved forward and relieved Rees of his musket. He did not resist. He did not *think* these men were killers, but he didn't know. Besides, they were protecting their home and families and he could see the fear in their eyes and in the stiffness of their bodies. Maybe not as frightened as he and Lydia were – he could feel her trembling next to his arm – but anxious about what danger they might bring to their home. Sometimes, fear could cause a man to lash out without thinking and be sorry afterwards, so Rees did not want to give them any reason to strike.

Besides, he reassured himself, with Tobias as their guide they most certainly would not be harmed. Right?

Lydia reached over and clutched his arm. When he glanced down at her, she looked up with a face as white as milk under the mud and insect bites. Her eyes were huge. But she managed a shaky smile. Together they followed Tobias and the other men through the thick underbrush deeper into the swamp.

They reached the village as night was falling. The concluding leg had taken significant time although Rees suspected they hadn't traveled a great distance. The ground had continued to dry, and pine trees became more plentiful. They walked until confronted by a thick wall of thorny greenbrier vines. Everyone stopped for a moment of rest.

'Just got to get through the canebrake,' muttered Toney.

'Follow me,' Tobias said, turning to Rees. 'There's a path.'

There may be, Rees thought, glancing at the expressions on the men. But it would not be an easy one. All of them were steeling themselves for this, the final and ultimate challenge. Huffing out a breath, Toney took the lead through the narrow and spiraling path through the brambles. Even following Tobias as closely as they dared did not spare Rees or Lydia from numerous cuts and scratches.

The ground sloped up slightly. They slid through the protective barrier and climbed the short slope, stepping in the circle of buildings that were barely visible in the gloom. A fire burned in the center, the orange flames reflecting from the face of a woman who stood over the fire. Smoke eddied out from the burning logs and Rees could already feel the difference in the number of mosquitoes around him. Lydia dropped heavily upon the ground and put her face into her hands.

Scipio and Neptune grabbed Tobias and urged him toward the fire. 'You want to see Jackman? Come along.'

Rees, his legs almost too shaky to hold him, collapsed next to Lydia. She leaned against him and closed her eyes in exhaustion. Rees felt like doing the same; he was so tired he no longer felt afraid. But he knew if he relaxed, he too would fall asleep and he did not want to do that until he knew they were safe. Instead, he looked at the young man guarding them.

'What's your name?' Rees asked, his voice rusty with disuse.

'Cinte,' he replied, sounding startled. He was very fair and his hair glittered with flashes of gold when he turned his head. Rees guessed he was probably little more than twenty. 'Here they come.'

A group of people were slowly approaching. Backlit by the fire, they were only silhouettes. Rees stood up and pulled Lydia to her feet. If he were going to be executed, he wanted to be upright.

His leg muscles had stiffened while he sat and he felt the pain of the long walk through the swamp. Just standing made his muscles quiver. At least that was the explanation he gave himself for the trembling that made him almost too weak to stand.

The group of people halted in front of him. Rees had the sense they were inspecting him. Since he faced the fire, he was visible in the flickering firelight but he could see nothing of their faces and could not guess what they thought.

One of the figures, a woman in a head scarf, detached itself from the group and approached Lydia. She opened her eyes and for a moment the two women stared at each other.

'What's your name?' one of the men asked Rees.

He started and brought his attention back to the band of men. The speaker stood a little forward of the others and Rees could see the gray threading his hair. 'Are you Jackman?'

'Yes. Who are you?'

'My name is Will Rees.'

'Why're you here?'

'Tobias is a friend of mine. I've known Ruth since we were kids. I came to help them go north, to the District of Maine.' As he spoke, Rees felt some of the tension ease.

'These people know where we are,' Scipio put in, staring at Rees with hostility. 'They're a danger to us and our kin.'

Jackman turned and made a sound. Scipio slapped his hand on his thigh but did not continue the argument.

Jackman turned to the woman. 'Feed 'em, please, Aunt Suke, while I think.' Turning, he limped to the fire, leaning heavily on a cane.

Rees extended a hand to Lydia and together they followed Jackman. Scipio and Neptune trailed them, so closely Rees twitched with nerves. He knew Scipio saw him as a danger and feared he would lash out at the slightest provocation.

The fire and a few dish lamps bathed the camp's center in a dim rusty light. Jackman gestured to a log. Rees and Lydia took their seats.

The woman turned and handed them both bowls of soup, redolent with strange spices. With no spoons on offer, Rees tipped the bowl so that the savory soup could run into his mouth. After a few seconds, Lydia did the same.

'Thank you, Madame,' Rees said. 'It's good.' Instead of being energized by the food, he felt even more tired.

'You can call me Aunt Suke, child,' she said.

'You not be thinkin' of believin' him,' Scipio cried. In the firelight Rees could see details about Scipio and the other men that had not been visible earlier. Scipio was missing an

ear. Just a few ragged stubs remained. And when he turned
to demand an answer from Jackman the firelight picked out
the ridges on his back through his ripped shirt.

'Tobias swears for him,' Jackman said softly.

'Tobias!' Scipio started to say something else, but Jackman
shook his head at him. Appearing out of the darkness, Tobias
walked with Ruth.

Rees rose clumsily to his feet.

Ruth was clearly pregnant, at least five or six months, Rees
guessed. He could clearly see her trim brown ankles under
the ragged hem of her dress. But a new ribbon – blue, Rees
thought, although it was hard to see the color – had been sewn
around the frayed neckline. She still cared about her appearance. She smiled at Tobias but the space between her brows
was pleated with worry. When she saw Rees looking at her,
she put her hand on her belly and bowed her head, reluctant
it seemed to meet his gaze. She seemed embarrassed. He
suddenly wondered if she really wanted to go north with Tobias
or not.

'Ruth?' he said.

When she met his gaze, her eyes were full of tears. 'Oh,
Mr Rees. He involved you in our business?' She threw Tobias
an angry glance. He lowered his eyes to the ground.

'Oh damn,' Rees muttered. Had they made the difficult and
dangerous journey for nothing?

'Come here, you sweet thing,' Scipio said, opening his arms.

'You leave her alone,' Tobias said, stepping in front of
Ruth.

'But Ruthie wants to stay here, with me, don't ya, Ruthie?'
As Scipio stood up, Ruthie smiled at him. But, before she had
an opportunity to speak, Tobias surged up with a roar and
flung himself at the other man. As Jackman shouted at them
to stop, punches smacked into flesh with a meaty sound. Scipio
was taller and heavier but jealousy and anger energized Tobias.
Staggering back, his nose streaming blood from a blow that
had landed squarely on his face, he picked up a stick and
lashed at Scipio with it, striking his arm and cutting it.
Glistening in the flickering light, the blood began running
down Scipio's arm. Ducking and weaving, he danced forward

and wrenched the stick from Tobias's hand. Laughing, Scipio tossed it aside.

Tobias hurled himself forward once again and they went down to the dirt. They rolled over and over, punching, kicking and biting. The firelight shone on the arms and backs of the fighters, reflecting in flashes of copper. Scipio shoved Tobias aside, but he came back, pounding at the other man. Scipio shifted away, rolling into the fire. The kettle rocked on its stand as sparks flew into the air. Scipio yelled loudly; his shoulder had gone into the burning embers, and with a heave he pushed Tobias to the side. But the smaller man would not surrender and, throwing himself to his knees, began pounding at Scipio, slapping, punching, kicking and biting.

Jackman picked up his cane and limped forward and tried to catch hold of Scipio. Cinte jumped in to help. Rees moved forward to pin Tobias's arms to his sides and drag him away. For his pains, he suffered a clout to his cheekbone from one of Scipio's blows. When Neptune joined the fray, helping Jackman and Cinte drag Scipio away, the fight was over. Tobias shrugged out of Rees's grasp and stood to one side, wiping his bloody nose on his sleeve. Scipio too bore battle scars. Besides the arm that had been scraped and burnt, his good ear now streamed with blood. Tobias had bitten it. Although he had not succeeded in tearing it away, blood ran down Scipio's cheek and neck and on to his shoulder.

Tobias went to stand by Ruth. She stared at him in embarrassed horror and shifted away.

'Clean up while I ponder what to do,' Jackman ordered the two combatants, his voice vibrating with anger.

'Come here,' Aunt Suke said. Exasperated, she pointed at a space next to her. 'You boys don't have good sense.'

As Tobias sat down on the ground in front of Aunt Suke, Lydia said, 'Sit by me, Ruth,' and patted the log next to her.

Scipio said incredulously, 'That boy a woman?'

'That's how we know they safe,' Aunt Suke said, turning a mocking smile upon him. 'No slave catcher bring his wife.'

As Rees went to sit beside his wife, Aunt Suke put out a hand to stop him.

'Wait,' she said. 'I need your help.' Such was the strength

of her personality that Rees did stop and wait for further instructions.

She looked at Tobias first. The blood had already stopped gushing from his nose but it was swollen and his eye was almost completely shut. Taking his face in her hands, she turned it this way and that to catch the best light. Then she raised his shirt and examined the cuts and bruises marring his torso. 'You'll live,' she said at last. 'I'll make a poultice for you.'

Shooing him away, she gestured at Scipio. Although he stood almost six feet and outweighed the woman by at least one hundred pounds, he obeyed her, coming to sit at her feet like a naughty child. She looked first at his ear. 'If Tobias bit harder,' she said, 'you'd a lost this one too.'

'You'd match,' Cinte said, laughing. 'Two torn ears.' Scipio joined in, his robust guffaws rolling through camp. Rees, who couldn't help but smile, wondered at the bond he sensed between these two men.

'Did you lose the other one in a fight also?' Rees asked Scipio.

He shook his head. 'No.'

'Here, hold his arm,' Aunt Suke told Rees. When she disappeared into a hut, Scipio continued.

'One of the times I ran away,' he said, 'an' they caught me, they nailed my ear to a post.' Rees gasped. 'They do that,' Scipio continued, 'to keep the runaways home. But I pulled free. Nothin' can hold me,' he added with quiet pride.

Rees could find no words. One heard about the evils of slavery, especially in Maine, a state full of abolitionists. But he'd never really thought about the reality of it. Now, although the reactions of those around him told him Scipio's story was true, Rees struggled to accept it.

Aunt Suke came out of the hut with a small brown bottle and what looked like mashed leaves in a cup. 'Hold 'im tight now,' she said to Rees. 'To the light.' She handed the bottle to Scipio. 'Take a drink of the laudanum. This'll sting.' He took a healthy swig and she removed the bottle from his hands. Then she began dabbing the leaf mixture on the scorched and bloody wound on Scipio's arm. He groaned and tried to twist away. 'Some turpentine to clean it. And now . . .' Singing a wordless melody, she smeared a thick paste that smelled strongly of lard over the burn. 'That'll feel better and help it heal. You be fine.'

Scipio jumped up with alacrity but he didn't voice a complaint.

'I've decided,' Jackman said. 'You, Scipio, go back to your job at the canal.'

'The canal?' Rees repeated, whispering to Aunt Suke. He was beginning to feel he had truly left his own world, the one he understood, behind. This was an unknown land.

'White men be digging a canal. Only the biggest and strongest survive that work.'

'I make the shingles,' Scipio said. 'Fastest shingle maker they got.'

'Stay there until they finish for the winter,' Jackman continued. 'By then we'll know what Ruth want to do.'

'Aw,' Scipio said. 'That's more 'n a month from now.' But he didn't argue. Jackman was older than the others, probably Rees's age, and carried himself with the authority of the head man.

'First you had to mess with Sandy and now Ruth, another man's woman. We can't have it.' Jackman shook his head. 'We can't be fightin' among ourselves.'

'Too bad if other men can't keep their women,' said Scipio, looking across the fire at Tobias. 'You like that ribbon I bought you, Ruth?' Tobias took a step forward to the sound of Scipio's roaring laughter. Ruth caught Tobias's sleeve and held on.

'You know better,' she said in a low voice.

'Who's Sandy?' Rees asked Aunt Suke.

'My niece. She run off from the Sechrest plantation all the time so you'll probably meet her.' Suke shook her head. 'Scipio does love his women. But Sandy? No, he's not interested. She too young. He just messin' with Cinte.'

Rees glanced at the fair-skinned man. He was laughing too and as Rees watched he slapped Scipio on the uninjured shoulder. So why did Scipio want to mess with him? And why didn't Cinte seem to mind?

'I want you gone by sun-up, hmmm,' Jackman continued.

'All right.' Still chuckling, Scipio looked at the other men. 'How about a game tonight?' He took some bone dice from his pocket and rolled them in his large palm.

'I'll go too,' Cinte said, rising to his feet. 'Keep my brother company.'

That answered one of Rees's questions.

'How about it, Neptune?'

'No.'

'You'll double that runnin' away money,' Scipio coaxed. 'And you, Toney?'

'I'm in. For a little while. Until I start losin'. I swear, those dice be loaded.'

'Cinte? You got more money than any of us,' Scipio said. His brother shook his head and turned away.

'C'mon, Neptune. Don't be no fun with only two.' As Scipio did his best to persuade Neptune to join the game, Rees turned to Cinte.

'Do you work on the canal too?' he asked, eyeing the other man's slender build and fair skin.

'No. I make banjoes. And I got one to deliver to one of the other shingle makers at the Ditch.' With that statement, Cinte ran down the slope to a distant hut.

'What's a banjo?' Rees asked himself.

This was truly a foreign place.

FOUR

Rees awoke the following morning to the sound of a crowing rooster. Lydia had pulled linen sheets from the satchel and spread them out upon the rough bench which served as the bed. Rees, shrouded in the linen until only his hair showed, had ended up on the wooden floor.

Aching, he slowly pushed himself into a sitting position and looked around. In the darkness the previous night he had been unable to see his surroundings. He was in a small hut, barely ten feet by twelve, and furnished solely with two wide benches set on adjacent walls and a table with two stools. Although wooden planks formed the floor, they were muddy and rough with bark. One of the straw-covered benches was empty; Ruth had already awakened and left. She had retired by herself. Tobias, frowning and disgruntled, had gone down the slope to the men's cabin.

On the other platform the sheet-wrapped mound that was Lydia lay unmoving. Rees wiped a grubby hand across his face and unwound the sheet from his body. He had slept poorly. The raucous laughter of the men gambling outside had kept him awake – that and the steady whine of mosquitoes in his ears. He struggled to his feet, using one of the stools to help him rise. A stabbing pain ripped down the left side of his back. He stretched and tried to twist. The pain subsided to a throb.

He went to the door and looked out. The hut had been elevated a little above the ground on posts, so he looked across the camp into the swamp. Pine trees dotted the village and the morning mist curled around the trunks in a thick white wall. To Rees, it felt as though this little village was entirely cut off from the rest of the world.

Ruth sat by the edge, grinding corn. She looked up with a smile.

'Over here,' Jackman called, waving. He and Aunt Suke sat by the fire. As Rees walked to them, she looked up. In the gray light her skin shone a smooth medium brown. Many braids hung from beneath her red scarf. She did not return his smile.

'Come and eat,' she said, gesturing to the pan shoved into the ashes.

Rees obeyed, wondering what would happen now. Jackman gestured to a log that served as a seat. Rees squatted, his knees protesting as he dropped. Aunt Suke handed Rees a piece of corn pone and bacon on a wooden slab. Although the corn pone looked gritty from the fire, Rees bit into it hungrily. A bowl of soup was not sufficient for a man of his size.

There was no coffee. Aunt Suke handed him a pottery mug of some strange tasting tea. He took one sip and put it aside.

Chicory, as a substitute, was bad enough but this brew was undrinkable. It tasted like leaves.

Rubbing her eyes, Lydia came down the steps and joined him at the fire. She declined the corn pone but accepted both the bacon and the tea.

While they ate, Tobias approached the fire, carrying a gun. Ruth jumped up and disappeared behind the cabins. Tobias stared after her longingly.

'That looks like my musket,' Rees said, glancing at Tobias.

'It is,' he replied, looking at Rees. 'Jackman told me to bring in some game – more mouths to feed. Neptune took one – he's already out hunting – and Scipio took the other.' He glanced around the camp. 'Was that Ruthie running off?'

When no one answered, he looked around once more before continuing on his way. As he disappeared into the brambles, Ruth tiptoed cautiously around the hut. 'Is he gone?' she asked. Rees looked at her, wondering what was wrong. Did she no longer care for Tobias? Maybe she wanted to stay with Scipio now? Surely she did not wish to remain in the South, far from Maine.

Lydia was wondering the same thing. 'I hope we didn't make this terrible journey for nothing,' she murmured to Rees. He nodded. His plan, to return home immediately, seemed doomed to failure.

When Ruth joined them by the fire, Lydia said to her, 'You do know you don't have to stay with Tobias. You can stop with us or with the Shakers until you know what you want to do.'

Ruth offered a half-nod that told Rees nothing and then changed the subject. 'I'm not eager to see those long Maine winters,' she said, her hands protectively cupping her pregnant belly.

'Oh, you'll adjust again,' Lydia replied with an encouraging smile.

'But what's happening with you?' Ruth began banking the fire, reducing it to a mound of coals. 'Tobias told me you aren't in Dugard anymore.'

'We've moved toward the coast and the Shaker community of Zion. David still lives at the old farm in Dugard with another of our sons. We adopted several children and have a little girl of our own.'

'Tell me everything,' Ruth said, smiling for the first time. 'Oh, but I have work to do.'

'I'll help you,' Lydia said, jumping up. She directed a speaking glance at her husband before following Ruth away from the fire and into the hut in which Rees and Lydia had slept the night before. To the sound of Lydia's voice, dirt began flying out the door, propelled by a broom.

Rees also was not allowed to linger by the fire. Once he'd eaten, Jackman began limping away on his cane but turned after a few steps and looked over his shoulder. He did not quite have the nerve to ask a white man to help him. Rees understood this and rose to his feet. 'The corn is in,' Jackman said, 'but the yams need weedin'. If you don't mind, hmmm?' They walked east, out of the cluster of huts. Rees looked curiously at Jackman's feet. He was missing the last few toes on his left foot. Rees did not feel as though he knew the other man well enough to ask. But Jackman saw the direction of Rees's glance.

'Frostbite,' he said, replying to the unspoken question. 'When I went through my first winter, I didn't know nothin'. But now . . .' He looked around with pride. 'We've done good.'

'How long have you been here? I mean, since you ran away?'

Jackman stared into space, thinking. ''Bout seven years.'

'That's a long time,' Rees said in amazement. 'The slave catchers can't be very good at their jobs.'

'They don't like the swamp,' Jackman said with a grin. 'Some of us maroons been here longer, longer than me, and some a lot less. Scipio now, first time he ran away, he got caught in two weeks.'

'Was that when he lost his ear?' Rees asked. Jackman shook his head.

'That came later. Third or fourth time he run away. Now they have a reward out for him. Two hundred dollars, hmmm?'

Rees whistled softly. 'Two hundred dollars is enough to buy a farm with cash left over.'

Jackman nodded. 'He made 'em look bad.' Stopping, he

pointed. 'Here's the fields,' he said with evident pride. Rees looked at the corn stalks rustling faintly in the breeze. There couldn't be more than two acres here, hardly enough to feed even the few members of this camp. He did not see any of the crops Lydia grew in her kitchen garden: spinach, turnips, beets and the like. And, although Rees knew there were chickens and he saw a pen with small dark cattle, there were no sheep. And he saw no pigs. Where had the bacon come from?

'Yams over here,' Jackman said, pointing.

Rees followed Jackman through the cornfield. The irony of traveling hundreds of miles and struggling through the Great Dismal to do farm work was not lost on him. He could have stayed home and done the same.

Rees worked all morning until the hot sun drove him into the shade under a tree. How did the people here survive under this heat?

'Coolin' down now,' Jackman said, joining Rees. 'Now we into fall, hmmm?'

'Cooling?' Rees repeated in astonishment. Even in the depths of the summer, on the hottest day, Maine never experienced such a temperature. Jackman laughed and offered Rees a wooden cup of water. The water was dark and Rees suspected it came directly from the swamp. He tried not to think about it as he drank. It wasn't cold either, but it was wet.

'Jackman! Jackman!' Tobias ran into the field and raced through the cornstalks. He was sweating hard and his eyes were wide. Although he called for Jackman, Tobias looked at Rees.

'What happened?' Rees asked, putting down the cup.

'It's Scipio.' Tobias stopped and gulped. 'He's dead.'

'Dead!' Jackman glanced at Rees and then back at Tobias. 'What? Are you sure? What happened? Where is he?'

'He's been shot,' Tobias said. 'I found him in the swamp with a great bloody hole in his back.'

Both Rees and Jackman glanced in unison at the musket in Tobias's hand.

FIVE

Jackman asked Aunt Suke to find another of the men to help, Toney or Peros. Rees, who hadn't seen this Peros, looked at Jackman in surprise. 'He be hidin',' Jackman said, glancing at Rees. He touched his face, very conscious once again of his white skin.

'But where is he? They?' Rees asked.

'This,' Jackman gestured at the cluster of huts, 'isn't the only village, hmmm?'

Rees looked around at the dense wall of green surrounding them and wondered how many of these communities were hidden here in the Great Dismal. There could be hundreds and no one outside would be the wiser.

Almost an hour passed before Aunt Suke, accompanied by the two men, reappeared in the village. 'Toney and Peros,' Jackman said. Rees nodded. Toney he remembered from the previous day. Peros, even more raggedly dressed than his companion, was shorter, slim and light-skinned.

After one horrified glance at Rees, he fixed his eyes on the ground. Almost, Rees thought, as though Peros thought the white man would run mad and slaughter everything in his path. And when it came time for them to leave, he pressed closely to Jackman and said, 'He can't come.' Peros's eyes flicked at Rees. 'What if he calls the slave takers on us?'

'He's got to come,' Tobias said. 'He's studied murder. He'll find Scipio's killer.'

'Maybe it's a trap,' Peros whispered, flicking a suspicious glance at Rees.

'Nah,' Toney said. 'He Tobias friend.' Peros's eyebrows rose in astonishment.

With a sigh, Rees stepped away, leaving them to discuss him in private. He went to find Lydia. She was not in the hut they shared with Ruth but in a different hut nearer the fields. The two women were washing greens in a wooden pail. They both looked up when Rees's shadow darkened the door, but Lydia did not speak until he came in and sat down on a bench. Then, seeing his face, Lydia asked, 'What's the matter?'

'It's Scipio,' Rees said. Ruth turned with a sudden intake of breath and stared at him. He didn't know what to say. Should he tell her Scipio had been shot and killed? 'Jackman and the others are going to find him.' With another glance at Ruth, Rees took the easy way and did not confide the entire truth. 'They don't want me to accompany them.'

As Lydia joined her husband on the bench, Ruth said, 'They are afraid. Almost every white person here turns their hands against us and they know nothing else.'

'What else?' Lydia said, putting her hand on Rees's. 'Why do you want to go with them?'

'Because . . .' Rees began but it was Aunt Suke who finished the sentence as she stepped into the cabin.

'Scipio is dead. Murdered.'

With a little scream Ruth sank down on the floor. Lydia hurried to her side.

'I'm sorry for your loss.' With a quick glance at Rees, Lydia added, 'Do you love him? Did you?'

'No. I knew him for what he was: a man who would never settle down.' Ruth lifted a face streaked with tears. 'But he was fun. Always smiling and ready with a joke.'

'The men be waitin' for you,' Aunt Suke said to Rees.

'Tobias persuaded them?' He rose to his feet.

'Yes. He swore for you. Don't you disappoint him now.' She shook her head, the braids moving beneath her scarf. Rees was struck by her beauty; those amber eyes against that smooth coffee-colored skin and the high cheekbones that hinted at another heritage, Indian maybe. But he would never compliment her. Her eyes shone with a fierce intelligence and a determination never to be taken lightly.

'I'll do my best,' Rees promised her. Of course he would. Solving murders was what he did. And he couldn't make Tobias a liar.

He started for the door but then turned back to kiss Lydia. He didn't want her to think his admiration of Aunt Suke – and

Lydia would surely notice it – meant anything. She jumped, startled, but tolerated his embrace.

'I know you will,' Aunt Suke said. 'You one of the seekers. You be studyin' this and won't stop until it's ended, one way or the other.' He glanced at her in surprise but nodded.

'No, I won't,' he said. As he stepped through the door, she touched his sleeve lightly.

'Be careful,' she warned him. 'I saw the signs; I knew death be coming. And I don't think he done yet.'

Disconcerted, Rees offered her a short nod before leaving the hut and joining the other men by the fire.

They walked down the slight slope to the wall of thorns. They passed through that directly into thick swamp. Rees resolved to stick close to Tobias and Jackman; he knew he would never be able to find his way back to the camp without guidance.

The humidity seemed much worse here than in the village. And the bugs! Rees had liberally applied Lydia's salve, but the insects, the yellow flies especially, seemed untroubled by it. The vegetation pressed around them in a wall of green. Rees shuddered. He had never realized how claustrophobic forest could be.

In silence, they threaded their way over the damp ground, through the trees and thick underbrush, the only sounds a faint grunt now and then and the rhythmic thud of Jackman's stick. Rees tried to step where Tobias stepped but even so his shoes were soon coated and heavy with mud. Traveling shoeless, like Jackman and the others, was clearly more sensible.

He wasn't sure, but he thought they were traveling through the swamp by way of a different path than the one he had followed Tobias in on. He knew it when they stopped at a body of water, black as night and shaded by the growth around it. The trees, cypress, with those bulbous trunks, grew all around them. Rounded bumps protruded from the ground in every direction, ready to trip the unwary. Despite the water glittering all around them, Rees could barely see the sky when he looked up.

'Is this a lake?' he asked.

'Lake?' Jackman looked at him and shook his head. 'No. Just one lake in the swamp. We go fishin' in it sometimes. This just water.'

Two pirogues, little more than hollowed logs, were tied to a dead tree where the deeper water began. Tobias and Rees climbed into one. Toney remained on the shore while Jackman and Peros climbed into the other. Tobias handed Rees a paddle as Toney untied the rope. Then, with a powerful thrust of the paddle, he sent them into the pond. Rees glanced over his shoulder in time to see Toney untie the second pirogue before jumping into it, squeezing himself into the back.

'Paddle,' Tobias shouted from the front. Rees obeyed and the small vessel began moving through the black water.

'Did Scipio take one of these boats too?' Rees asked.

'No,' Tobias said. 'He and Cinte would have walked west of here, walked the whole distance. But this is faster.'

Afterwards, when Lydia asked him about it, Rees found this journey hard to describe. It seemed almost dreamlike. Silent, except for the faint splashing of the oars and the cries of the birds, the pirogue slid quietly through that strangely tinted water. It was warm and humid, but not as hot as it had been. A heron drifted down from the sky for a fish and turtles lay on the tiny spits of land that passed as the bank.

He was glad when Tobias broke the silence. 'We'll pull over here.'

Rees nodded, glad to see they were returning to land.

As they approached a piece of drier ground – which looked almost identical to the area they'd left – a large tortoise slipped into the water with a splash. 'Relieved that's not an alligator,' Tobias said, half to himself. Rees began paddling much faster, slowing only when the bottom of the log scraped against the bottom. The water through which they'd floated was shallow and here it was less than a foot deep. Tobias jumped out and tied the craft to a branch. Rees struggled out of the water, wetting his feet even further in the fluid mud, and clambered over a massive fallen tree to join Tobias. A few minutes later, the other pirogue slid in beside the first.

Once everyone was on land, Tobias took the lead. He kept

stopping, looking up at the sky. Finally, Rees said, 'Do you know the way?'

'Sort of,' Tobias replied. 'I walked out last time. I know Scipio is around here somewhere.'

They floundered through the underbrush for some time before Tobias saw something Rees did not. 'Now I know,' he said and set off in a southerly direction. Although he seemed to be following landmarks, Rees could see no difference at all between this patch of the swamp and any other.

They came upon the body quite suddenly, although Rees realized then he'd been smelling the faint taint of blood for some time. The metallic odor was almost drowned out by the smells of earth, water, and green vegetation.

He stared down at the prone figure. Just last night this man had been vividly alive; laughing and joking as he threw the dice. Now he lay dead, shot in the back. 'He didn't deserve to die like this,' Rees muttered. 'The coward who killed him couldn't even look him in the face.' He knelt, the soft wet ground soaking through the knees of his breeches, and swatted away the flies covering the wound. 'Powder burns,' he said as he bent over it. 'Scipio's killer stood close to him when he fired.'

'How'd you know that?' Jackman asked suspiciously.

Rees looked up and caught the men staring at him in appalled surprise. 'Well, I—' he began. But Tobias spoke first.

'I told you, he's studied murder,' he said. 'He's famous for finding killers.'

Jackman turned a narrow-eyed look upon Rees. 'Studied murder, hmmm? Like a sheriff?'

'Something like,' Rees agreed. He didn't think the sheriffs he'd known would agree, but the description was close enough to serve.

'Seems like a strange skill to have,' Jackman commented as he returned his gaze to the body. 'Powder burns, you said? Does that mean he knew his killer?'

'Maybe,' Rees said carefully, although he thought it likely. 'But not definitely.' He looked around. Although some of the leaves were yellowing and turning brown at the edges with the change of seasons, the foliage here was still thick and almost impenetrable. Because of the dense underbrush around them, the men had formed a tight circle around Scipio. 'Someone could have slipped up behind him without being seen. He never had a chance.'

'Jacob maybe,' suggested Toney. 'Scipio had words with him.'

'Jacob's overseer at the canal,' Jackman explained to Rees as he touched the wound on the back. The flies rose in a blood-drunk cloud away from his hand. The blood around the bullet hole was drying and the body had stiffened.

'He's been dead a few hours,' Rees said. With a heave, he turned the body over.

Curious about the lumps in Scipio's pocket, Rees reached in and closed his fist around the dice. He pulled them out, feeling the slight pull to one side. The dice were loaded, as Toney had warned. Rees dropped them in his pocket and continued his examination.

Damage to Scipio's eyes indicated insect activity had begun. Tobias turned away and vomited in the grass when a beetle scuttled across Scipio's cheek. 'But not many hours,' Rees said. Most of Scipio's eyes remained.

'Has to be the slave catchers,' Peros said. 'You know they be after him.'

As soon as Peros said the words 'slave catchers', everyone became very silent. Rees looked up. By the intent expressions on their faces, he had the sense they were listening for the sounds of baying dogs or shouting men.

'But they be long gone,' Jackman said, looking around him nervously. 'Otherwise we be chased too.'

Tobias suddenly straightened. 'Where's Cinte?'

'Do you think . . .?' Peros began, gesturing to Scipio.

'Cinte couldn't kill a fly,' Jackman said scornfully. 'Certainly wouldn't hurt his brother, hmmm?'

'Besides, Cinte always take the other way,' Toney said. 'Sell his banjoes to the slaves on the Sechrest and Grove plantations.' He grinned and added slyly, 'Visit Sandy too.' Jackman sighed.

'Let's go,' Peros said, glancing around. 'It not be safe here.'

'Right. We're not safe,' Jackman agreed. 'But first, look for the gun. Scipio carried one.'

They dispersed, searching through the thick undergrowth for it. Peros, the smallest and thinnest, found it lying half-submerged in a pool. He brought it back and handed it to Jackman who examined it unhappily. 'We only own two,' he said. 'Or three, counting yours.' He glanced at the one Tobias held.

Rees held out his hand. 'May I?' When Jackman, eyeing Rees with both reluctance and renewed suspicion, handed it to him, he sniffed the barrel. It had been fired and recently too.

Had Scipio tried to protect himself? Or had his murderer wrested the musket from Scipio and shot him with it? 'You can smell burnt powder,' he said, returning it to Jackman. He smelled it.

'He could've fired at some animal,' he said hopefully.

'How come you not smellin' Tobias's gun?' Toney asked, staring at Rees. 'Scipio and Tobias fought over Ruth. Maybe he did it.'

'Now wait a minute,' Tobias said as Rees reached for the gun.

'It's a fair question,' Rees said.

'I was hunting. I shot at a deer,' Tobias protested as Rees sniffed and smelled the tell-tale odor of black powder. He nodded slightly at Jackman.

'Where is it then?' Peros demanded.

'I missed.'

'We'll talk about this later,' Jackman said. 'In camp. After we bring him home, hmmm?' he added, gesturing at Scipio.

There was no question of leaving the body where it lay. Without speaking, everyone knew it had to be brought back to camp for burial. Rees handed the musket to Jackman and joined the other men in lifting Scipio to their shoulders. They could not have managed if the body had relaxed into floppy softness. Since he had stiffened lying straight, it was almost like carrying a very heavy board.

But angling something so big through the verdant swamp was difficult. Scipio's limbs caught on every branch, every twig, jerking the men who were carrying the body to a stop. Worse, the sky began to darken. With a gust of wind, the clouds above opened up and the rain poured down so furiously that no one could see more than a hand's breadth in

front. Lowering the body to the ground, the men took shelter
under the trees. It helped – some. At first the rain felt warm
but as Rees's clothing became saturated, he began to shiver.
But he didn't complain. The men from the village were
dressed only in rags and they suffered far more. Toney and
Peros stamped their feet and clapped their hands against
their arms.

Fortunately, the rain lasted only ten minutes or so and then
stopped as abruptly as it had started. The sun came out again
and the air warmed, quite pleasingly Rees thought now. But
it was not as hot as it had been.

'We better hurry,' Jackman said.

'We're close to the boats,' Tobias said, his voice rough
with disuse.

They picked up their burden once again and continued on.

At the stream they ran into another problem: how to fit
the living and the dead into the pirogues. No one wanted to
sit with the body in the pirogues. After some jostling around
and some loud discussion, Rees and Tobias took Scipio's
body in one of the boats while the other three took the
second. Rees sat with Scipio's head in his lap, the sightless
and filmy eyes staring up at the sky until Rees closed them.
He could paddle only on the starboard side; the position and
weight of the body made it impossible to lean left. Tobias
perched awkwardly over Scipio's bare feet and paddled for
all he was worth.

As the pirogue glided into the black water Rees felt
melancholy steal over him. Another murder. Men, it seemed,
could not prevent themselves from murdering their fellows.
And here was Scipio, a man so determined to escape his
bondage he'd lost an ear; a young man making a new life in
the swamp, murdered.

If it had not been for Lydia, waiting for him at the camp,
Rees thought he might just turn this boat around and head
north to his home and family.

SIX

It was late afternoon by the time they struggled into camp with the body. Shadows were stealing out from under the trees and creeping across the village. Rees was surprised by the rush of relief he felt when he saw the huts and fire, and the meat roasting over the flames.

The women, who were clustered around in the center, surged forward, crying out questions, as the men lowered the body to the ground. Rees stretched. His back hurt and his arms and legs were scored with insect bites, scratches and cuts. He looked around for Lydia.

'Will.' She ran forward and hurled herself into his arms. Although still clad in boy's clothes, she had braided her hair into a long rope down her back. She smelled clean and fresh. He squeezed her tightly. For a moment they stood together and then, as though recalling the anger between them, she pulled back. 'What happened? You were gone so long.' Stepping away, she examined him. 'There's blood on your breeches.'

'Scipio's blood. It was a strange journey.' Rees didn't think he would ever be able to describe it. 'He was shot in the back.'

'We need to put the body somewhere,' Aunt Suke said behind them. Rees turned. Suke was speaking to Jackman. 'In a hut or something to protect the body from the animals.'

'Should bury him tomorrow, hmmm?' Jackman said. He glanced longingly at the meat roasting over the fire. 'The body will corrupt—'

'No. We keep him and don't have the funeral until Cinte comes home. He has to say goodbye to his brother,' Aunt Suke said firmly.

'We don't even know if he'll come back,' Jackman argued. Shaking her head, Aunt Suke frowned at him. 'Don't suck-teeth at me,' Jackman said. 'This is the fact: Cinte might be recaptured.'

'Or dead,' Tobias put in glumly.

Rees turned away from the argument. 'What's happening here?'

'As you see,' Lydia said, gesturing around her. 'Neptune returned. He shot one of the wild pigs.' She tugged her husband toward the fire and the roasting meat. 'You must be hungry. Come and eat.'

Rees realized he was ravenous. But somehow it didn't seem right to eat with Scipio lying dead behind him. 'We can't . . .' He gestured at the body. 'It's not right.'

'We'll put him in Quaco's hut,' Aunt Suke said. 'He don't use it anyway.'

'For how long, hmmm?' Jackman shook his head. 'We can't leave the body to rot.'

'A day or two. Just to give Cinte a little time to come home.'

'And what if he don't?' Jackman asked, his voice rising in frustration. Aunt Suke stared over his head for several seconds.

'Cinte not be dead,' she said finally. 'He'll come home.'

'We'll wait two days only,' Jackman said firmly. 'Then we bury him.'

'We'll bury him after his funeral,' Aunt Suke said.

'Two days,' Jackman repeated.

This time Aunt Suke inclined her head but she did not say yes or no and Rees wondered if Jackman's wishes would be met. Aunt Suke was a powerful woman. She turned to Rees. 'You and Toney take the body to the hut, please. You the strongest men here.'

Toney glanced at Rees, shocked by the woman's casual request of a white man. But Rees, who might have been asked to do something similar by his wife, or even by the Shaker Sister Esther, nodded and lifted Scipio's feet. As Toney lifted Scipio's shoulders, Aunt Suke picked up a burning brand to light the way.

'Jesus!' Toney grunted as Scipio's heavy body began to slip. Tobias ran to help.

The hut was situated a distance away from the others, down a slope and closer to the trees and the water of the swamp. Even from the outside Rees could see this building had long been uninhabited. The path to it was overgrown and as the party approached a flock of birds took flight from under the rafters. Together, the three men carried Scipio's body to the hut and put him on the bench. The stiffness was beginning to ease off and Rees thought Jackman's concern was valid; it wouldn't take long for the body to corrupt in this warm weather.

None of the huts contained more than the bare essentials but this one seemed particularly devoid of comfort. Ruth had displayed a few treasures in the hut in which Rees and Lydia now slept; a cracked china bowl, a string of beads and a fine hairbrush. In here, even in the flickering illumination of the torchlight, Rees could see only dust and cobwebs.

'Where's Ruth?' Tobias asked Aunt Suke as the men left the hut.

'In my cabin,' she replied. 'She helpin' me.'

Tobias turned and hurried up the slope. He disappeared into Aunt Suke's hut. Rees and Toney followed more slowly, returning to the village center.

'You'll want to wash your hands before eating,' Lydia said. 'There's a barrel around the back. Ruth showed me – here, come.' Rees followed her out and around to the back of the hut. A poor cooper had made this barrel; the staves did not fit as tightly together as they should, and the water was leaking through them. 'Bathing in the swamp is best.' Lydia spoke rapidly, filling up the silence. 'There's a place, down the hill, past the men's cabin.' She gestured in that direction. 'Everyone usually bathes in groups. But not after dark. Something could come out of the water. Everything here seems to eat people.' She took the lid from the barrel, revealing black water that glittered slightly. 'This is some of our drinking water. Give me your hands.'

Rees obeyed and as Lydia poured the water over them, he scrubbed his hands several times with the harsh soap. When he was sure they were clean he accepted the towel to dry them. The silence between them was not the easy quiet they'd once enjoyed.

'What did Ruth tell you?' Rees asked, rushing into speech and keeping his gaze fixed on his hands. He looked up as Lydia sighed audibly.

'She loves Tobias but she cannot return home to Maine with him. She refused to say anything more.' Lydia shook her head. 'I am not sure what happened here in Virginia. And Ruth won't tell me.'

'I guess this was a wasted trip,' Rees said.

'Maybe not. If she still loves Tobias, and she says she does, then we have a way to persuade her.' She paused and watched Rees dry his hands for a few seconds. 'When you're done,' she continued, 'I have something to show you.' Rees nodded, his heart sinking. There was a tone in her voice that warned him he would not like this.

'Show me now,' he said.

She directed him to the hut they slept in. She'd rigged up two mosquito bars over each of the benches using the linen sheets. 'It should at least keep the mosquitoes from us,' she said.

Rees stared at the two beds in dismay. 'But where will Ruth sleep?' he objected.

'She will be staying with Aunt Suke in her cabin,' Lydia said. Although she spoke firmly and met his gaze, she twisted her hands together until the knuckles went white.

Rees sighed. Although, on the surface, their marriage continued placidly and with no obvious signs of trouble, he knew Lydia still felt the hurt left from last spring. No matter how many times he'd reassured her that nothing had happened between him and the rope dancer, he had not managed to breach the wall Lydia had erected. It wasn't that she hadn't forgiven him exactly, but she was afraid to completely trust him again. She'd frozen him out. He felt the distance between them keenly and felt alternately guilty and annoyed by it.

'Lydia.' He paused, not sure what to say. 'If it weren't for you, I would have gone home. You're the reason I came back here.' He paused and swatted at the mosquito buzzing in his ears. 'I don't like the swamp.'

'I don't either.' She smiled tentatively. 'But this isn't the time to talk. Go eat.'

Rees hesitated but when Lydia grasped his sleeve he allowed himself to be pulled out of the cabin and toward the fire.

When Neptune saw them coming, he immediately rose to slice a chunk of the pork from the haunch over the fire and drop it in a bowl. He handed it to Rees with a flourish, grinning in pride. Rees acknowledged the food with a nod and blew on the pork to cool it.

'What . . .' Lydia stopped and started again. 'We were all worried when you didn't come back right away.'

'It was a hard trip.' Rees paused, unsure what else he should say. She'd been through the swamp and knew both the beauty and the cruelty of it.

'They said,' Neptune began in a hushed voice, 'Aunt Suke said Scipio was shot.'

'He was,' Rees agreed. He watched the blood drain from Neptune's white skin, leaving it a sick ashy pallor.

'Slave takers?' Neptune whispered.

'Maybe.' Rees didn't think so though. Wouldn't slave takers have taken the body? But he didn't want to say that. Instead, he cast around for another topic. How old was this young man sitting across the fire? Sixteen? Eighteen maybe. 'Did you do well with the dice last night?'

'Nah. Lost every penny of my runnin' away money.' Now the red flush of anger swept up into his cheeks. 'I swear, Scipio has the luck of the Devil.'

Rees thought of the loaded dice in his pocket but said nothing. Toney had warned Neptune; what good would it do to remind him of that now?

Toney had no such scruples. 'Told ya,' he said as he walked past. 'As soon as you lose once, walk away.'

'What will you do now?' Lydia asked Neptune softly.

'Don't know.' Neptune stared into the swamp. 'Run anyway, I guess. Go to Norfolk. There's Quakers there to help.'

'You can work at the canal,' Toney suggested, adding mockingly, 'they'll be wanting another shingle maker now.' Lydia frowned at him as he disappeared down the hill. Rees popped the final chunk of meat into his mouth.

'How well did you know Scipio?' he asked Neptune. Neptune stared at Rees for a long moment. Then, holding up his hands as though warding off a curse, he hurried away.

Rees looked at Lydia. 'Does he know something?'

'I believe he is just scared,' she replied.

Rees thoughtfully wiped his greasy fingers on his breeches

and stood up. Maybe he was imagining it but he smelled decomposition as well as his own sweat. 'I need to bathe,' he said.

'Not by yourself,' Lydia said anxiously.

'Toney is already down there,' Rees said. 'Probably Tobias too.'

As Rees started towards the men's hut and the trees beyond it, Lydia reached out and grasped his sleeve. 'Wait. I can't follow you. Let me fetch your clean clothes.' She disappeared into their hut, reappearing a moment later with his oldest breeches and a linen shirt. She also carried the same tattered towel he'd used before – still damp – and the crock of soft soap. She handed them to Rees with a smile.

SEVEN

Toney was already in the water. He rose to the surface, the water rolling off his powerful shoulders and sparkling in his hair. When he turned, Rees saw the tell-tale scars left by the lash – but nowhere near as many as had marked Scipio's back. Tobias quickly stripped off his clothing and dove into the water. Rees undressed but he followed more cautiously, first dipping a toe in the water and then walking in carefully lest he startle a snake.

'Nothing will come near us,' Tobias shouted. 'Not with all the splashing.' He emphasized his statement by sending a wave toward Toney.

The water felt wonderfully cool. Rees ducked his head under and came up with a gasp.

They don't want for water, at least, he thought.

The air felt cold on his bare wet skin and he broke out in goosebumps. He quickly scrubbed himself with the soap and went back under the water. He would have to climb out of the water soon anyway, so he gritted his teeth and rose out of the pond. The water streamed off his body. Although it looked black in the ponds and under the trees, it appeared clear when it rolled down his skin.

He quickly toweled himself dry and dressed. While he was drying his feet, Tobias joined him on the shore. Tobias quickly dressed as well.

'What do you know about Neptune?' Rees asked Tobias.

'Nothing. He was newly arrived when I left for the north.'

For a few moments the two men sat in silence watching Toney splash around.

'Is he from the . . . what . . . the Sechrest plantation?' Rees asked.

Tobias shook his head. 'He came up from the Deep South, Georgia, I think. His wife was sold away and he followed her. She lives somewhere around here. Maybe on Grove?'

Rees turned to look at Tobias. All of these men had a story – and probably Aunt Suke did as well. Although Rees knew his friend Esther, the Shaker Sister from Zion, had escaped slavery and traveled north on foot for freedom, he had not understood that many of her people could tell similar stories. What had Tobias survived to reach his Maine home?

'Did you walk all the way to Maine?' he asked tentatively. Tobias shifted and turned to look at Rees.

'Mostly. Not always. The Quakers helped. I rode some in wagons, especially once I left Virginia.' He paused a moment, remembering. 'It was worst in Richmond. So much unrest, thanks to Gabriel Prosser. But it wasn't as bad for me as some others.' Turning, he shouted at Toney. 'Hurry up.' Rees knew the subject was closed.

Toney spent another minute or so in the water but it was too cold for prolonged immersion. And it was growing dark. Although the sun had not yet set, the shadows under the trees were reaching out to envelop the entire swamp.

Rees watched Toney climb out of the black water on to the bank. As he dressed, Rees asked, 'Did you know Scipio well?' He could not mistake the suspicious glance Toney threw at him.

'Not well at all,' he said as he hurried across the bank.

Tobias and Rees scrambled to their feet and ran after Toney. He had lied – Rees was pretty sure of that – and he wondered why.

When the three men returned to the center of camp only Jackman sat alone at the fire. 'Where's Lydia?' Rees asked.

'And Ruth?' Tobias said.

Jackman pointed to Quaco's hut. Rees and Tobias walked to the other side of the fire and stared down at the busy women.

Under Suke's direction, Ruth and Lydia were carrying armfuls of aromatic leaves into the hut. Rees continued down the slight slope and peered into the hut. The women were sprinkling the leaves over the body; the astringent spicy scent filled the hut. 'It will help cover the smell of corruption,' Aunt Suke explained when she saw Rees. He nodded. Of course. Without ice, without lime, without anything that might halt the body's decay, other measures had to be adopted.

'We'll put him to rest when Cinte returns,' Aunt Suke said decisively.

She had won the argument with Jackman. Despite the seriousness of the situation, Rees grinned. Men and women and their relationships were the same everywhere. Jackman would not be allowed to bury Scipio until Aunt Suke approved.

'You'll find the man who did this,' Aunt Suke said, eyeing Rees sternly.

'Of course,' Rees said, knowing Aunt Suke would not let him forget his rash promise.

'I'm countin' on you,' she said. It sounded like a threat.

Rees glanced at his wife just as an involuntary yawn caught her unawares. Blinking, she reached up to cover her mouth.

'Time for bed,' Rees said. He was tired too.

'Where are your dirty clothes?'

'By the water.'

'Oh, Will,' Lydia said reproachfully. 'Someone might take them. Clothing, cloth of any kind, is scarce here.'

'I'll get them,' he promised.

When they reached the camp, and Lydia went up the stairs into the hut, Rees continued on, past the hut and the fire across from it, and down the slope to pick up his discarded clothing. By now it was almost entirely dark and spooky. Something screamed close by and Rees heard the soft plop as an animal jumped into the water. He bundled up his dirty clothes and ran to the center of camp.

*   *   *

Rees had trouble falling asleep in his solitary bed. Despite the linen sheet screening him from the biting insects, he could hear them buzzing outside. Besides, it did nothing for the bites Rees had already suffered. He itched everywhere. The cuts and scratches inflicted by the underbrush he had pushed through stung. And it was cold. The thin ragged blanket assigned him was not enough to ward off the night's chill. He missed Lydia's warm body beside him. He vowed to talk to her as soon as possible.

And then there were his attempts to question Neptune and Toney. They had avoided his questions as though they were poison. Could one of them be the guilty party? Could both? Or was everyone drawing together to protect the murderer? And why would they do that?

Finally, Rees drifted off into an uneasy slumber but the sound of voices outside woke him. After tossing and turning for several minutes and feeling more and more wakeful with each passing second, he finally gave up. He crawled out from under the tent and went to the door. The coals of the fire burned a dull red, just bright enough for him to see two figures sitting side by side on the log. One was Jackman. Rees could see the stick Jackman used and although the syllables coming out of his mouth were not understandable, he inserted a 'hmmm' every now and then. The other man was just a shadow. Rees couldn't tell which of the other fellows he might be.

Rees was just considering going down the steps and speaking to them when the unrecognized man rose to his feet. A few more non-comprehensible sentences and he turned to go. As he passed by the hut he turned and looked at Rees. For a moment they stared at one another. Rees had never seen this man before. Dressed in skins and with a beard that hung almost to his waist in graying ringlets, he snarled at Rees and broke into a run. Within seconds he had disappeared into the darkness.

Rees looked back at the center of camp, but Jackman too was gone.

EIGHT

When Rees awoke alone the next morning – Lydia was already gone – he was not sure if the strange figure he'd seen the night before was real or a dream. Jackman would know. Rees crawled out from underneath the linen curtain and went to the door. He paused on the top step and looked around.

It was just past dawn and the light fell softly upon the camp. A bird erupted from a tree nearby with a raucous cry. Although something bubbled in the small pot over the fire and there was a jug of molasses beside it, no one sat by the fire. Rees went down the steps and examined the food. No coffee or even tea, a drink he usually scorned. But there was corn mush and molasses. He had not expected to see this dish, a breakfast he connected with his childhood, here. He helped himself and sat down to eat.

He was scraping the bottom of his bowl with the wooden spoon when Jackman came up and over the slope from the fields. Although Rees smiled and acknowledged the other man with a wave of the spoon, Jackman's solemn expression did not lighten. He limped to the camp center and sat in his usual place.

'I saw something last night,' Rees said. 'I don't know, maybe I dreamed it. But I thought I saw a man dressed in skins—'

'Quaco,' Jackman said. 'He live in the swamp. A slave ship crashed on the coast and he escaped into the swamp.'

'How long has he lived here?' Rees asked, recalling the man's beard.

'I don't know. More 'n seven. He saved my life. Found me in the swamp and kept me alive with beetles and turtles.' Rees gasped and Jackman nodded. 'He live wild. He refuse to wear white men's clothes and live wild. Won't speak English, only Ibo.'

'What did he want here, then?' Rees asked.

'We trade. He be bringin' game, be takin' corn, molasses, sometimes rum.'

'And where do you get rum?' Rees asked. 'Or bacon?' Jackman smiled.

'We trade with camps closer to Sechrest or Grove plantations. Or, sometimes we sneak in at night, take what we need.'

'You steal it?' Rees asked.

'We take,' Jackman corrected. 'My family worked for those things.' He pointed at the molasses to which Rees had helped himself. 'You eatin' it too, hmmm?'

Since that was true, Rees had no response. Jackman hesitated, chewing his lower lip. Finally he said, 'Um, Rees?'

Oh no, Rees thought. What now?

'I been thinkin',' he said. 'Tobias fought with Scipio. He went out with a gun.'

'Doesn't mean he's guilty of murder,' Rees said, instantly protective of his friend.

Jackman nodded gravely. 'True.'

'Neptune also went out into the swamp, also with a gun.'

Jackman nodded. 'True again.'

'And,' Rees continued, 'Scipio cheated Neptune out of the money he'd saved. That sounds like a good reason to kill someone to me.'

'But he brought in meat,' Jackman argued. 'I don't think he'd 'a had time to kill a wild pig, dress it, bring the meat back into camp *and* shoot Scipio.'

'Neptune had a gun. And it was recently fired,' Rees said although he acknowledged Jackman's point. 'Quaco?'

'Best weapon he own is a scythe. Besides, there be no reason. Quaco barely knew Scipio. Although,' Jackman added thoughtfully, 'both Ibo. Don't know if Scipio speaks Ibo though. Spoke Ibo.'

'What about Cinte?' Rees was beginning to feel a little desperate.

'He speaks Ibo—'

'No, I mean, could he have killed his brother? They left together.' He'd seen the vicious fight between Tobias and Scipio but didn't want to believe his friend had been moved to murder. Would Neptune kill Scipio over that money?

Jackman sighed. 'I want to say no, Cinte would never do that. But I know he has a temper. And I done heard stories . . .' His voice trailed away as he stared into space. 'I've seen too much of the evil men do to one another to swear Cinte be innocent. But why? Did you see bad blood between them?'

'No,' Rees admitted. 'I'd say Cinte admired his brother.'

'Right. Where's the why of it? And Cinte carried no gun. It would make more sense if Scipio shoot Cinte.'

Rees nodded. He couldn't imagine the slender stripling overpowering his bigger and much stronger brother.

'Besides, Cinte always sneak off to see Sandy at the plantation. He think we don't know. But he never miss an opportunity.' Jackman shook his head. 'Most likely he left his brother as soon as he could.'

'Couldn't be jealousy, could it? Scipio and Sandy—'

'No. She wasn't interested in him. Too old and too poor. Nor Cinte neither. More's the pity.'

Rees wondered about this Sandy. He would like to meet the girl but since he didn't see the possibility of that happening, he turned his attention to the more pressing problem. 'What happens to Tobias now?'

Jackman sighed. 'I don't really know. I suppose, for now, he better stay here in camp, hmmm? I'll watch him, until we figure out what happened.' He looked over at Rees. 'Tobias better hope you as good at finding murderers as he thinks you is.'

And how was he going to do that? Rees wondered. He would continue to try, but after both Toney and Neptune had evaded Rees's simple questions – did they know Scipio well – Rees doubted anyone would answer any questions. And why should they? Rees had no official standing and no leverage. And how would he speak to Sandy? Or to the overseer with whom Scipio had had words? Or anyone else, in fact?

'Maybe a slave catcher shot Scipio,' Jackman suggested hopefully. 'Someone not connected to this village at all.'

Rees nodded doubtfully. 'Maybe. I wondered that too, at first. But see, here's what I was thinking. A slave catcher, if he killed Scipio, would want that two hundred dollar reward. But the body was just left lying there.'

Jackman nodded. 'To collect the reward, the killer would have to take the body. Or something from it. To prove that Scipio was dead, hmmm?' He paused.

'You think it was personal?' Rees asked. That was his opinion, in fact.

Jackman nodded. 'I don't think his murder be about the reward at all.'

Rees sat back. He had seen the dislike between Scipio and Tobias. Could he have committed the murder? For the first time, Rees seriously considered the possibility. Tobias was a reserved fellow, so Rees did not know him that well. Although he didn't want to believe it, yes, Tobias could have killed the man he saw as a rival. Anger and jealousy were always powerful spurs.

Women's voices sounded from somewhere across the camp. Rees stood up and saw Ruth and Lydia following Aunt Suke out of the woods behind Quaco's hut. All three carried baskets full of greenery. They came up the slope and went into Aunt Suke's home.

When Lydia and Ruth exited, they both came straight to the fire. Lydia dished out a bowl of mush for Ruth and then for herself. Yawning, she sat down and poured molasses liberally over her food. As Ruth did the same, Lydia said to Rees, 'Aunt Suke pulled us out of bed before daybreak to hunt herbs in the woods.'

'Herbs?' Rees repeated. All he saw when he looked at the mass of vegetation was green weeds.

'Aunt Suke is a healer,' Ruth said unnecessarily, taking the molasses from Lydia and drowning her mush with it. Ruth was a wonderful baker, at least she had been, and now Rees remembered she had a sweet tooth.

When she put the jug down Jackman picked it up, pulled out the stopper and peered inside. 'Almost gone,' he muttered. 'Time for another raid on the Sechrest plantation.' And he looked very hard at Rees.

He regarded the jug in Jackman's hands and wondered if he could join a raid on another man's farm. He knew he would find it difficult to do so. Although Jackman viewed it as taking what had been produced by his brethren, Rees saw it as stealing. But hadn't he eaten food that had been acquired that way? He wasn't sure of the right thing to do in these circumstances.

'Are we weeding the sweet potatoes again?' he asked Jackman.

'I have dishes to wash,' Lydia said, nodding at a battered keg, cut in half, and filled with slimy gray water.

'We have laundry to do too,' Ruth said.

Yawning once again, Lydia rose to her feet and shuffled to the keg with her wooden bowl. Turning, she stretched out a hand for Ruth's bowl. She pushed it through the water and jumped back with a little scream.

Rees leaped to his feet. 'What's wrong?'

Without speaking, she turned back and held up the bowl, full of water and with a dead mouse inside.

Jackman laughed. 'You in the swamp now.'

'Here,' said Ruth, pushing her ungainly body upright. 'Let's empty the water and add fresh. The pot is empty; we'll heat water in it and that will help clean it and give us hot water.'

NINE

'We'll weed while it's cool,' Jackman said. Leaning on his cane, he limped by Rees's side to the field. Cool? No, Rees thought, but he held his tongue. It was cooler today than it had been previously, although by Maine standards it was still as hot as a midsummer's day. He experienced a stab of homesickness. In a month or so Maine would see its first snowfall, probably a dusting but perhaps not. The air would be cold and crisp, and Rees would spend much of his time chopping wood for the oncoming winter.

'Does it ever get really cold here?' he asked.

'Course. We see snow. But not this early. In another month

– November or so – we'll see frost. Maybe some ice on the water.'

Rees had not realized how much a man of the north he was until now.

As they passed Quaco's hut, Rees smelled the faint taint of corruption leaking from under the mound of leaves covering Scipio. Even at a distance of fifty feet. Cinte had to arrive home soon, before Aunt Suke was forced by natural processes to allow the burial. Rees had no way of knowing how far this camp was from the canal or how long it might take Cinte to transact his business and return.

And that was *if* Cinte remained free and alive.

Meanwhile, Rees had a murderer to find. As he started walking again, Rees said to Jackman, 'I have to talk to Quaco.'

'He had nuthin' to do with Scipio's death,' Jackman said without turning around. 'I told you, Quaco couldn't have murdered Scipio.'

'He might have seen something,' Rees said.

Without answering, Jackman continued walking. Rees chose to drop the subject for now but knew he would have to return to it again.

Jackman and Rees passed over the ridge and started walking between the corn rows. Although the cornstalks were brown, the various squashes were still bearing. The leaves were only beginning to brown. But still, despite the over-bearing smell of the lush vegetation, the stink of corruption lingered in Rees's nostrils.

As they approached Tobias, Rees saw he had been weeding like a demon; the heaps of discarded plants marked his passage along the rows. He had taken off his shirt and sweat glistened on his back. Rees saw the lash scars; Tobias too had been whipped although not as brutally or as often as Scipio. A spasm of sick fury took hold of Rees on behalf of this man, his friend. How could anyone justify owning another human being and treating him so?

'God damn them!' he said between his teeth.

'Steady,' Jackman said, pausing. Rees stopped beside him.

'But they—' He gestured with his hand toward Tobias.

'Your anger won't help him now. It'll only point out the

whippin's and remind him he couldn't stop it.' Jackman flicked his eyes at Rees 'It's humiliatin' for a man to know he can't protect himself, hmmm? Ignore the scars. Let Tobias keep his dignity.'

Rees tried to imagine himself held down, unable to prevent the strikes of the lash, and shuddered. 'Why don't more of you run north?' he asked in a low voice. When Jackman did not immediately respond, Rees added, 'Why didn't you?'

'Our families are here. My wife,' he pointed at the edge of the swamp, 'still lives at Sechrest plantation. And some of us, me for example, can't go. I can't run.' He tapped his foot with his cane. Looking around him with some pride, he added, 'So, we have our own farm here.'

'But you're always in danger from the slave catchers,' Rees pointed out.

'Yes. But they don't usually come this far in. We been here seven years now. We have it good. Some of the maroons closer to the plantations dig caves. Spend all their days underground. Here we're outside, livin' and answerin' to no man.'

Rees mulled that over for several seconds. Finally, he blurted, 'Then why doesn't your wife—?' He stopped, realizing he was prying. Jackman shrugged.

'Bein' free means the freedom to starve, hmmm? Some people are too scared to take that chance and some days I don't blame 'em.' Raising his stick, Jackman shouted, 'Tobias. Hey.'

Tobias looked up and, spotting Rees, quickly grabbed his shirt and put it on, turning aside his face so Rees couldn't see his expression. Tobias was ashamed. Rees pretended he'd seen nothing and said, as he came upon the other man, 'Looks like you've spared me this job, Tobias. Thank you.'

When Tobias didn't speak, Jackman said, 'Hard work taketh away wrath, hmmm.'

'I didn't kill Scipio,' Tobias said, glaring at Jackman. When the headman didn't speak, Tobias turned beseeching eyes upon Rees. 'You believe me, don't you?'

Although Rees wasn't sure he did, he said yes.

Jackman didn't answer. He looked around at the squashes. 'Not much summer left,' he muttered.

'Jackman!' The call came from the top of the ridge. It was

Neptune, waving his arms to attract attention. 'It's Sandy. She's here.' Jackman sighed. Without glancing at either Rees or Tobias, he began trudging through the fields, back the way he'd come, toward Neptune. Rees, who wanted to meet Sandy and ask her about Cinte, followed. Tobias started to say, 'But what about—?' He stopped talking and hurried after the other two men.

'It's her baby,' Neptune said as they approached him. 'He sick.'

The first thing Rees noticed about Sandy was her clothing. She wore shoes and, instead of faded rags, was attired in a neat pink gingham gown with a brown cord around the hem. Her dark hair, although now tousled by travel, had been arranged in ringlets over her ears.

She was very pretty with large, long-lashed dark eyes, a small pert nose, and full pink lips. Her complexion was a creamy white – Rees had seen farm workers in Maine tanned far darker than she.

'My baby,' she wept.

Aunt Suke flipped back a corner of the blanket to reveal a small white face blotched with red. 'Stay back,' she told Rees and Lydia. 'He's sick.'

'They have the smallpox at the plantation,' Sandy said. Unlike the men who had brought her here, and who had melted back into the swamp as soon as they saw Rees, she glanced at him, unafraid. 'I'm Sandy Sechrest.'

'Will Rees,' he said, gesturing first at himself and then at his wife. 'My wife, Lydia. I had smallpox as a child.' He'd been too young to remember but his mother had told him often enough.

'I have had it, as well,' Lydia said as she crossed the yard.

'Are you sure it is the smallpox?' Aunt Suke asked, examining the toddler's face and chest. Sandy shrugged.

'A lot of people are sick,' she said.

Aunt Suke carried the child to her hut, Sandy following closely behind.

'I suppose you think Sandy is very beautiful,' Lydia said, a tremor in her voice. Rees turned to look at her.

'She is pretty,' he agreed. 'But how old do you think she is? Fifteen or sixteen? Just a year or two older than our daughter. Sandy is a child.' If pressed, he would have chosen Aunt Suke as the more beautiful of the two. She had the advantage of exotic looks and a fully formed personality. But he thought it wiser not to confess this opinion. Since his attraction to the rope dancer last spring, he and his wife had not recovered their easy and affectionate relationship. He was glad now to see Lydia smile. Lowering his voice, he said, 'You don't like her?'

'I don't know her. But she is . . . arrogant in the power of her beauty over men.' Lydia sounded more pitying than disapproving. Rees glanced at her curiously, but before he could question her the door to Aunt Suke's hut opened. Sandy, ejected from the hut, drifted toward the group.

'Sandy,' Rees said. She looked up, her sad expression changing to a faint smile.

'He want to ask you some questions,' Jackman said. 'About Cinte.'

'Cinte?'

'He left a few days ago,' Rees said. 'Did you see him?'

'Did he visit you at the plantation?' Jackman put in.

Sandy shook her head. 'No. But I wouldn't have seen him. I left home several days ago. I visited my Aunt Bet first an' she told me to come here. So, even if Cinte stopped, I wasn't there.' She turned to look over her shoulder at Aunt Suke's closed door. 'Everyone's down sick.'

Rees nodded and exchanged a disappointed glance with Jackman. They still had no word of Cinte and no way of knowing what might have happened to him.

The door to Aunt Suke's hut opened and she stepped outside. 'Abram be sleeping,' she said, coming forward to put a hand on Sandy's arm. 'Don't worry, child. He don't have the smallpox. It something else, something not so dangerous. He must be kept in darkness so you both should stay with me for a few days before goin' home.'

The tension went out of Sandy's shoulders and she flung herself into Aunt Suke's arms. 'Thank you, thank you. Aunt Bet told me you'd know what to do.'

'You'll be here for the funeral,' Aunt Suke said.

'Funeral? What funeral?' Sandy asked. Aunt Suke frowned at Jackman and the others.

'You didn't tell her?'

Jackman shrugged.

'Who?' Sandy reached out and put her pale hand on Jackman's darker arm. 'Who?'

'Scipio,' Aunt Suke responded. Sandy stared at her aunt for a few moments as though she were trying to understand.

'Scipio?' she repeated dumbly. 'Not Scipio.' Aunt Suke nodded. Sandy burst into noisy tears. Aunt Suke pulled the girl into her arms and began patting her back.

'What happened?' Sandy asked. Aunt Suke flashed an accusing glance at Rees.

'Not sure yet.'

Rees looked guiltily away from her gaze, feeling that he should have somehow already solved Scipio's murder.

'Does C–Cinte know?' Sandy sobbed.

'We waiting for him to return,' Aunt Suke said. Sandy sobbed harder.

Rees, feeling awkward, stepped back a few paces to join his wife. Before he could say anything, Aunt Suke looked at Lydia over Sandy's head. 'Would you help Ruth start the laundry as we planned? I'll come as soon as I be finished here.'

'Of course,' Lydia said, stepping away from her husband. She followed Ruth, who had already started down the hill with her basket of dirty clothes, almost running. Rees saw his shirt and breeches in the pile disappear past Quaco's hut.

Rees stared after his wife, involuntarily taking a few steps in her wake. She'd left him without a word or a smile. He felt the emotional distance between them keenly, and it stung.

'Women,' Tobias said. Rees glanced at the other man, catching an expression of yearning on his face as he stared longingly after Ruth, and clapped Tobias sympathetically on the shoulder.

TEN

Cinte arrived a day later, appearing on the camp side of the thicket as the others were sitting down for the midday meal. Sandy saw him first and jumped up with a little scream. Like Jackman and Aunt Suke, Rees and Lydia followed Sandy's pointing finger to the figure approaching the camp.

Cinte approached the fire with leaden steps, frowning with concentration. As Neptune and Tobias started toward Cinte, Sandy called his name. He looked up. Breaking into a wide smile, he began to hurry.

'What are you doing here?' he asked Sandy. He seemed unaware of both the men. 'I stopped at Sechrest; they said you was gone.'

'Abram is sick,' Sandy said. 'I brought him here, to Aunt Suke.'

Tobias helped Cinte remove the sack on his back as Neptune reached for his arm. But Cinte only paid attention to Sandy. He grabbed her hands and held them tightly until she gently but firmly pulled them from his grasp. Rees, looking at Cinte's red-tinged hair, wondered if he had fathered Sandy's fair-skinned babe.

'How'd you get past Peros and Toney, hmmm?' Jackman asked.

Cinte laughed. 'I know the back way, a' course.'

Jackman still looked unhappy and Rees didn't blame him. Slave catchers could appear in the village just as easily as Cinte had.

'Was it successful, your trip to the canal?' Aunt Suke asked, shaking her head at Neptune. He was grabbing at Cinte's arm and trying to break into the conversation. 'Let Cinte settle a bit,' she added softly, turning to frown at Neptune.

'Yes.' Cinte took his pack from Toney and opened it. He pulled out a paper of tobacco, a jug of rum, a bag of rice and, finally, a bar of soap and a packet of herbs, both of which he handed to Aunt Suke. 'I got cash money too, for the banjo I sold. And orders for two more.' He shot a pointed look at Sandy, but she looked down at the ground and pretended she didn't see it. Rees looked at Lydia who was watching Sandy and Cinte with concentrated attention. Since she was much better at understanding the nuances of relationships, he hoped she could explain what he had just witnessed.

'Come and eat,' Aunt Suke said, gesturing to the fire and the center of the camp.

'How is the canal comin'?' Jackman asked.

'Makin' headway,' Cinte replied as he took the bowl of stew from Aunt Suke.

'White man's folly,' Jackman said. 'Spend a lot of time digging ditches through the swamp so they can float their boats.' Then, realizing he had spoken in front of a white man, he threw a nervous glance at Rees, who simply nodded.

For a moment everyone was silent, waiting for someone else to speak first. Ruth looked as though she might weep. Tobias took her hand.

'What's a banjo?' Rees asked Cinte.

'A musical instrument. Here, I'll show you.' Jumping to his feet, he raced to the westernmost hut. Everyone sitting in the circle exchanged glances. 'You have to tell him,' Sandy hissed.

'Let him rest a bit,' Aunt Suke said, adding sternly, 'don't you tell him, girl. Not yet.'

Cinte returned with two objects in his hands. One was a long neck ending in a smooth bowl. The other had the same structure but skin was stretched across the bowl and strings ran from the bottom, up the neck to the top. Pegs stuck out on both sides of the top.

'They're beautiful,' Rees said truthfully.

'I prefer hickory for my banjoes,' Cinte said. 'Oak is too heavy. Maple is a good second choice.' He ran the fingers of his left hand over the strings. They made a jangly yet harmonious sound. Bending his head over the instrument, he listened as he turned the tuning pegs. Once he was satisfied, he used his fingers to pick out a melody.

'Amazing,' Rees said, forgetting for a moment the terrible news they still had to impart.

'I make 'em and I know how to play, but Scipio is the master . . .' His voice trailed away, and a startled expression crossed his face. 'Where is Scipio?' When no one answered he looked around at the group. 'What's the matter? Everyone been strange since I got home.'

'Child,' Aunt Suke began.

'Scipio dead,' Jackman said.

'Dead? I don't believe it.' He cast a quick look around the circle. 'Is this a joke?'

'Someone murdered him,' Neptune said, leaning forward. Sandy gasped and stared at Aunt Suke accusingly.

'Why didn't you tell me?' she demanded.

'Shot,' Neptune continued. 'In the back.'

'No.' Cinte shook his head. 'It can't be. I don't believe it.' Tears began running down his cheeks.

'We got the body,' Jackman said.

'I want to see him. I have to see him.' Cinte put the banjoes aside and stood. 'Where is he?'

'Maybe you shouldn't . . .' Jackman began.

'He won't believe his brother is dead until he sees him,' Aunt Suke said. Jackman flapped his hand at her.

She rose to her feet. Gesturing to Cinte, she started down the slope, east toward Quaco's hut. Rees quickly joined her and after a minute Lydia followed.

The stink of corruption was noticeable a distance away from the hut and it only grew stronger as they approached. Cinte put one arm across his nose as he went up the steps. Rees watched Cinte brush the leaves away from the face. Stepping back, he uttered a howl like an animal. Aunt Suke went in and took his arm to draw him outside. But he shook her off and ran up the slope, directly to Sandy. Aunt Suke watched him from the doorway. She sighed and, shaking her head, went back inside to adjust the aromatic herbs over Scipio's face.

'Cinte is in love with Sandy,' Rees said, watching Cinte reach for the girl, clutching at her like a drowning man.

'Yes. But she doesn't love him,' Lydia said. 'She's fond of

him, I think. As fond of him as she was of Scipio. But she doesn't love him.'

'She just a foolish girl,' Aunt Suke said as she left the hut and shut the door behind her. 'The old mistress at Sechrest, Miss Minerva, spoiled her. Treated her like a pet. Almost a friend. Since Sandy a seamstress, they talk about fashion all the time. Well, Sandy grow up beautiful. Next thing you know, she with child.'

'Abram,' Lydia said. Aunt Suke nodded.

'Who's the father?' Rees asked.

'Sandy won't say. Could be the old master, Robert, but I think it his son Gregory. Sandy start prancing around like she better 'n everyone else. Won't even look at Cinte. He could take her north.' Aunt Suke shook her head, her face creased with worry. 'Now Miss Minerva die and Master Robert marry a new wife and she already starting to pick on Sandy. Miss Charlotte jealous, you see. And Sandy think she safe.'

Rees and Lydia turned in unison to look up the slope. Both Cinte and Sandy were weeping but she was holding him away from her, out of her embrace, with her hands on his shoulders.

While the men went to the graveyard to dig a grave, Aunt Suke directed the women to the banks of the swamp to finish the laundry. 'Everyone should wash and put on clean clothes for the funeral and the burial,' she said firmly. 'As a sign of respect.' Lydia joined the women, looking quite odd in a boy's breeches with a laundry basket in her arms. After a few seconds, Rees followed them down the slope, past Quaco's hut, and over a narrow path to the black water beyond.

Drying clothes festooned the tree branches and shrubs. Ruth was already kneeling by the water, slapping the soapy body linen with a board. She was singing something rhythmical, a nonsense song accented on the beat with the thud of the paddle. Aunt Suke handed Lydia a sliver of soap, carefully shaved from the bar brought into camp by Cinte. Although Rees knew Lydia had not washed clothes in this manner before – the Shaker Sisters used a large wash tub and copper cauldrons of heated water – she took the soap and joined Ruth by the stream.

Lydia began submerging the clothes, piece by piece, into the water. When they were saturated, she ran the sliver of soap lightly over the cloth. Then the clothing went to Ruth to be pounded with the paddle before rinsing. Dyed by the black water to a light brown, the clothing still did not look clean.

'Go help the men,' Aunt Suke told Rees. 'Less you want to take up a shirt and start soapin'?' Rees shook his head and, spinning around, he started up the slope. The sound of pounding followed him, growing fainter with distance and the thick muffling effect of the vegetation around the camp.

Rees followed the sound of voices and found the men in the small cemetery outside the village, on another knob of dry ground. A fence of twigs sunk into the ground marked the perimeter of the graveyard. The graves themselves were marked with wooden crosses made of sticks. Carved bone or wooden items, feathers, even a metal coin or two with a hole punched through it hung from the crosses. Rees stared at them.

'Charms,' Jackman explained. 'To protect the spirits of the dead and speed 'em on their way.'

Rees nodded although he wondered what superstitious nonsense this was.

Cinte was digging the grave, shoveling as fast and furiously as a madman, the dirt flying on to the small hill in an almost continuous shower. When he began to tire, Jackman insisted the young man surrender the shovel to another. Toney jumped into the shallow hole while Neptune helped Cinte climb out.

Once the other men had each taken a turn, Rees volunteered to help. Neptune handed him the shovel and, jumping into the hole, he began to dig. The soil was stone free but heavy with moisture and after only a little while his back and arms ached. His hands were starting to develop several blisters. But he continued on, digging until Jackman said 'enough'. By then the shadows of late afternoon were beginning to crawl over the graveyard and the grave was several feet deep. Rees looked at the white swellings on his hands and hoped the wounds would have time to heal before he had to work on the loom again.

'Here.' Toney, his dark skin filmed with perspiration and glinting gold in the sun, leaned down with his hand outstretched. Rees grasped it, his wounded hands stinging with Toney's salty sweat, and climbed painfully out of the hole. When a breeze sprang up ruffling the leaves, Rees stood still with his arms wide and let the air cool him.

'Aunt Suke sent me,' Lydia said, walking up the slope toward them. 'It's time for supper.'

Rees turned to look at his wife. He stared. He'd gotten used to seeing her in breeches and a shirt. Now she was wearing a dress of brown gingham. It was faded and worn, and too big for her, but it was a dress.

'So many of these graves are for babies,' Lydia remarked, looking around her at the small crosses. 'So many.'

'I hope Ruth—' Rees stopped and glanced anxiously at his wife.

'I know,' Lydia agreed with a nod. Neither one wanted to admit they were afraid she would continue to refuse to leave with them. Childbirth was always dangerous, but here? Lydia shuddered involuntarily.

Rees turned and examined the new grave. More digging should be done; it still was not deep enough.

'Come on,' Lydia said, tugging at his hand. 'Someone else can finish this. Let's eat before all the food is gone.' Rees nodded, groaning. Besides the blisters on his hands, the muscles in the backs of his legs and his lower back ached. And his skin stung with sunburn. The sun here was so much stronger than it was in Maine.

As Lydia fell into step behind the group, Rees threw one last glance behind him at the shadowy grave. Then he hurried to catch up.

Aunt Suke was in Quaco's hut, attending to Scipio. When Rees peered in, he saw her using chalk to coat the soles of the corpse's feet and the palms of his hands. 'What are you doing?' Rees asked.

'My mother told me they always colored a dead body's soles and palms,' she said. 'They didn't use chalk.' She cast a rueful glance at the white chunk in her hand. 'But I do my best to keep to the old ways.' She sighed. 'Tell Jackman I be up directly.'

Rees joined the quiet group sitting around the campfire and accepted a bowl of stew. From the amount left in the pot he guessed that most of the people here had little appetite.

Aunt Suke was not the only absence. Rees looked around and spotted Cinte, seated in front of the men's hut, sobbing as he carved something from one of his leftover pieces of hickory.

'He's making his brother's cross,' Sandy said, her own eyes filling with sympathetic tears.

Rees felt moisture burn his eyes as well. It wasn't fair – it wasn't fair at all – that Scipio should make it to a bit of freedom only to be murdered.

ELEVEN

Despite Cinte's naked grief, he approached Sandy after supper and asked her to walk with him. Rees watched them as they walked away from the campfire. Although he couldn't hear the couple, he could see from Cinte's impassioned arm waving that he was making some emphatic case. Sandy kept shaking her head. Rees felt for both of them: for Cinte who was so obviously in love with the girl, and for Sandy who did not feel the same.

'I wish she'd say yes,' Aunt Suke muttered. Lydia looked at the other woman questioningly. 'Cinte can make a living making banjoes. Gregory Sechrest never goin' to take care of her.'

'Why won't she say yes?' Rees asked.

'Because she young and foolish,' Aunt Suke said flatly.

'She think Cinte not good enough for her, hmmm?' Jackman said.

'Cinte'll never have enough money for her,' Neptune said.

'He could,' Jackman said. 'Up north. And they fair enough to pass.'

'Pass for what?' Rees asked in confusion.

'White. They can pretend they white and get treated white.' Neptune, so pale Rees wondered if he too could pass for white, stood up so abruptly he kicked dirt at the fire and sparks rose into the air. Turning, he strode to the hut he shared with the other single men and disappeared within.

'I'm sorry,' Rees said, even though he didn't know what he'd done wrong.

'Passing be complicated,' Jackman said.

'Neptune look too African to pass,' Aunt Suke explained. 'White skin but African features.'

'One drop of African blood and you considered black,' Jackman added.

'Besides,' Toney put in, 'if they go north as white folks they have to leave their families forever.'

Rees nodded, pretending he understood. None of what he'd just heard made any kind of logical sense to him.

'No point discussing this,' Aunt Suke said brusquely. 'I think marrying Cinte would be wise, but she won't hear of it. Too taken in by young Master Gregory. She seem to think she be young and beautiful forever. She spoiled.'

She rose abruptly to her feet and began gathering the used dishes.

'I'm sure she has her reasons,' Ruth said in a soft voice.

'She's young,' Lydia said soothingly. 'She may change her mind as she grows up.'

'If something else don't happen to her first,' Aunt Suke said, her voice quivering.

Rees tried to imagine the fear and sorrow Aunt Suke was feeling but couldn't quite grasp it. In his view, something bad had already happened; Sandy had had a baby with no chance of giving Abram a father.

'Do you think that Gregory is toying with her affections?' Lydia asked, her thoughts mirroring Rees's.

'I know he is,' Aunt Suke said. 'Offering her pretty jewelry and that after his mother spoiled her with pretty clothes. It can't last. I know it.'

'And here she comes,' Jackman said as Sandy ran toward them. She seemed on the verge of tears. Although at first she ran toward Aunt Suke, the cry of her fretful baby drew her instead toward the hut. Sandy disappeared inside and after a moment Aunt Suke followed.

Cinte, his shoulders slumping in defeat, followed Sandy for a few steps before turning and heading down the slope to the men's hut.

'I'll see to him,' Toney said, rising to his feet. Rees went after him and caught him by the elbow.

'Toney. What do you know of the brothers?' he asked softly, hoping a different question would pry out some information. Toney looked at Rees.

'They good together.' Pulling his arm free, he ran down the slope after Cinte.

Sighing in frustration, Rees returned to the fire. Lydia had risen to her feet and was staring at him. He put Lydia's arm through the crook of his elbow. He felt the slight tug of her resistance but she did not pull away. They said their good nights and went to the cabin. It was time for bed.

Sleeping on a hard bench only exacerbated the soreness of an afternoon spent digging a grave. Rees fell asleep quickly, but his sleep was a restless one, punctuated by wakeful periods. He simply could not get comfortable. Finally, long after dark had fallen and the camp was still, he rose and went to sit on the steps of the hut. During one of the times when, tossing and turning on the hard bench, he'd tried to fall asleep once again, he thought he'd heard footsteps walking outside. But now all was quiet. The fire had been banked and when he looked around it appeared everyone was inside sleeping.

Rees shifted on the steps; they were just as hard as the bench on which he'd been sleeping. Or trying to. What was he even doing here? He'd expected to leave – with Ruth – by now. But she still did not want to go, and he'd foolishly promised Aunt Suke he would look into the murder. In fact it was beyond foolish, because no one here, except Aunt Suke, seemed interested in identifying the murderer. So far, everyone was stonewalling him.

After a moment, he stood and stepped off the stairs. It was

cooler now; humid but cooler. Rees walked around to the back of the hut and washed his face and hands in the barrel. As he was drying his face on his shirt, he heard something. He paused and listened. Among the noises of the night he heard a faint grunting. He peered around the back of his cabin but the back of Aunt Suke's hut protruded even further to the rear and he could see nothing. The darkness was absolute. Now very curious, he walked around the backs of the buildings and stared into the night.

Quaco's hut, fifty feet or more distant, was a dark shape. Nothing stirred. Rees swept his eyes over the eastern edge of this encampment but saw nothing until he spotted something – or someone – moving to the south.

He couldn't tell who it was, no matter how he strained his eyes to peer through the gloom. Here in the swamp, the night-time darkness had a solidity to it that was impenetrable. Rees couldn't see even a glimmer of a pale shirt, the light brown of tow linen, which everyone wore. Everyone but Quaco. Of all the men, he was the only one who did not wear a shirt and breeches, choosing instead to cover himself with animal skins.

Had Quaco met with Jackman again? Or was he trading with Jackman for food? But Rees couldn't see enough to know. After a few more seconds peering into the night, he gave up and returned to his seat on the front steps. Despite Jackman's reassurances, Rees still thought Quaco could have murdered Scipio. He certainly went where he pleased with no one the wiser. Rees decided he must talk to Quaco, whether Jackman protested or not.

Now that Rees had washed himself, he found he was wide awake. He did not feel like returning inside the stuffy shack just yet, despite the steady drone of the insects around him. It was peaceful out here. Rees looked up at the waxing moon. It would be All Hallows' Eve in three weeks. He would be gone by then. And late October was hard to imagine here. For a man who had spent his life in Maine, where early October was cold, here it still felt like summer.

A bird call nearby, very sudden and very loud, made Rees jump. Most of the noises in the swamp were muted by the thick vegetation, the water and the spongy ground, but this bird sounded as though it had flown right over Rees's head.

He stood up, preparing to go inside the hut, but a flare of light on his left drew his attention. Someone carrying a candle had come out of the men's hut. In the faint light, Rees could see pale skin. Either Neptune or Cinte then. With an audible belch, he disappeared around the back of the hut. Rees thought the figure was too tall to be Cinte, who was as small and slight as a boy. So that person was probably Neptune. Rees was sure of it when the young man lifted his face to the sky before extinguishing the candle and disappearing into the hut. For those few seconds, the light was sufficient to make Rees's identification certain. Now he considered Neptune. He certainly had had reason to murder Scipio, who had won all of his hard-earned money from him.

'Better get some rest,' Aunt Suke's voice came out of the darkness. She came up the slope from the swamp with a lantern in one hand and a basket resting on the opposite hip. 'Tomorrow we bury Scipio.'

'You were in the swamp now?' Rees asked in amazement.

'Some herbs are the most powerful when picked by the light of the moon.' Aunt Suke's voice came out of the darkness. The candlelight picked out the curve of one cheekbone. 'Go on to bed now.'

Instead of obeying, Rees stood up and crossed the shadowy ground. 'Aunt Suke,' he said, 'tell me about Scipio.'

She put her basket down. 'You lookin' to see who might have killed him?' she said with a shrewd glance in his direction. He nodded.

'As you requested,' he said. 'Not that I've received any help at all.'

For a moment she stared into the darkness. Then, with a sigh, she said at last, 'Most anyone. He liked his women. Well, you seen that. He cheated at dice.'

'Seen that too,' Rees said.

'He could be provoking. Taunted everyone but me 'n Jackman. Mostly the other men took it in good part. But I saw Toney punch Scipio once. And Peros ran in the other direction when he saw Scipio coming.'

'Neptune?' Rees asked.

'Him too. Scipio taunted him; Neptune has white skin but not white enough to pass.' She sighed heavily. 'Jackman was right to send Scipio back to the canal. Scipio upset everyone.'

'And then there's the reward,' Rees said.

She snorted. 'Most of us don't care about that.' Picking up her basket, she said, 'Go to bed. Rest for tomorrow.'

Rees started for the cabin but after a few steps he turned. 'Thank you for speaking with me. No one else is willing.'

'I asked you to help,' she said. 'And the others . . . well, give them time. You only been here a few days. They don't trust you yet.'

'You did,' Rees said. He couldn't see her face but he heard the rustle of her clothing as she turned.

'They can't look past the color of your skin. I see into a person's soul.'

Thoughtfully, Rees returned to his own hut. He didn't know which made him more uneasy, the distrust of the men surrounding him or Aunt Suke's assertion that she could see through him.

But Aunt Suke was right; tomorrow would be a long and difficult day. He pushed his other concerns aside. He would need his rest.

As he climbed the steps a snarling scream, like a woman's agonized shriek, pierced the night air. The hairs rose on Rees's arms.

'Bobcat,' Aunt Suke said as she opened her cabin door.

The night no longer felt so peaceful. What was he doing, out here in the darkness? Rubbing his hands over his pimpled arms, Rees stumbled over the last step and went inside. Lydia, clad only in her petticoat, was sleeping peacefully. Rees glanced at his solitary bed and shook his head. He crawled under the blanket beside his wife and put his arms around her. She murmured a sleepy protest. Suddenly very tired, Rees closed his eyes and slept.

TWELVE

Rees's odd night-time adventure seemed like a dream when he awoke the following morning. Lydia was gone but she had put his washed and dried, although wrinkled, clothing by the bench. Rees put them on and went outside.

Only Jackman was seated by the fire at the center of the camp. He was shiny with moisture and water droplets glittered in his hair like glass beads. 'Where is everybody?' Rees asked.

'Bathing.' Jackman pointed at the slope which led past the men's hut toward the area where Rees and Toney had bathed a few days before. Rees stared at his hands. Soil from digging Scipio's grave yesterday still rimmed his nails. The blisters, fringed with dirt, had come out in all their puffy white glory. They stung. Maybe cool water would help take away the burn. And he could use another bath. He turned and started for the swamp.

He could hear the bathers before he saw them; the splashing and muffled laughter. Didn't they realize today was Scipio's funeral? But when Rees stepped through the screen of trees and saw the dark water beyond, he understood. They'd never had much chance to play so now, despite the seriousness of the occasion, Neptune and Peros were flinging handfuls of water at one another and howling with laughter. Only Tobias, always the outsider, and Toney, older than the others and of a more sober disposition, were keeping their distance.

Rees approached Cinte who was seated on the bank. He offered Rees a sad smile and handed him a sliver of soap. Dark circles shadowed Cinte's eyes and he'd bitten his lip so often he'd left a bloody cut. He looked worn down by grief. 'Look at them,' he said, gesturing at the others. 'Playing around.' He picked up his ragged breeches and half-heartedly swirled them in the water. The white dust upon them came off and formed a scummy pale streak in the black liquid. 'And my brother murdered.'

'They don't mean any harm,' Rees said. 'Don't think less of them.' Then he paused and eyed the men playing in the water. Which of them could be the murderer?

Cinte sighed. After a few seconds he nodded. 'I guess. If Scipio were here and I was lyin' dead, he'd be jokin' and splashin' water at everyone. He never missed a chance to have some fun.' Rees put his hand on Cinte's shoulder, wondering at the bitterness in his voice.

'You seemed . . .' Rees paused, struggling to find the right word. 'Close. Affectionate even.'

'We grew up together, till he was sold away to Grove.' Cinte smiled. 'We didn't get along as boys. He made my life a misery, callin' me ghost boy and milk jug and such.' He pulled on his wet breeches and tattered shirt. 'Sometimes he made me so angry.'

'Sounds like brothers,' Rees said. He thought about his sister Caroline. Crazed with resentment and malice, she had almost caused Rees's and Lydia's deaths. For their own safety, his family had to flee their farm and seek refuge with the Zion Shakers. 'It's surprising, isn't it, how you can love someone so much and at the same time they make you so angry you can almost hate them?'

Cinte shot Rees an astonished glance. 'That exactly how it be,' he said. He sounded as though he didn't believe a white man could feel the same as he did. For a few seconds he stared over the water. 'Scipio defended me too, sometimes. He always be big and strong. And when I was ready to run – I wanted to make a life I could take Sandy to – he came with me. Showed me the way.'

'You'll miss him,' Rees said. Cinte's face crumpled and, standing up, he pulled on his ragged pants and fled. Rees could hear him sobbing as he pelted up the hill. Rees's own eyes moistened in sympathy and he wiped his sleeve across them. He'd meant what he'd told Cinte about loving and hating at the same time. Sometimes he still missed his sister.

But there was no point in thinking about it. Stripping off his clothes, he stepped into the cool water. He did not want to be splashed or engage in any of the play, but he didn't go very far away from the others either. The scream he'd heard last night reverberated in his head and although he knew a bobcat was unlikely to come into this pool, he remembered Tobias's warning about snakes and alligators.

'I've got to leave and help Ruth,' Tobias said now, just as if he'd heard Rees thinking about him.

Of course he did, Rees thought as he waded through the water toward his friend. Tobias spent every minute he could find with Ruth, even though she'd made it plain she did not want his company.

'I've been meaning to ask you,' Rees said. 'Do you know why Ruth refuses to come home with us?'

Tobias glanced around at the other men but no one was paying attention. 'I don't know,' he replied in a whisper. But his gaze darted away from Rees's.

He does know, Rees realized. Or at least suspect. What had happened between Ruth and Tobias?

Before Rees could press Tobias, he started for shore, saying loudly, 'Ruth and me are going to help Aunt Suke shroud Scipio's body.'

Saying Scipio's name out loud depressed the mood. With a quick glance at the others, Neptune ducked under the water once again before joining Tobias on the bank. After a moment Toney followed. Peros spent another minute or so splashing around – until he saw Rees approaching with a determined expression. Then Peros fled, splashing through the water as quickly as he could, until he stood next to Toney on the muddy shore.

Rees did not want to remain in the opaque water by himself. He hurriedly rinsed off the soap and scrambled out. He brushed most of the water from his body with his shirt and quickly dressed. Then he gathered up his discarded clothing and joined the other men as they climbed the slope. He was not the most patient of men, but for now he had no choice but keep his questions to himself.

As they approached the village center an anguished scream split the air. Rees took a few steps toward the wild cry, just in time to see Aunt Suke lunge from the hut in which Scipio's body had been placed.

'He's gone!' Aunt Suke shouted. 'Scipio's body done disappeared.'

THIRTEEN

After a few seconds of shocked paralysis, Rees broke into a run. He topped the rise, sprinted past Jackman, and raced toward Quaco's cabin. Aunt Suke stood at the bottom of the steps. Although she was no longer screaming, she was twisting her skirt in her hands. The door to Quaco's hut hung ajar, partly open and partly closed, and from the outside the mound of leaves still appeared to be covering a body. Rees bounded up the steps and flung the door wide.

Light flooded the interior through a hole in the back wall where at least two boards, probably three, had been removed. From this position, it was apparent that the leaves covered cornstalks heaped up into a semblance of a body. The area where Scipio's head had lain, and from which Aunt Suke had brushed away the leaves, lay a stuffed burlap sack. Rees pulled at it. Pieces of branches, leaves, and acorns flooded out upon the bench.

Rees walked to the back of the hut and looked through the opening. At least one of the roughly cut boards lay on the ground. Although Scipio's body was gone, and Rees really hadn't expected to see it lying on the ground, the vegetation behind the cabin had been crushed by a weight. Scipio's weight probably. A faint silvery trail of trampled brush led away from the hut, north into the swamp.

Rees grunted and went to the door. As he went down the steps, Jackman limped to the hut. Pointing with his cane, he asked, 'Scipio truly gone?'

'Yes,' Rees said.

'Why?' Lydia asked, patting Aunt Suke's back to comfort her. The healer had her arms clenched tightly across her chest. 'Why take a dead body?'

'My grandmother would blame angry spirits,' Aunt Suke said in a subdued voice. Lydia threw a quick glance at her husband, but he did not need her prompting to speak.

'No angry spirit took Scipio's body,' he said. 'A human agent stole it and took it into the swamp.' Aunt Suke turned to face Rees.

'You sure?'

Rees nodded. 'I can see the trail. The killer dragged Scipio into the swamp on one of the boards he tore from the back of the cabin.'

Jackman stamped his cane hard into the dirt. 'I'll be . . . Someone done stole that boy's body for the reward,' he said.

Rees thought, recalling the people he'd seen wandering abroad the previous night. Aunt Suke he dismissed, at least for now. But Neptune? Rees had seen him outside last night. And he'd been in the swamp, with a gun, when Scipio had been shot. Rees decided he would question him today.

Then there was Quaco. Rees didn't realize he'd spoken aloud until Jackman replied in a sharp voice.

'He didn't do it. He don't have no reason.'

'How much was the reward?' Rees asked. 'Two hundred dollars?'

'And what would Quaco do with money?' Jackman scoffed. 'He wants nothin' to do with white men. He don't wear white men's clothes, eat white men's food or even speak white men's language. What good would money do him?'

Rees hesitated. Although he thought Quaco could use the reward to buy his freedom, maybe return to Africa, he chose not to argue the point. Instead he said, 'He might have seen something. He visits this village after dark, doesn't he? I heard something last night; I think someone removed the body then.'

Jackman stared into space and Rees could see his mouth moving. He wanted to protect Quaco, as well as the other men, but he couldn't fault Rees's logic.

'We need some answers,' Aunt Suke said, scolding Jackman. He glanced at her and, after a moment, nodded his head.

'I'll ask him,' he said.

'Let me,' Rees said. 'I know the questions I need the answers to.'

'He won't talk to you, hmmm? And he don't speak English anyway.'

'You can translate, can't you?' When Jackman did not reply, Rees added, 'He may be our only witness. It stands to reason the man who took Scipio's body is also the killer. So, if we want to catch him . . .' He let the suggestion hang there. After a few seconds, Jackman nodded reluctantly.

'I'll hang the flag. He can meet us in the swamp. If he choose to. He don't obey me, you know. He does what he want.'

Knowing he had wrung as much of a concession from Jackman as possible, Rees thanked him and turned his attention to the hut. Since he had already examined the interior, he walked around to the back. He hoped to find something there that would help him.

The hut's floor had been elevated about three feet from the ground, a distance not too great to jump. As Rees had noted before, the vegetation here had been trampled almost flat. But he didn't see any footprints or scraps of cloth; nothing that would help. That's when he realized only one of the boards removed from the back of the hut was still here, lying on the ground.

After a careful examination of the undergrowth all around the cabin, Rees guessed that the killer had lashed the other boards together to form a sled. The body had been tied to it for easy transport. That would explain the wide trail of broken stems and flattened leaves going downhill, a line of destruction far greater than what could be explained by drag marks from a body. Rees surveyed the damage leading down the incline and shook his head in reluctant admiration. The killer must have been very determined; even with the sled pulling a body of Scipio's size and weight through the tangled vegetation could not have been easy. Who among the men in camp was strong enough? Toney? After Scipio, he was the tallest and strongest. Or could it have been two men working together?

Wishing his Iroquois friend Philip was with him, Rees started following the trail down the slope.

Keeping a close eye on his feet lest he step on a snake, Rees tracked the trail of crushed vegetation into the swamp. At first the path was obvious, but as he went further away from the village, and away from the small area of dry ground,

the marks in the ground vanished. As long as trampled underbrush and broken stems guided his way he could follow. But
when the killer began floating the body through the pools, and
the imprint of the boards disappeared under the black water,
Rees began to struggle. Once he reached a large expanse of
water glimmering under the trees, he was blocked.

He looked around in frustration but there was no indication
where the murderer – and the body – might have gone. Rees
turned, intending on retracing his steps. He realized for the
first time that he was alone in the swamp. There was no sign
of the village and he could hear only the sounds of insects
and bird calls and the wind through the leaves.

For a few seconds panic threatened to engulf him. Then
he realized he could see the marks of his passage through
the woods. His footsteps, now filling with water, were still
visible. He began following them, finding a broken branch
on one side or bent leaf on the other as he went. Finally,
after what seemed like hours, the forest thinned. Open sky
shone blue through the topmost branches. He hurried toward
what he thought must be a clearing. He saw a gray wall
ahead of him, a fence of boards. As he approached what
appeared to be a palisade, he realized he was looking at the
back of Quaco's hut.

'Give me a Maine pine tree forest any day,' Rees said aloud
as he went up the grade. Lydia was waiting for him by the
hut. She moved to intercept him.

'Where have you been?' She brushed back her hair with a
shaky hand. 'I wouldn't have known where you were gone
but for Aunt Suke. You could have been lost.'

'I followed the trail left by the killer.' Rees elected not to
mention his moment of panic. 'Don't worry; I was fine.'

'What were you saying just now?'

'Nothing. Homesick,' he said, realizing only after he'd
spoken how true it was.

'I miss the children.' Sighing, Lydia looked away. Rees
thought he saw the shine of tears in her eyes. 'We've been
away days longer than I expected we would be.' Rees nodded.
He guessed they would be away for longer still, but didn't
want to say so out loud.

'I wish you'd gone with someone. Or at least told someone. You could have been lost forever.'

'I wasn't lost. I always knew where I was,' Rees lied. He paused, wondering how much to admit.

'What?' Lydia looked at her husband very sharply. He exhaled.

'I didn't tell someone or bring them with me because I don't trust anyone. Anybody here could be the murderer.'

'There's me,' Lydia said quietly. 'You could have told me.' Rees stared at her for several seconds.

'But . . .' He stopped. He could have pointed to her long skirts but he knew that would be only an excuse. She was correct; he should have told her. Of everyone here, she was the only one he trusted.

'I feel . . .' She paused, staring into the sunlit trees as she gathered her thoughts. 'You only remember me and our family when it's convenient. Otherwise, you choose to put us aside and behave as a single man would.'

'That's not true,' Rees objected, feeling her words sting.

'Yes, it is.'

'I just get so curious.'

'Does that explain the rope dancer?' she snapped. Rees flinched.

'A mistake I've begged forgiveness for many times,' he said, annoyed because he knew she was right.

'And you would have left me home this time if I hadn't insisted.' Lydia sighed. 'Are we—?'

'There you are,' Sandy said, breaking into the conversation. Both Rees's and Lydia's heads turned in unison. Sandy stood just outside Aunt Suke's hut, her toddler on her hip. His skin was still mottled with a red rash, now scaly as it healed, but he was laughing and gurgling. Astonished by the child's fair hair and skin, even lighter than he'd realized, Rees stared. 'Aunt Suke asked me to find you. Breakfast's ready.' She put the little boy on the ground. He began staggering toward Lydia.

'Good,' Rees said, realizing he was very hungry. He started up the incline but then, remembering Lydia's words, he stopped and turned around. Flushed with tangled feelings of guilt and anger, he held out his arm. Instead of taking it, she bent down and swept Abram up into her arms. He wailed and reached out to his mother. Sandy took him. 'Lydia?' Rees said. After a moment's hesitation, she slipped her hand into the crook of his elbow.

Sandy went ahead as Lydia and Rees walked more slowly. When they caught up to Jackman, they slowed their steps even further to match his. He threw a quick look at Rees. 'What did y'all find, hmmm? I saw you go into the swamp.'

'The murderer – or murderers – took Scipio's body out of the back of the hut,' Rees said. 'Two or three of the boards were removed and lashed together. I suspect Scipio's body was tied to those boards and pulled out into the swamp. Probably into some hiding place.'

'He got away then,' Jackman said.

'I didn't find the body,' Rees admitted. 'But it had to be someone from the camp. He knew where Scipio was.'

'Possibly.' Jackman paused. 'Simple way to know; who's missin' from camp?'

'Missing?' Rees repeated.

'If someone took Scipio's body for the reward, he'll be missin' from camp. No one is goin' to take Scipio's body and come back here, are they?' Rees looked at Jackman in approval.

'Of course not,' he agreed. 'Good thinking.' All they had to do was see which of the men had left camp. Then they would know the identity of the killer. It seemed so easy.

FOURTEEN

While Aunt Suke dished out bowls of hominy, Rees and Jackman kept their eyes fixed on the men coming to breakfast. A somber Cinte arrived first, but he was quickly followed by Toney and Peros. Tobias ascended the slope last – but he carried a string of freshly caught fish, already gutted and scaled. He handed the fish to Aunt Suke and sat down beside Ruth. She rose to her feet and moved to the other side of the circle, leaving Tobias and Cinte seated next to one another. Stricken, Tobias caught his lower lip in his teeth, but he didn't speak.

That was everyone but Neptune. Rees and Jackman exchanged glances. But just as Rees was ready to declare Neptune the murderer, in he raced. 'Are we havin' a meetin'?' he asked when he found himself the focus of several eyes.

'Where have you been?' Jackman demanded.

'Thinkin'.' His gaze swept around the circle of men. 'About the murder.' His eyes lingered on Tobias, who was staring longingly across the circle at Ruth.

Tobias started and blurted angrily, 'How many times do I have to tell you, I didn't kill Scipio.'

Neptune shrugged but he didn't apologize.

'That's everyone,' Rees said, turning to Jackman in consternation.

''A course, other men know of our village,' Jackman said. 'Some of them shingle makers like Scipio.'

Rees imagined some ghostly figure lurking around the village, first to shoot Scipio and then slipping into the hut to steal the body. He supposed it was possible. Unlikely, but possible. It was certainly a more palatable scenario than assuming Tobias was guilty. 'I knew it wouldn't be simple,' Rees muttered.

'When is my brother's funeral today?' Cinte asked Aunt Suke. Everyone froze and for a moment it felt to Rees as though time itself had stopped moving.

'Where did you go this morning after bathing?' he asked carefully. 'You left earlier than the rest of us.'

'Into the swamp. I went to cut some hickory for my next banjo. It helped clear my head.' Something of the stillness with which the others were holding themselves seeped into Cinte's awareness. He blinked a few times before saying, 'What happened?'

Jackman and Rees looked at one another. Neither wanted to be the one to speak.

'Someone stole Scipio's body,' Aunt Suke said gently.

'Stole? What do you mean, stole?' Cinte looked from one person to another.

'His body is missing from Quaco's hut,' Rees said. 'Someone
tore some boards off the back and spirited his body away.'

'No, no, no!' Cinte jumped to his feet. Pacing, he began
sobbing noisily. Rees glanced at Lydia. From a proper
Bostonian family, and raised to abhor such public displays of
emotion, she was staring at Cinte in mute disbelief.

Neptune rose to his feet and put his arm around Cinte's
shoulders, murmuring into his ear for comfort. After a few seconds
Cinte shrugged the arm away. Aunt Suke whispered something to Sandy and she rose to her feet. Going to him, she
took his arm and began speaking to Cinte in low soothing
tones. He turned and grasped her tightly, sobbing into her
shoulder. Although tears were running down her face and
she held her arms out, they remained stiff and straight. She
did not embrace him.

Rees could not watch them; him clutching her and yearning
for a comfort she was unwilling to give. It was too painful,
and reminded him too powerfully of his own hurtful behavior.

Turning to his wife, he whispered, 'I'm sorry. I'll try to
do better.'

Lydia directed a startled look upon him. 'This is hardly the
time,' she said in a low voice.

Rising to her feet, she joined Ruth and Aunt Suke. Rees
could not help glancing at Tobias. They exchanged a glance
of shared understanding.

'I'm goin' down, check the flag,' Jackman said to Rees.
'Y'all want to come?'

Rees jumped to his feet and followed Jackman down the
slope.

The scrap of white cloth Jackman had hung at the edge of the
swamp was gone. As Jackman began limping along the edge
of the vegetation, Rees asked, 'What now?'

'We find the flag.' Jackman limped as quickly as his injured
foot would allow, his cane thudding softly on the soft ground.
'Quaco always put it in the same place.'

They left the village behind, stepping into the thick green.
Rees immediately felt as though he had left all civilization
behind. But when he looked over his shoulder he could see

light through the trees, the sunlight pouring down upon the fields.

Although they were not far from the village, it felt as though they were deep in the swamp. The scrap of white hung on a branch, the pale cloth obvious against the green. Rees couldn't see Quaco at first; he was hidden within a thick clump of vegetation. 'Quaco?' Jackman said, following it up with a string of syllables that bore no relation to any language Rees had ever heard. A response in the same language came from behind the leaves. Jackman glanced at Rees and said something else. With a quivering of vegetation, Quaco's dark face peered through the greenery. He was much shorter than Rees, so short he wondered if Quaco was kneeling or squatting. Ritual scarring dotted his forehead. But it was his glare, filled with hatred, that shocked Rees the most.

'What do you want me to ask him, hmmm?' Jackman shot a glance at Rees.

'He was at the village last night, yes?'

Jackman turned the question into more of those strange words and Quaco, never removing his gaze from Rees, nodded.

'Did he go into the center of the village?'

Quaco shook his head. He responded with one clipped sentence.

'He says no,' Jackman translated. 'He says he never left the southern end. We exchange goods there,' he added, explaining for Rees's benefit.

'Did he see anyone near the hut? His hut?'

This time Quaco's response was a bit longer. Rees did not need Jackman's translation; Quaco was shaking his head as he spoke.

Although Rees could not explain why – Quaco never removed his angry aggressive gaze from the white man before him – Rees suspected the man in the bush was not being truthful. Something was off. 'Ask him if he heard anything,' he told Jackman.

Frowning and reluctant, Jackman nonetheless complied but Quaco did not respond. Instead, the leaves moved back into the space where his face had been and, with a few soft sounds, he disappeared into the swamp.

'He's gone,' Jackman said.

'I see that. Does he know someone took Scipio's body?' Rees asked, his voice rising with frustration. Jackman nodded.

'I didn't expect him to talk to you,' he said, a hint of disapproval coloring his voice. Rees should, his tone implied, be grateful Quaco met with him at all.

'He knows something,' Rees said, wondering if the wild man had heard enough to know who had broken into the hut and taken Scipio's body.

'Maybe.'

'Do you know where he lives?' Rees wanted to find Quaco and shake all the truth from him.

'No. No one does. He come and go as he please.' Jackman frowned at Rees. 'He told you all he's goin' to, hmmm?'

That was most likely true. For a moment Rees struggled with the desire to demand a search. But even if he could force Quaco into agreeing, and that wasn't certain, a search would probably not succeed, and it would irritate Jackman as well. Rees did not want to do that. Like it or not, Jackman was the headman here. Rees had to find another way to find the man who'd stolen the body. With a sigh, he nodded in compliance.

Rees wrestled with the problem as he followed Jackman through the trees, past the animal pens and into the fields.

'Does everyone here speak that language? Ibo, is it?'

'No.' Jackman laughed. 'Cinte pretty good. Scipio a little. But Toney from the Deep South and he don't know his father's language. And Peros speak somethin' else; he a Bushman.'

Rees, who had always viewed the black population as one solid homogenous mass, stared at Jackman in amazement. He had never thought of them as separate cultures with different languages and customs.

'Mos' likely the murderer one of the other shingle makers,' Jackman continued after a moment of silence. 'You'll never find him.'

'If the murderer is there, then I need to go to the ditch and ask questions. Speak to the foreman, that Jacob you mentioned, and anyone else who might be involved,' Rees said.

Jackman stopped walking and turned a horrified look on Rees. 'No. You lost your reason? You can't do that.'

'If I don't,' Rees said, 'Scipio's murderer will go free.'

'Hundreds of men work there. You don't know which ones is a maroon and know about us.'

'I have to try.' Rees considered pointing out that Jackman couldn't stop him but decided not to. Yet.

'Y'all get lost?'

Rees inclined his head in assent. 'Someone will have to guide me.'

'Who? He be risking capture. And what's to prevent you from betrayin' us?'

'You know me now. Do you truly believe I would do that?' Rees asked, offended.

'Better Scipio's murderer go free than the rest of us get captured,' Jackman said stubbornly, his voice shaking with passion. Rees turned to look Jackman in the eye and took an involuntary step forward. Jackman, face twisting with alarm, stumbled backwards. His bad leg gave way and he tumbled to the ground.

When Rees extended a hand to help the other man up, he hesitated.

Rees had not understood the depth of Jackman's fear before then. Of course, Rees thought, *he* would never break his word. But Jackman had no reason to trust a white man. Shocked, Rees stepped back. He felt strangely ashamed and angry too. He was not a slave owner and he prided himself on keeping his word.

'I would never betray you,' he said. 'I gave you my word. But this is your village and I will abide by your decision.' He couldn't help adding, 'Although I think you're wrong.'

'Is everything all right?' Tobias shouted. Looking up, Rees saw Neptune and Tobias standing on the ridge at the top of the fields and watching.

Jackman reached out and clasped Rees's hand. When he was on his feet again, he looked over his shoulder and said, 'We fine.'

Together they climbed the slope.

All the women – Aunt Suke, Ruth, Sandy and even Lydia – were gathered outside the healer's hut. Abram, clad in a shabby long-sleeved dress, was toddling from one woman to another and giggling as each woman turned him and sent him staggering across the circle. Although only a few healing blemishes marked his cheeks, his hands were still red with rash.

Aunt Suke was passing around a clay pot of something white. Lydia too was chewing, a meditative expression on her face. Rees peered at the substance in the pot; it looked like chalk or clay. 'Eat more,' Aunt Suke said to Ruth. 'You with child . . .' Her words trailed away when she saw the men approaching.

'What is that?' Rees asked suspiciously, staring at the white piece in Lydia's hand. Almost guiltily, she put it back in the bowl.

'White clay,' Aunt Suke said. She glanced at Lydia; she shook her head slightly. Rising gracefully to her feet, Aunt Suke said, 'We heard y'all shoutin'.'

'He wants to go to the canal,' Jackman said. Lydia gasped and turned a horrified glance on her husband.

'Through the swamp?' she asked, her voice rising. No one answered her.

'I want to question Jacob,' Rees corrected. 'And any of the men who might know of this village.' Aunt Suke regarded him for a moment.

'Go to the fire,' she said finally. 'I'll meet you there.' She took the pot of clay and disappeared with it into her hut.

Jackman looked at the men and jerked his head toward the fire.

FIFTEEN

'I say it's impossible,' Jackman said when Aunt Suke joined them. She squeezed in between Sandy and Jackman. When Abram reeled to her, she patted his head and sent him back to his mother.

'Do you want the murderer to escape justice?' Rees asked the head man. He frowned and shook his head in distress.

Aunt Suke turned her level gaze upon Rees. 'Why?' she asked him. 'Why do you want to go?'

'It is possible Scipio's murderer came from outside,' he replied. 'Jackman thinks so anyway.'

'Of course,' Jackman said. 'Scipio's murderer not one of us.'

Rees and Lydia exchanged a glance. Neither of them agreed with Jackman.

'Are we havin' a meetin'?' Cinte asked, coming up the slope to join them. Rees shifted over to make room on the log. Although Cinte was no longer pacing and crying, his face was still flushed and swollen.

'Rees wants to go to the canal,' Jackman explained. 'Talk to people there.'

'What?' Cinte turned to look at Rees. 'You'd do that?'

'Maybe the murderer is that Jacob, the overseer,' Rees explained. 'Or one of the other shingle makers who know about this place here.' He gestured around him. 'I want to talk to them.'

'Y'all won't make it,' Cinte said with certainty. 'Not without help. And even then . . .' As Abram, giggling and with arms outstretched, staggered to him, he impatiently pushed the child away. The little boy would have fallen if Rees hadn't grabbed him and put him back on his feet. Sandy jumped up and swept her child into her arms. She glared at Cinte.

'It's too dangerous,' Jackman said. 'I can't let you go.'

'He must,' Cinte said. 'For the truth.'

'I don't want his death on my conscience,' Jackman said.

'That it then,' Cinte said mournfully. 'My brother's truly gone. We can't even bury him.' His eyes filled with tears.

Lydia clutched at her husband's sleeve and breathed a sigh of relief. But Aunt Suke, turning to Rees, inspected him thoughtfully.

'You feel this is necessary?' she asked him.

Rees nodded. 'I do. If only to prove the innocence of everyone here. But this is your village.' He looked at Jackman, acknowledging his authority with a nod. 'My wife and I are only visitors.'

'I want justice for Scipio. We all do.' Jackman looked around at his small band. 'But we must protect this camp. Our freedom. And the freedom of all those who reach us, hmmm?'

'No justice for my brother,' Cinte said bitterly.

'Let him go,' Aunt Suke said. When Jackman began to argue she lifted her hand commandingly. He fell silent. 'We need to know the identity of Scipio's murderer. What do we be, as a people, if we let a murderer go free? What is our freedom, so hard-won, worth if we allow such a crime to go unpunished?' She looked at every person sitting with her, meeting their eyes with a fierce gaze of her own. No one dared speak. 'Allowin' fear to prevent us even tryin' to find a murderer will lay a stain on us. If this man think he can find the murderer, we should help him. Anyway, he the right color to question that Jacob.'

'But what if he don't come back? What if he tells them about us?' Jackman flung his hand toward the swamp in a gesture encompassing the white world.

Aunt Suke smiled and threw a glance at Lydia, sitting with her hand tucked into Rees's arm. 'He love his wife. He'll come back for her.'

'He'll get lost in the swamp,' Tobias said anxiously, speaking for the first time. 'He doesn't know the paths.'

'I'll need a guide,' Rees agreed. Nobody volunteered. Cinte bit his lip and stared at his bare feet.

'I'll take him,' Tobias said at last.

'No,' Jackman said emphatically. 'You good friends. Besides . . .' He didn't add that Tobias was one of the men suspected of murdering Scipio, but his meaning was plain.

'We both will be leaving our wives behind,' Tobias argued.

'Ah, y'all don't know the swamp anyway,' Cinte said, raising his eyes.

'Then who, hmmm?' As Jackman looked at the other men, Toney turned his gaze to the swamp and Peros suddenly found a nearby bush very interesting. Cinte looked at Sandy.

'Will you wait?'

'She be here a few more days,' Aunt Suke said when Sandy did not speak. 'Her baby not well enough to travel yet.'

Heaving a huge sigh, Cinte said, 'I'll go. It's my brother murdered. More 'n anyone, I want his killer caught. Besides, I know the swamp best.'

'Now, wait a minute—' Toney began. Cinte talked over him.

'I go to the canal and sell banjoes all the time.'

'That's true,' Jackman agreed.

'But we need to leave right away,' Cinte said, looking at Rees. 'Get gone, get home sooner. We shoulda left this mornin'. Now we'll be sleepin' in the swamp.'

'How long will it take?' Rees asked.

'A day and a half. If we hurry. Scipio . . .' He stopped and swallowed convulsively. 'He could make it in less 'n a day.' As his eyes reddened he added with a smile, 'Those long legs of his.'

'Eat first,' Aunt Suke said. 'This be the last hot food until you return. And I'll put up some food to carry.'

'Take the pennyroyal salve,' Lydia said to Rees as she rose to her feet. 'Keep the bugs away. I'll fetch it.' She disappeared into the hut.

Cinte pulled Sandy to one side. 'Will you wait until I get back before goin' home?' he asked.

'I don't know.' Her eyes went to one side. 'I have to return to Sechrest. They'll be lookin' for me.'

'Please.'

Sandy bit her lip. 'All right. I'll try.' Rees saw the girl's reluctance but Cinte grinned with happy relief. Despite her numerous refusals, he had not given up hope she would marry him.

Shaking his head, Rees followed his wife into the hut.

Lydia had spilled the contents of his satchel on the bed. From the litter of freshly dried clothing, she plucked the jar of salve and the drawstring bag of coins and handed them both to Rees. He shook most of the coins into Lydia's hands.

'I'll take some,' he said. 'But I'll leave the majority with you.' He thought that if he did not return from this dangerous trip, she would have enough funds to reach home. He put the salve and the drawstring bag into his satchel.

'If you don't come back for me, I might not ever escape this dreadful place,' Lydia said, as though he'd spoken his fears aloud. 'Don't forget our children, Will.'

'Of course I won't,' he said with false heartiness. 'Don't worry. I'll return in a few days. Three at the most.' Then he hugged her tightly to him. 'Don't worry,' he repeated.

'I won't,' she said. But he knew she lied. And he was glad that she cared enough to worry for him.

Before they left the cabin, she reached up and kissed him.

Aunt Suke had heated up the hominy from earlier that morning. Rees choked down a few mouthfuls, tasting the bitterness of the lye. By now, it was as solid as a brick and there was no milk to dilute it. Cinte was already waiting, a banjo strapped to his back on top of a sack. Aunt Suke gestured to Rees and made a circling motion with her finger to turn him around.

'Something to eat,' she said as she pushed a few items into his satchel. 'You be fine with water.' She chuckled a little. 'All through the swamp. Here some ash pone, some cooked beans, and a few sweet potatoes.' Rees felt the weight of his pack increase with each offering.

'Let's go,' Cinte said. 'You know we can eat from the swamp.'

Rees turned to look at Lydia. She stared straight into his eyes for a few seconds before spinning around and running into the hut. Tobias, his face creased with worry, held his hand up in goodbye.

Then Rees followed Cinte down the slope, through the brambles, and into the swamp.

SIXTEEN

Cinte set a rapid pace but Rees followed easily. His legs were longer for one thing but, even more importantly, it was cooler now and he felt less sluggish. Fall was coming. The leaves were turning and beginning to fall. And Rees began to realize that Cinte, and probably all of the people who walked through the swamp, did not strike out randomly through the vegetation. It looked as though Cinte was following a definite path.

'How do you know where to go?' Rees asked. Cinte turned to look at Rees.

'There are trails. The animals always know. We follow their trails.'

Rees looked around him at the ground he and Cinte walked over but it looked no different to him. Cinte laughed. 'You have to learn to see the signs. Learn the paths.'

They walked a little while in silence before Rees spoke again. 'How did you meet Sandy?' Cinte threw a quick glance at him.

'Known her since we were babies. Both born on Sechrest plantation.'

'So, you grew up together?' Rees asked.

'Sorta. She a house slave. Miss Minerva – she dead now, from lockjaw – took Sandy into the house and taught her sewing. But I still seen her, at church and funerals and weddings.' Cinte smiled. 'She was a funny-looking girl.'

'She's a beauty now,' Rees said. Cinte nodded emphatically.

'And sweet. We be gettin' married soon.'

Rees did not reply. He thought of Sandy's obvious reluctance and her baby, fathered by a different man. He suspected Cinte would be doomed to disappointment.

'Do you have any ideas who might've killed my brother?' Cinte asked.

'No,' Rees said. 'Do you?'

'Not really. Everyone liked my brother.'

Rees recalled Scipio's booming laugh and zest for living and nodded. 'I believe it,' he agreed.

'What about the shingle makers? Who might also know of the village?'

'I show you them,' Cinte promised. 'There's only a couple.' He paused for a few seconds before adding, 'I don't know why any of them would slog through the swamp to murder Scipio though. He helped them. But Neptune now? Scipio won his runnin' away money. That makes more sense to me.'

Rees nodded slowly.

By late afternoon, the shadows were creeping over the swamp. Rees had stopped paying attention to his surroundings. As long as he followed Cinte, the footing remained fairly dry. Rees was beginning to think longingly of the food in his pack

when suddenly Cinte turned and grabbed Rees's arm so tightly
his nails went through the linen shirt.

'What—?' Rees began.

'Quiet,' Cinte commanded, dragging the other man under
the root ball of a downed tree. It smelled of wet leaves and
damp dirt but at least it was relatively cool. Rees imagined
insects dropping upon him and crawling under the collar of
his shirt. He shuddered.

'Listen,' Cinte whispered, his lips barely moving.

Rees held his breath, straining to hear. Dogs bayed in the
distance and then, as the barking grew louder, he began to
hear the sounds of men. Although Rees couldn't understand
the words, he could hear the shouting. A few minutes later the
echo of a gunshot reverberated through the trees.

Cinte was trembling uncontrollably. When Rees looked
over, he saw Cinte's head was bent and he had wrapped his
arms around his knees.

They waited long after all sounds of the slave takers ceased
before leaving their shelter. It was growing dark. Rees knew
they wouldn't be able to travel much further today.

Since Cinte was still frightened; he did not light a fire. They
had to make do with stale corn pone and the remains of a cold
sweet potato. As Rees took the food from his satchel, Cinte
leaned forward and spoke for the first time in an hour or more.

'Save half for tomorrow,' he said. 'You'll be just as hungry.'

Rees nodded and meticulously divided the food in half. In
reality he was not very hungry right now. Although no longer
as terrified as he had been the last few hours, his stomach still
had not settled.

'Slave takers?' Rees asked softly. Cinte nodded.

'Although they don't go into the swamp as far as our village
– haven't yet so far anyway – they come into the swamp
regular. Especially here where the slaves be workin' on the
canal. Sometimes they catch a maroon. Sometimes just a man
who take it into his head to run.'

Rees tried to imagine living with such fear day after day
and shivered. He would like to think he could be as brave as
Scipio, who had kept running away until he succeeded, but
doubted he could be.

Rees and Cinte did not approach the construction area until the following day just after noon. They had been able to hear the activity for some time before that: men's shouts and a rhythmic chant. By then Rees was hungry and footsore. His shoes had gotten wet early on and had never dried. Although he'd brought extra stockings south, they were with Lydia in the hut in the village.

The pennyroyal salve had proven only moderately effective and Rees was covered with bites.

Although he had done as Cinte suggested and divided his food stores in half, he'd eaten the remaining brick-hard ash pone for breakfast. Now he was so hungry he felt faint.

'Don't worry,' Cinte consoled him. 'We'll eat in camp. And there's a store.'

The only thing that kept Rees going was visualizing that store.

Cinte halted a good distance away from the canal, too far away to see the open space with the felled trees. 'Go straight from here,' he told Rees.

'Aren't you coming?' Rees asked nervously. Cinte shook his head.

'I don't want to meet Jacob.' He pointed right. 'I be travelin' east, to the digger camp.'

'I'd rather you came,' Rees said. Cinte looked at Rees almost pityingly.

'Jacob knows I be an escaped slave. Most of the overseers here, they tolerate me. But that could change.'

Rees stared at Cinte who was as fair as Rees himself. So fair, in fact, he had stopped thinking of Cinte as a black man. He was just Cinte. 'But you . . .' Rees stopped. He did not know what to say.

'Don't matter how white I look,' Cinte said bitterly. 'Don't you know? One drop black blood make me black. Sandy too.'

Rees shook his head in disbelief. 'No one would know – or care – in Maine,' he said.

'We not in Maine. And Jacob knows me. He might turn me over to the slave catchers, depending how he feels.' Rees recalled hiding from the slave catchers the previous day and nodded in understanding. Cinte smiled. 'Now you

see. I'll meet you at the store.' Turning, he vanished into
the undergrowth.

Rees faced the sounds of men working and began walking
toward the noise.

Once he could see the empty sky where the trees had been
cleared, Rees traveled more quickly. Soon he could see the
empty space on the other side of the underbrush. Finally
he stood just within the thick vegetation. Two more steps
and he would leave the safety of the swamp behind.

Two white men were standing a few feet ahead of him.
One, the talker, carried a rolled scroll and was dressed in
the newly fashionable trousers. The other, clad in muddy
boots up to his knees and a tattered shirt, was smoking a
cigar. Although he appeared to be listening to the man Rees
assumed was the surveyor, his eyes never left the ditch and
the men laboring inside it. As he looked at those diggers,
Rees felt ashamed for complaining about his discomfort.
They stood chest high in swamp water swirling with mud.
Foot by painful foot, they were shoveling a narrow trench
through the soggy soil. And they weren't alone in the
water either. Someone shouted and a few seconds later a
snake, lifted up by the shovel, came flying on to the bank.
The snake opened its mouth, revealing a white interior.
Cottonmouth. The cigar-smoking man stepped forward and
shot the creature in the head. The report of the pistol shot
reverberated through the trees. Rees could not prevent the
tremor that ran through him.

How many of these men digging here died from these
conditions?

He must have made a sound because the two men standing
in front of him turned to look behind them.

Swallowing nervously, Rees stepped out of the underbrush.
'I'm looking for Jacob,' he said.

The cigar smoker's eyes swiveled to Rees as he took the
cigar out of his mouth. 'You found 'im.' He waved the cigar
around his head. 'Damn flies,' he said. 'Only thing keep 'em
away is smoke.' A heavy black beard covered his chin and
throat and Rees wondered how he could stand it in this
heavy humid air. 'Who are you and what do y'all want?'

Rees had been considering a variety of approaches but had discarded every one. Now he said simply, 'I am looking for Scipio.'

'Which one? Got five or six here.'

'Must be the Scipio who didn't show up,' the surveyor said. 'From Grove plantation, yes?'

'Ah. Big Scipio. That so?' Jacob asked, turning to Rees.

'Yes.'

'Must be he did somethin' real bad you come all the way down here lookin' for 'im,' Jacob said. He looked around. 'Did you walk here?'

'No. Brought my wagon. But had to leave it at – uh – Grove plantation. It was a longer walk than I expected,' Rees added truthfully. Jacob grinned.

'I see. They sent you here.' Sticking the cigar back into his mouth, Jacob spoke around it. 'Well, you had a wasted trip.'

'I guess Scipio isn't at Grove either,' put in the surveyor.

Rees shook his head. 'So, he's not here either?' Just as though he didn't know Scipio was dead.

'Lazy bastard ain't turned up for a couple of days,' Jacob said.

'Lazy?' the surveyor interjected. 'I thought he was one of your best and fastest shingle makers. He helps the others make quota.' Jacob scowled at him.

'Is there anyone I can talk to?' Rees asked. That was his true purpose for visiting the canal.

'Any of you seen Big Scipio?' Jacob shouted at the men in the ditch. A chorus of 'no' greeted his question and Jacob turned his attention back to Rees. 'Your best bet is to find his brother and ask 'im.'

'Cinte?' Rees said and then wished he hadn't spoken when Jacob threw a sharp glance at him.

'You know 'im, huh?'

'Light-skinned?' Rees asked vaguely, trying to recover. 'They told me at Grove Scipio had a brother.'

'That's one of the Cintes. Got a whole mess of 'em. Scipio's brother makes banjoes? He comes around here sometimes. Ask 'im. He might know. Although they argue plenty.' Jacob grinned, exposing stained and broken teeth. 'If you know where *he* is.'

Rees knew where Cinte was in a general way but elected not to mention it. Instead, shaking his head, he asked, 'Would you please direct me to the store?'

Jacob looked surprised but pointed at a roughly made bridge, hacked logs tied together, over the ditch. Nodding his thanks, Rees made his way over the soggy ground. The conversation started up behind him once again. The discussion, as far as Rees understood, was the path of the next leg of the canal.

As he crossed the rickety span Rees looked down at the trench and the men laboring within it. Some of them glanced up at him but most of them kept their eyes on their shovels and the water that swirled around them chest high.

The walk to the store took longer than Rees expected. He followed the ditch for almost ten minutes before he saw the first signs of a camp. First one cabin, little more than a lean-to, and then another. Some were roofed with shingles, other with branches, but all of the habitations were linked by the rough bridges over the muddy ground. Swamp vegetation had grown up in the spaces between the structures.

Although some of the shacks exhibited signs of occupation – a metal cup hanging from a string, a carved stool, a quilt flung to the bottom of the bed – they all were so decrepit they appeared ready to fall down. These primitive buildings would certainly not provide decent shelter through the winter; that explained why the digging stopped then.

Rees stared over the city of hovels and wondered how many men lived here. Forty or fifty? Maybe more? It was hard to tell. Were most of them slaves? Another question Rees filed away to ask Jackman when he returned to the village.

Then he saw the store, tucked into a clearing cut into the swamp. It looked better built, but only just. Like the shacks, it seemed impermanent. Would the entire camp be picked up and moved as the ditch progressed?

Rees followed the path of scrap wood through the camp to the store. As he approached, he could smell food. Meat, he thought, saliva rushing into his mouth. Someone nearby was cooking. He hadn't expected such a homey aroma, not here.

Two men, one with his arm wrapped in bandages, sat just outside the door. They watched Rees as he approached but they did not speak. Rees went through the open door.

Posters were pasted on the walls on either side of the door. When Rees looked through them, he saw the one advertising for the sale of Scipio's capture. The reward, in big letters, occupied the first line.

The man standing behind the counter was white. He glanced at Rees incuriously and returned to his whittling. Rees found a jug of molasses and a five-pound sack of cornmeal and put them on the counter. He added a small amount of salt, twisted up in paper and almost as hard as stone. He was sure Aunt Suke would appreciate the seasoning.

Then he saw the coffee beans. Drawn to them, he stood over them for several seconds. He knew he shouldn't buy a luxury like coffee but the hunger for it was too powerful to ignore. He weighed out a pound and added it to the collection of items on the counter. Then he rooted through the store until he found a coffee grinder and a small coffee pot.

He could almost taste the coffee now.

'Psst.'

Rees looked up. Cinte was gesturing from the doorway. Rees hastily paid for his purchases – it took almost all of the money he had with him – and bundled them into his satchel. Then he went outside to meet Cinte.

'Hurry up,' he said. 'Diggers coming back from the canal now.'

Rees hurried after Cinte, the coffee pot and the grinder rattling together in his satchel.

SEVENTEEN

Cinte led Rees through the camp, almost to the very back. These structures looked the oldest. More of them were roofed with shingles and the walls seemed sturdier. A few of the lean-tos also had small porches with floors made in exactly the same manner as the bridges. Furniture made of logs from felled trees and cut to seat height were arranged upon the wood floor.

Cinte gestured to one of the stools, taking one of the others himself. 'Ask your questions quickly,' he said. 'They all be going to supper soon.'

'Who are these men?' Rees asked. 'Scipio's friends?' Cinte nodded.

'They all from Grove plantation.'

'Slaves?'

Cinte looked at Rees as though he were stupid. 'A' course. They all hired to dig, just like my brother hired to make shingles. But Birame and Chopco still slaves so they dig.' Rees didn't fully understand, but before he could ask any further questions two dark-skinned men approached from the west. They walked as though exhausted and mud coated them in a second skin. They did not seem surprised to see a white man sitting on the stool in front of the shack so Rees guessed Cinte had gotten word to them somehow.

They sat down and waited, eyes on the floor. 'Birame,' Cinte said, gesturing to the short skinny man. 'And Chopco.' He was taller and pudgy with a round face.

'Have either of you left here?' Rees asked. 'Left the dig the last few days?' Both men shook their heads. Rees could not tell if that was true or not. He tried again. 'You know Scipio?'

'He stays here sometimes.'

'We friends,' Chopco agreed.

'Do both of you know the village in the swamp?'

'Been there,' said Birame. 'Scipio took us once.'

'But we's couldn't find it again,' said Chopco with an emphatic nod. 'Not without Scipio showin' us the way.'

'Usually Scipio take off walkin' so fast we couldn't follow even if we wanted,' said Birame.

If they wondered why Rees was asking these questions, they didn't say.

'Has Scipio been back here recently?'

'No. Not for a coupla days'

'Almos' a week,' Birame put in. 'Not since the reward went up.'

'Massa Jacob real mad.' Chopco grinned widely and then, realizing he was still talking to a white man, looked down at the floor again.

'Why? Did he want the reward?' Rees looked from Birame to Chopco and back again. Birame shrugged.

'Prob'ly,' Chopco said. 'But Scipio the best shingle maker aroun'. Massa Jacob most likely turn 'im in at the end of the season.'

'Winter,' Cinte clarified.

Rees nodded. He asked a few more questions but the answers didn't change and he finally gave up, feeling that the visit had been very unsatisfactory.

As he and Cinte walked through the camp, Rees said, 'I'll meet you about where we parted in the swamp. I want to ask Jacob another question.'

Cinte glanced at Rees in surprise but then he nodded. 'All right. I'll meet you there. But hurry. It's best we far away as possible from the ditch by dark.'

Rees made his way back to the store. The diggers were congregating around several large crude wooden tables loaded with food. Rees saw pork, chicken, a big pot of grits and what looked like biscuits. He was suddenly so hungry he felt like joining the line.

He looked around, finally spotting Jacob standing with a group of white men. All of them held tin plates heaped with food.

Of course, Rees thought, they eat first even though it is the slaves who did all the work.

Since he needed to ask the overseer additional questions, Rees rook a deep breath and tried to smooth out his expression. Fixing a bland smile on his face, he approached Jacob.

'Still here?' the overseer asked. Rees nodded.

'I have a few more questions.'

Jacob wiped his mouth on his sleeve. 'What?'

'When Scipio stopped coming to work, did anyone else leave?'

'Why you want to know that?' Jacob eyed Rees suspiciously.

'One of the diggers told me Scipio stopped coming after the reward was posted.'

Jacob's head went back and he stared at the tall trees. 'I guess that's true,' he said after a moment, his gaze returning to Rees. 'I didn't think of that. I wish Mr Hamilton waited until after the season.' He looked at Rees. 'You thinkin' someone went after 'im and caught him for the reward?'

Rees did not reply. That was not exactly what he was wondering but it was close enough.

'The reward ain't been claimed,' Jacob said. 'Not yet anyway. And none of the diggers went missin' in the last few weeks.' He paused and thought some more. 'I can't tell you about the shingle makers. Most of 'em,' he grinned, 'well, they work their own schedules anyway.' Rees guessed Jacob meant that the shingle makers were already escaped and hiding in the swamp. 'But I can tell you,' the overseer continued, 'the quota for shingles still been met. Even without Scipio. So most of the others been comin' to work.'

'You don't keep account of them?' Rees asked. Jacob shook his head.

'Only the slaves. We hire them, so we're accountable to their owners, you see.'

Rees understood. The labor of the maroons was kept hidden, an open secret between the escaped slaves and the overseers who appreciated their work on the shingles for meeting the quotas. The system made a certain kind of sense although Rees found it offensive. More and more he admired Tobias's courage in returning to this society where every hand was raised against him. Rees resolved to spend more energy helping Tobias recover his wife.

'Can I get back to my supper?' Jacob asked, interrupting Rees's thoughts.

'Of course. And thank you.' Wishing Jacob had invited him to partake in some of the rich smelling pork and the biscuits, Rees shook Jacob's hand and withdrew. He was conscious of all the eyes following him as he retraced his steps to the bridge over the canal. He was soon out of sight of the camp.

The sun had dropped so low shadows stretched across the canal to the edge of the swamp on the other side. Rees recognized the location where he'd stepped out of the trees; a discarded cigar end marked the place where Jacob had stood.

Rees stepped through the greenbrier thicket shielding the swamp and began following the path he'd made earlier.

He walked for some time as evening took hold but saw no signs of Cinte. Finally, fearing that he would lose the trail in the dark, he stopped where he was. The temperature was rapidly dropping, and he knew it would be a cold night. He did not dare light a fire for fear of the slave catchers, who would surely wonder what he was doing in the swamp.

The moon rose, not completely full but enough to shine a silvery light upon Rees. Cinte erupted from the vegetation. Startled, Rees jumped to his feet with a gasp.

'Sorry,' Cinte said. 'Sit down.'

'Where the hell were you?' Rees asked, too angry to be polite.

'I got us some food.' Cinte held up a wooden bowl. The fragrance of slow cooked pork swirled enticingly into Rees's nose. Suddenly he was too hungry to think of anything but food.

'I know the cook,' Cinte added. Although Rees could barely see the other man in the thickening gloom, he could hear the grin in Cinte's voice. 'I'll just fix up a fire.'

'What about the slave catchers?' Rees asked.

'They won't be this close to the canal, and not this late neither.' Cinte handed Rees the bowl of pork and what looked like a sweet potato and then he knelt. He cleared a space and took some hickory fragments from the sack on his back. 'Always use hickory,' Cinte said. 'Or oak. The smoke stays low to the ground.' After a few minutes of struggle, a few red sparks glowed to life in the tinder bundle in his hand. Rees could hear Cinte blowing and within a few seconds, the tinder sent up a flame.

'You've done this a lot,' Rees said. It could take twenty minutes or more to light a fire; Cinte had succeeded in maybe five.

'Scipio used to say it was my only talent,' Cinte said. 'Now, watch that smoke there. It goes off low.' He took back the bowl from Rees and took out his dinner knife. The flickering light from the fire ran up and down the blade in sparks of orange and yellow. He cut the meat and the sweet potato in half. Rees took out his bowl and Cinte dumped his share into it. They sat down by the fire and ate in silence.

Rees did not believe he had ever tasted anything so good. The meat was tender, smoky with just a little charring, and seasoned with spices he could not put a name to. The sweet potato, although they had no butter or gravy, was soft and sweet. Rees almost licked his bowl.

'One thing you gotta say about the Great Dismal Swamp Company,' Cinte said with a satisfied belch, 'they feed the diggers good.'

'I've never eaten anything like this before,' Rees said.

'The hog is put in a hole,' Cinte said. 'Covered with leaves and set on fire.'

Although Rees knew the process had to be more complicated than that, he was too full and too tired to ask questions.

'Did you learn anything from Jacob?' Cinte asked.

'Not a thing,' Rees said. He felt as though he could sleep all night and all the next too. 'Did you get the money you were owed?' He yawned.

'Most of it,' Cinte said. 'And another order for a banjo.'

'Good.' Rees leaned his back against a tree and, with the smoke keeping the insects at bay, he fell asleep.

EIGHTEEN

Rees and Cinte arrived at the village just before dusk the following evening. As they neared the camp, Cinte speeded up. Rees was too tired to hurry but he tried to keep the other man in sight. He did not trust his ability to find this small cluster of buildings on his own.

By the time Rees straggled in, Cinte had already divested himself of his pack and was seated by the fire eating. It felt strange to return. Claustrophobic but also familiar. Lydia stood up and took a few steps forward but halted, still constrained by the coldness between them. Rees had no such reserve, however. He took several giant steps forward and wrapped his arms around her. 'I am so glad to see you,' he whispered in her ear.

She hugged him and then pulled herself back from his arms. 'You stink,' she said bluntly.

'Did you learn anything?' Jackman asked. Rees shook his head.

'It was a dead end,' he said. He looked at Jackman for a moment and then his gaze traveled around the circle of male faces: Toney, Peros, Tobias. And Neptune. Any one of them could be Scipio's murderer. Rees thought it unlikely Jackman could have manhandled Scipio's body out of camp, and he discounted the women for the same reason. Maybe Peros. But Toney, Neptune and, yes, Tobias could all have managed to do it.

Rees rummaged in his satchel and pulled out the paper of salt. He handed it to Aunt Suke with a flourish. She smiled, her eyes lighting up. Handing Abram to Ruth, Aunt Suke sprinkled some of the salt into the pot and stirred it energetically. 'Sit down and eat now,' she said.

Rees took out the jug of molasses and the soap. 'I should bathe first,' he said. 'And then . . .' He took out the small coffee pot, the grinder and the beans.

'Coffee?' Lydia asked. She did not sound very happy.

'I don't know when I had coffee last,' breathed Jackman, pleasantly surprised.

'Thank you,' Aunt Suke said. 'That be thoughtful. You sure you don't want to eat first?'

'Where's Sandy?' Rees asked, suddenly realizing she was missing from the circle. Cinte looked up, suddenly alert.

'Oh, she went home to Sechrest,' Aunt Suke said.

'She promised she would wait for me,' Cinte wailed.

'She'll come back for Abram,' Aunt Suke said serenely.

'But she promise.' Cinte stood up.

Feeling that he could not abide more drama right now, Rees turned to Lydia. 'I'm going to bathe now, before it gets too late.'

'I'll bring your clean clothing down to you,' she said, rising to her feet. Rees extracted the soap from his satchel and started down the slope to the water.

It was already very dark under the trees and the black water looked like ink. Rees stripped off his clothing and stepped into the stream. Goosebumps popped out on his skin; the water was far colder than he expected. And he was afraid of meeting one of the venomous snakes, so he did not go any deeper into the water than his ankles. He quickly splashed himself with water. Every scratch, every insect bite stung. And when he soaped up the pain was worse. He rinsed off very quickly. By the time Lydia came down the hill Rees was using his breeches to dry off. She handed him his clean clothes, although, since they were dyed brown by the swamp water, they did not look clean. She turned her back while he dressed.

'Surely you learned something,' she said. 'Tell me what happened.'

Rees reflected on his experiences the past few days. 'Jacob, the overseer,' he said, 'told me he hadn't seen Scipio for several days, not since the reward was posted.'

'Do you believe him?'

'I do,' Rees said finally, after some thought. 'His annoyance with Scipio for threatening the quotas seemed genuine.'

'Could he have found the village without help?'

'I don't think so. Scipio's two friends, who I also questioned, said they could not find their way here without a guide. And they'd been here once.' He paused and added after a few seconds, 'I doubt I could find my way without help. The men have taken a different way every time.'

Nodding, Lydia turned around. 'You looked rough when you came home. Scratched and bleeding.'

'And itchy. The salve only helps a little.' Rees swatted at the swarm of insects descending upon him. 'Let's go back to the fire. The smoke helps more than anything else.'

Lydia nodded but she didn't move. 'You know what that means,' she said. Rees felt his heart sinking; he hadn't wanted to put words to the logical conclusion.

'I know. The murderer is here in this village.' He paused and then added softly, 'Cinte thinks Neptune . . .'

Lydia nodded sorrowfully and reached out to take his arm. For the first time in many weeks, since Rees's indiscretion the previous spring, he felt his wife softening toward him. In harmony, as sweet as it was unexpected, they walked up the slope together.

Aunt Suke waved them to the fire, a bright orange in the gathering shadows. Rees could smell coffee and as he approached the fire he saw the pot keeping warm on the side. Only Jackman and Tobias were still seated on the log. Jackman lifted his cup of coffee in silent thanks.

Rees looked around for Cinte. He was a distance away, standing with Neptune who had put a consoling arm around his shoulders. Toney and Peros had moved away from the fire and were talking and laughing.

'I'll return soon,' he said to Lydia and walked quickly to Toney and Peros. The smaller man hurried away but Rees caught Toney's arm before he could take more than a few steps.

Shaking off Rees's hand, Toney said, 'What?'

'I wish people would stop running away,' Rees said. 'Aunt Suke asked me to look into Scipio's murder and the body's disappearance. But I can't do it if people don't speak to me.'

Toney grinned involuntarily. 'Aunt Suke a powerful woman,' he agreed. Sighing heavily, he added, 'What do you want to know? And, before you ask, I didn't kill Scipio.'

'I heard you fought with him.'

'Scipio fought with everyone. He couldn't help being provokin'. He be like a kid sometimes, not a grown man.'

'But you diced with him,' Rees said.

'Until he started playing his tricks on me.' Shaking his head, Toney added, 'I warned Neptune.'

'Who do you think might have murdered Scipio then?'

'I don't want you pinning the murder on someone,' Toney replied quickly.

'I would never do that,' Rees said angrily. 'If I was black, would you think that?'

Toney stared into space for several seconds. 'I might. But not immediately,' he admitted. 'All right. Only two I see havin' a good reason is Tobias and Neptune. Is that good enough for you?' He walked away, Rees watching. He didn't like Toney's answers. Although Rees had already thought of

Neptune and planned to question him tomorrow, he did not want to suspect Tobias. But he accepted the fact that he had to.

Rees sat down beside Lydia and Tobias and helped himself to coffee. There was no milk but a chunk of sugar sweetened it up quite well. He offered his cup to Lydia but, wrinkling her nose, she shook her head.

Rees looked at Tobias. 'You look unhappy,' he said.

'Thinking of Gabriel Prosser,' Tobias said. 'It must be about October tenth. His hanging was scheduled for October tenth.'

Rees looked into the distance, trying to count up the days. But he had lost track of time and wasn't sure. 'Just about,' he agreed. But he knew that wasn't the real reason Tobias looked so glum.

'Where is Ruth?' Rees asked.

'With the baby,' Tobias replied. He did not sound happy.

'She's putting Abram to bed,' Aunt Suke said, dishing out a bowl of stew and handing it to Rees. 'She be very good with him.'

'Pretty soon she'll have a baby of her own,' Tobias said.

Rees felt Lydia's involuntary flinch and turned to her with a curious expression. She shook her head at him and stood up to take her supper from Aunt Suke's hand.

'Tobias,' Rees said. 'How well did you know Scipio?'

'We were at Grove plantation,' Tobias said. 'And right away he went after Ruth.'

'Went after?' Rees asked.

'Telling her she was pretty. Trying to get her to walk out with him.'

Rees thought of the baby Ruth carried and wondered. Was that Scipio's baby?

'Why all these questions?' Tobias asked. 'You don't think I had anything to do with Scipio's murder, do you?' Angrily jumping to his feet, he raced to the hut and joined Ruth inside.

Rees looked at Lydia. He resolved to ask her what she knew as soon as they were in private. No chance presented itself until an hour later when they retired for the night. Perched on the bench that made his bed, Rees looked over at Lydia. She paused in arranging her sheet.

'What?'

Although Rees wanted to speak about the rancor between them, he did not dare. Instead he said, 'When did Sandy leave? And why? She as good as promised Cinte she would wait for his return.'

'She left as soon as you and Cinte were out of sight.' Lydia sat down with the linen clutched in her hand. 'She was almost desperate to leave; couldn't wait.'

'She never intended to wait,' Rees muttered.

'No. I don't think she did. Sandy was so eager to leave she didn't even think about Abram. Fortunately for her, Aunt Suke was willing to keep him here.'

'Is she so smitten with the Sechrest boy?' Rees sounded disapproving, even to himself. What if Sandy was his daughter? She was barely a year or two older than Jerusha and he would not like it at all to see his daughter behaving so. And with a baby too.

Lydia did not respond immediately. Finally she said, 'I don't know. But I got the impression she's frightened of Cinte.'

Rees thought of the short, slight young man and snorted.

'I also spoke to Ruth,' Lydia said. 'She is still determined to stay behind when Tobias returns north.'

'But she loves him,' Rees said, mystified. 'You told me that.'

'Yes. But it isn't enough.' Lydia sounded so much as though she understood that Rees stared at her. But in this dark and windowless shack he could barely see her face.

'I don't understand why she is balking,' he said.

'She sounded firm when she told me she can't live with Tobias.'

'Cannot or will not?'

'She said can't. When I pressed her, she refused to say any more. Only that she would raise her baby here, in the swamp.'

'She must understand what Tobias risked, coming here for her,' Rees said, angry on behalf of his friend. 'Not just his freedom but his life.'

'I know. She does understand that. But there is something . . .' Lydia's voice trailed off. 'She will not tell me her reasons. Just that she can't go north and live with Tobias as man and wife.' Rees thought of his suspicion that Scipio fathered Ruth's babe. Still, that didn't seem enough . . .

'What do Sandy and Ruth want?' Rees wondered aloud.

For a moment Lydia was silent. Then she said, 'Something happened down here, something terrible. But Ruth won't tell me what.'

'Do you think we can change her mind?' Rees asked. If only they knew why Ruth was so set on that course. The sheet rustled faintly as Lydia shifted her position.

'I don't think so. I suppose there is a chance, but she seems pretty determined.'

'Tobias will be heartbroken,' Rees said, his voice cracking with sympathy.

'Yes.' After a second's silence she crossed the floor and joined her husband on his bed.

'I know he will be. He is a good man.' She leaned into him and he smelled, not of lavender, but some other herb. Rees was almost afraid to put his arm around her. The accord between them seemed too tenuous, too fragile to risk.

'I never meant to hurt you,' he said hoarsely. 'You must know I love you. I never—' Lydia placed her finger over his lips.

'We will talk,' she said. 'But not now.'

NINETEEN

Rees awoke just past dawn. The cabin was still dark but he could see a pink flushed light through the door. Lydia was still sleeping soundly beside him, her face rosy. Carefully, trying not to wake her, he crept out from under the sheet and went outside. Although it was very early, Aunt Suke was already at the fire preparing breakfast. She smiled at him but did not speak. Rees sat down on the step. He felt quietly happy and contented and, for the first time in several months, he was optimistic that all would be right between himself and his wife. Although he had not wanted her to accompany him, and he was even more aware of the dangers now, he thought in hindsight it had been a good idea. Lydia, it seemed, was beginning to forgive him.

He heard Abram crying and, a moment later, Ruth softly crooning to the baby. Tobias came out of the men's hut, quickly followed by Cinte, and they climbed the slope to the fire. 'Breakfast be just a minute,' Aunt Suke said. Rees guessed they were having cornmeal mush again – what he called samp and they called grits, for some unknown reason. The jug of molasses he'd bought at the store by the canal sat on one of the logs beside the fire. Aunt Suke passed him a handful of small nuts.

'What are these?' Rees asked.

'Goober peas,' Tobias answered.

'They good,' Cinte promised, helping himself to a handful. 'Animals love 'em.' Rees took a few and crunched them between his teeth. He had to admit they weren't bad.

'Where's the others?' he asked Tobias.

'Toney and Peros still sleeping,' he replied.

'But Neptune?' Cinte asked, looking around. 'I thought he'd be here.'

'Neptune?' Aunt Suke repeated.

'He's gone,' Tobias said. 'We thought he was already awake and here, at the fire.'

'I heard him go out,' Cinte added. 'He left hours ago.'

Rees exchanged a look with Aunt Suke as he rose to his feet. 'Where's Jackman?'

'Fishin'.'

'We'd better search for Neptune,' Rees said. He did not want that young man to be the guilty party, but feared it was so. It looked as though Neptune was on the run.

As Cinte retraced his steps, disappearing around the back of the men's hut, Tobias went behind Rees's and Aunt Suke's huts to search. Rees walked toward Quaco's hut and the fields that lay to the side. As he walked among the drying cornstalks, he met Jackman coming up from the water with a mess of fresh-caught fish. Fried, they'd make a fine breakfast.

'Did you see Neptune?' Rees asked.

Jackman shook his head. 'He missin'?'

Without answering, Rees walked all the way to the end of the fields. He looked in the pens with the short dark cattle. But there was no sign of Neptune at all.

When he returned to the center of the village and met the others, Cinte shook his head. Tobias said, 'There's no sign of him.'

'I guess we know our murderer, hmmm?' Jackman said, Rees nodded. He should have questioned Neptune again.

'It's still possible Neptune is innocent,' he said, although he doubted it. 'Let's look around the swamp outside. Maybe he went hunting? Or something.'

'Not likely,' Cinte said, glancing at Rees pityingly.

'He's prob'ly on the run, hmmm?' Jackman said.

'Worth a look anyway,' Tobias said.

'Breakfast take a few more minutes,' Aunt Suke said, shooing them away from the fire. 'Go on.' She looked at Rees. 'Find Neptune.'

'Spread out,' Jackman said. 'I know he ain't by the fields.'

So, as Rees and Tobias went north, through the canebrake into the swamp, Cinte headed to the men's hut to begin searching to the south.

Leaving the village felt like stepping into an untracked wilderness. Tobias looked around as though he wasn't sure which way to go. 'He could be anywhere,' he muttered.

'Now look,' Rees said. 'If Neptune was genuinely trying to escape, he would have chosen the quickest path to civilization. If it were me, I would take a boat and sail as far as I could before I took to this,' he gestured around him, 'and walked the rest of the way.'

Tobias stared at Rees and nodded. 'I guess old age does mean wisdom,' he said. Rees laughed and turned east.

As they started down the path to the pirogues, Rees saw a few broken stems. And then, in the muddy ground, the imprint of a bare foot. 'I think Neptune went this way,' he muttered to himself.

The swamp always looked the same, Rees thought; thick vegetation, water glittering around the tangled roots of the cypress and, occasionally, a pond. But he was learning to see the subtle differences that marked a safe trail through the soggy peat. And, helpfully, Neptune had left a trail of footprints and broken branches for them to follow.

'Look.' Tobias shouldered Rees aside and pointed. Rees stared in that direction but did not see anything. Tobias began moving as quickly as he dared over the muddy and leaf-strewn ground. Rees hurried after him, not spotting Neptune until he almost tripped over Tobias, who was squatting and almost invisible in the underbrush.

Neptune had fallen to the ground and was lying half in and half out of a shallow pool of water. Because he was wearing a tattered shirt and breeches woven of tow linen, the light brown of the unbleached fiber, he had blended into the turning leaves around him. His face was set in a rictus of pain and he was breathing hard. Vomit stained the ground.

'What happened?' Tobias asked. Rees could already see the problem: Neptune's lower right leg was grossly swollen, and his mottled skin was stretched tight and shiny halfway up his calf. Two bleeding holes just above his ankle marked the place where the snake had struck.

'Snake bite,' he said, groaning. 'Cottonmouth.'

Tobias turned to look over his shoulder at Rees and said, 'We've got to get him home.'

'I know,' Rees agreed. Neptune was too heavy to carry – and anyway, weren't the victims of snake bite supposed to be walked around? 'Help me get him to his feet,' he said.

With Tobias on one side and Rees on the other, they managed to lift Neptune to a standing position. He couldn't put any weight on his injured leg, and he seemed woozy and disoriented besides. 'We'll get you to Aunt Suke,' Rees promised.

'Why did you run away?' Tobias demanded. 'Don't you know you look guilty now?' Neptune muttered something. 'Did you murder Scipio?'

'I didn't kill 'im,' Neptune said distinctly.

Rees glanced at Tobias and shook his head. 'Don't make him talk. Not yet anyway.'

First, they had to keep him alive. Then Rees would find out why Neptune had run.

*   *   *

By the time they approached the wall of greenbrier, Neptune was almost unconscious, and the swelling had extended up his leg to his knee. Rees, pausing, looked at Tobias. Both of them were breathing hard and wet with sweat. 'I'll keep him here,' Rees panted. 'You run up to the village. Get help.' Tobias nodded.

'You have him?'

'I do.' But when Tobias stepped away and Rees took on all of Neptune's weight, he staggered. 'Hurry.' Tobias disappeared into the thicket.

Rees spread his legs wide for balance and looked down on Neptune's tightly curled brown hair. 'Did you murder Scipio?' Rees asked meditatively. 'Did you take his body? If so, where is it?'

But Neptune could not reply.

Although Cinte and Toney accompanied Tobias into the swamp only about fifteen minutes later, to Rees it felt far longer. Except for the sound of the wind through the trees, the rattling buzz of the insect swarm, and the loud bird calls, all was silent. Rees saw a family of deer with short cork-screwed horns glide through the trees and disappear. A loud crashing heralded a herd of feral pigs. They too headed toward the water.

Then Rees heard the movement of men, the crunch of their feet and a low mutter of conversation, as they came into the swamp to meet him.

TWENTY

They carried Neptune to Quaco's cabin and laid him on the bench. Aunt Suke shook her head and clucked when she saw him. Shooing everyone out, she went to work. First, she cut the snake bite open so the blood flowed. Rees wondered about that treatment; Neptune was already weak. But he was no healer. Then to the wound Aunt Suke added a poultice of leaves, so astringent Rees could smell them from outside. She covered that with a piece of white cotton.

'What is that?' Rees asked.

'Swamp cotton. Good for treatin' wounds,' Aunt Suke replied.

'Do you know why Neptune ran?' Cinte asked Rees, drawing his attention away from the activity inside the hut. Before he could reply, Cinte continued, 'Is he my brother's murderer?'

'Did he say somethin' to you?' Toney asked, crowding up behind Cinte.

Rees looked at their concerned expressions and shook his head. 'Sorry. He didn't say anything. He couldn't.' With an involuntary glance at Neptune, lying so still on the bench, he added, 'He's in a bad way. And I don't know how long he was out in the swamp.' Only Neptune's face was visible above the blanket. His normally pale skin was flushed red and he breathed in loud gasps.

'Will he live?' Rees asked Aunt Suke. She shrugged.

'Maybe. He young and strong.' But when she turned to look at him, she frowned and shook her head. 'It be in God's hands now. Nothing we can do.'

Rees exhaled and shook his head. He would dearly love to know why Neptune had fled. The most obvious explanation was that Neptune had murdered Scipio. But that didn't make sense. Why hadn't Neptune fled the camp before? Or, if he wanted to claim the reward, why had he left Scipio's body lying in the swamp, only to steal it from the village later? Rees shook his head. He just didn't see the why of Neptune's behavior.

'Cinte and Toney,' Aunt Suke said, coming to the door. 'Go and put up some boards over this here hole in the wall.'

'Do Jackman have nails?' Toney asked. Aunt Suke shrugged.

'Ask him,' she said. As Toney and Cinte started up the incline in search of Jackman, Aunt Suke gestured at Rees. 'Come inside. I need to show you somethin'.'

With a nod, Rees followed her inside.

Aunt Suke stood by Neptune and opened his shirt. A leather bag hung around his neck. It looked quite full, and when she lifted it Rees distinctly heard the clink of metal. She pulled the drawstring neck open and Rees looked inside at money, both dollar bills and coins. Lots of coins.

'I thought he lost his money to Scipio,' Rees said.

'He did.' Aunt Suke turned a worried expression to Rees. 'So where'd he get this?'

'Scipio?' Rees suggested with a nod. The reason for Neptune's flight from the village suddenly seemed much clearer.

'You think Neptune murdered Scipio for his money?' Aunt Suke said.

'Don't you?'

Aunt Suke sighed and shook her head. 'I don't want to believe it.'

'How much did Scipio win?' Rees cast his mind back. All he'd discovered in Scipio's pockets was a pair of loaded dice. 'There was no money on him when I found him.'

'I don't know. A fair bit. That boy been savin' up for years.'

'And Scipio took it all in one night.'

Aunt Suke nodded reluctantly. 'This looks like even more, though.'

'How much more?' Rees began. Then he stopped, realizing Aunt Suke probably couldn't count.

'I don't want to believe it,' she repeated. 'Neptune always been honest. Never been a liar or a thief.'

Rees did not argue but he thought the loss of what Neptune had called his 'freedom money' was a good motive for lying, stealing and murder – especially since it was clear Scipio had cheated the young man out of it with his crooked dice. Besides, Rees wasn't sure how much credence to put in Aunt Suke's opinions. She was whip-smart but she'd frequently demonstrated a vein of loyalty to those she claimed as hers, whether deserved or not. 'We should take the money to Jackman to hold,' Rees said instead.

'To hold?' Aunt Suke glared at him. 'Neptune not dead yet. He might wake up and look for that bag.'

Rees looked down at Neptune and wondered how venomous that snake was. When he touched Neptune's cheek, his skin was warm. And he was sweating and panting hard. How poisonous were cottonmouths? Rees pushed the poultice away from Neptune's leg. Although it was badly swollen and looked excruciatingly painful, so far, the leg had not turned completely black. Still, Rees thought Aunt Suke was being wildly optimistic.

'Very well,' he said. 'We'll keep an eye on him tonight. We'll know by tomorrow how likely he is to die.'

'How likely he is to live,' Aunt Suke corrected. But the glance she directed at Neptune was worried and sorry both. Despite her brave words, she held no illusions about his chances. 'Go up and eat some breakfast now,' she told Rees. 'You must be hungry. And I must recover this young man.'

With one final look at the young man lying on the bench, Rees turned. As he started for the door, Aunt Suke caught his sleeve. 'Find the murderer, Rees,' she said fiercely. 'We need to know the truth. Even if it's Neptune.' With a nod, Rees left the cabin. Lydia was sitting alone beside the fire, an empty bowl in her lap. She jumped to her feet when she saw her husband approaching.

'Where have you been?'

'Looking for Neptune. No one told you?'

'No. I woke up and you were gone.' The knuckles of the hand clenched around the wooden bowl were white.

'You were sleeping soundly,' Rees said defensively. Then he thought how it must have looked to her; as though he'd left her here alone. 'I'm sorry. A lot has happened. I'll tell you.' He looked at the hominy in the pot. 'Is this all that's left?'

'Yes. Toney and Peros ate most of the fish.'

With a sigh, Rees helped himself to a bowl of food. He looked around at the camp before sitting down. All of the inhabitants were busy elsewhere, and out of earshot. 'I'd only been awake for a little while when we discovered Neptune was gone,' he said in a low voice.

'Gone?' She turned to look into his face. Rees nodded. 'What do you mean, gone?'

'He ran off. We all went out to search. Tobias and I were the ones who found him. He'd been bitten by a snake. So, we brought him back here, to the village.'

'Is he all right?' she asked, a line forming between her brows.

Rees shook his head. 'No. He's in a bad way. And his leg . . .' He stopped and swallowed. Even if Neptune lived he might lose the leg.

'Did he say why he left?' Lydia asked.

Rees paused and glanced around them once again. 'No. He hasn't been able to speak. But Aunt Suke discovered he was carrying a bag of money.' He took a few bites of the bitter hominy. Lydia stared at him.

'Money. Where would he get money?'

'Well, one of the possibilities is that he murdered Scipio and took his money. You know, the money Scipio won from him in the dice game.'

'So why did he stay here, in the village? Why did he run now? He could have remained here, with the money, for a few more days. Then, when he left, we would not have been suspicious of him at all.' Lydia looked at Rees.

'Exactly,' Rees said, turning an approving look on his wife. 'I would have expected him to leave as soon as he murdered Scipio. He also could have taken the body and used it to claim the reward. But he didn't. Why not?'

'There has to be a reason,' Lydia said, a pleat forming between her eyebrows. 'How much does Neptune have in his bag?'

'I didn't count it.' Now Rees met her gaze. 'Why?'

'I'm thinking there are other explanations. I mean, Neptune didn't have more than twenty dollars saved up. So Scipio could not have had more than a dollar or two more than that.'

Rees thought back to the leather sack around Neptune's neck. 'He has a lot more,' he said. 'The bag was full. Maybe fifty dollars.'

'So, where did he get that much money?'

Rees shook his head. He had no answer. Yet. But her questions were percolating through his mind, sending his thoughts in other directions.

'Does anyone else know?' Lydia asked.

'Only Aunt Suke. And she says Neptune doesn't lie or steal.'

'That doesn't mean he isn't a murderer,' Lydia said, adding with an emphatic nod of her head, 'As we have seen more than once.'

'Yes,' Rees said in agreement. 'I just wish I had a clearer

idea of who might be guilty. Almost no one will answer my questions. So far only Aunt Suke and Toney have been willing to talk to me at all and he told me the bare minimum. Even Jackman has to be badgered into signaling Quaco.'

'Do you think Jackman . . .?' Lydia paused delicately. Rees thought again of Jackman's injured foot and the cane he used. But he didn't always use the cane.

'I wonder . . .'

With a giggle, Abram careened into Rees and put his muddy hands on his breeches for balance.

'Now Abram, don't go near the fire,' Ruth admonished the child as Rees stared at the handprints on his pants with dismay. But he didn't scold. Abram was at least a year younger than Sharon, Rees's youngest. He was just learning to walk, and he lurched around with the awkward clumsy stance Rees remembered from his daughter's first steps. Laughing, Abram headed straight for the fire. Exchanging a glance with Rees, Lydia rose to her feet to head the baby off. Rees quickly finished his breakfast and stood as well. There would be no more time for private conversation now.

TWENTY-ONE

Rees stopped in to check on Neptune several times during the day. The poultice of leaves and swamp cotton did seem to be reducing the swelling in the leg. But when Aunt Suke attempted to feed Neptune some spoonfuls of soup, he gagged and threw up. Suke jumped back just in time. Rees assisted her in laying the young man down upon the bench once again. As he turned to leave, Neptune grabbed him by the sleeve.

'He gonna kill me,' he said.

'Who's going to kill you?' Rees asked.

'Save me,' Neptune pleaded, his eyes rolling in their sockets. 'Don't let 'im kill me. Please.'

Rees cast a worried glance at Aunt Suke. She shook her

head mournfully and gestured to the door. Rees gently detached Neptune's grasping fingers and followed the woman outside. 'You can't believe what he says,' she said. 'He's not in his right mind. I seen it before. It's the poison.'

'Does that mean he's worse?' Rees asked anxiously. Aunt Suke shook her head.

'No. Not necessarily.'

Rees thought for a moment before asking, 'Who's "him"? Is Neptune frightened of anyone here?' Aunt Suke shook her head.

'I would've said no. But when Jackman and Cinte come visitin' Neptune terrified of 'em both.' She sighed. 'You can't believe him. It be the venom talking.'

Rees shook his head, thinking that Neptune, if he had murdered Scipio, had good reason to fear Cinte. If he suspected Neptune of murdering his brother, well, that could explain Neptune's flight from the safety of the village. But it was a tenuous theory at best. For one thing, it did not explain how Cinte had suddenly discovered Neptune's guilt. If he was guilty.

And Jackman. What about him? Neptune, at least according to Aunt Suke, was as frightened of him. Could he be the murderer? Maybe Neptune saw him? Rees shook his head impatiently. He couldn't see why Jackman would murder Scipio. But then, that applied to everyone here in this camp. Nothing made sense and he was becoming irritable with frustration.

Still, it was possible Neptune had reason to be afraid, although Rees would not share that thought with Aunt Suke. Instead, he planned to spend the evening hovering around this hut, just in case Neptune was genuinely in danger.

'Did Cinte and Toney cover the hole in the back of the hut?' Rees asked. Aunt Suke nodded and gestured to the hut.

'Go look.'

Rees walked around to the back. By now it was after noon and the sun was beginning to drop west. Although the back of the hut was now in shadow, Rees could still see the work that had been done. A roughly trimmed board, scraped but with patches of bark still on it, had been nailed into the hole.

The raw wood shone white against the weathered gray of the older boards. And the patch did not fit completely; two thin gaps on either side gave access to the inside of the cabin. Rees could see the sunlight that shone on the westward-facing front steps of the hut seeping through these slits. He hoped Neptune was not being tormented by flies and mosquitoes.

For extra security, Cinte had nailed some hickory scraps over the center of the board. Rees nodded in satisfaction. A guard at the front steps should protect Neptune.

He walked around to the front.

'Rees.' Aunt Suke hailed him from the cabin door. 'Jackman and Tobias gone fishing.' She said nothing else, but she raised an eyebrow meaningfully. Rees understood the hint. The village was running out of cornmeal and other staples and they had eaten the last of the meat days ago. With his injured foot Jackman was not an efficient hunter and Tobias, still under suspicion for Scipio's murder, was forbidden to carry a gun. So, fishing. As Aunt Suke had suggested, Rees decided to join them. He looked at her.

'Where are they?'

'Down past the cattle. You'll see a path.'

So Rees descended the slope and went past the pen for the cattle. He did see a path, winding through the thick vegetation to the black water below.

This was a slightly larger body of water than the stream on the other side; Rees suspected it ran into the waterway they had taken the pirogues on. Here the water formed a small pond. A water bird dove for a fish and came up with its prey held tightly in its beak. The water droplets sparkled on its wings as it rose into the sky. The ubiquitous cypress, juniper and white cedar grew thickly around the water. Everywhere he looked were the short and rounded protuberances rising from the ground. A large tree with a hole in the center grew from the water in front of Rees. He couldn't tell if one large trunk had split and healed or whether two independent trunks had grown side by side, joining together to rise as one into the sky.

It was beautiful, but in a wholly different way than the pine forests of Maine.

Jackman handed Rees a pole made of a long stick. Although the hook was metal, and appeared to be professionally made, the string tying it to the pole was common twine. Rees guessed some enterprising soul had either stolen or purchased the metal fish hooks.

Tobias was seated on a log, his hook already in the water. Rees sat beside him but couldn't settle. He rose to his feet and took a turn around the bank. He chose a log and deposited himself upon it. His hook and line went into the water. For a few seconds, he sat beside the other men. But he couldn't rest there quietly. He stood and stretched before sitting down once again. His blood simmered in his veins and he could feel his temples throbbing. The excitement of Neptune's flight into the swamp, and now Rees's fear for the young man's life, had sent his heart rate soaring. Neptune was important. Rees just didn't know how yet.

'If you can't sit still, go away,' Jackman said firmly, turning to glare at Rees. 'You scaring away the fish.' Tobias threw Rees a sympathetic glance as Rees dropped his pole and walked away from the pond.

He climbed past the fields, heading involuntarily to the hut where Neptune lay. Aunt Suke sat outside, a structure made of sticks in front of her.

'What're you doin' here?'

'I'm not good at sitting,' he said. 'How is he?' He tipped his head at the shack.

'He sleepin',' she said. 'I gave him some laudanum.'

'Did he say anything else?' Rees asked, sitting down beside her.

'All nonsense,' she said. 'One of Cinte's banjoes chasin' him.' She threw Rees a glance. 'He delirious.'

'How is his leg?'

'Still swollen. Hot to the touch.' She frowned. 'I don't like it.'

Nodding, Rees peeked through the open door. Neptune twitched and muttered in his sleep. To Rees's eyes, he didn't look any worse. He didn't look any better either.

'Do you know what kind of snake bit 'im?' asked Aunt Suke. Rees shook his head.

'Tobias thought it might be a cottonmouth. Neptune was lying in a pool of water when we found him.' He thought of the snake that had brushed by his leg when he'd first come through the swamp and shuddered. 'What are you doing?'

'Tryin' to set up a loom.' Aunt Suke gestured at the sticks and the yarn stretching from the top to the bottom. 'Miss Minerva gave Sandy the yarn before she passed. We all desperate for clothes.'

Rees inspected Aunt Suke. Once her bodice had been pink and her skirt brown but constant wear had left the dirty cloth faded almost to white. Rips had been mended until the fabric itself began to wear thin. And her hem was so tattered Rees had a clear view of her ankles and smooth brown feet.

'What about the swamp cotton?' he asked. 'Can that be spun into thread?'

'What do you think?' She handed him a handful of the white bolls. Rees touched one of them and it took off into the air. Like milkweed, each puff was light enough to travel a distance on a breeze. But when he felt the fibers he realized they were brittle and far too short to be spun.

He turned his attention to the yarn. The fibers were a mix of poorly spun tow linen and a variety of threads picked out of other clothes. Rees found it hard to imagine any cloth worth wearing coming from such poor thread.

And the loom! It was just a rectangle of sticks.

'It's not workin',' Aunt Suke said despairingly.

Rees examined the structure and the strands closely. Aunt Suke had tied each yarn to the top cross bar and the bottom. The tow linen and some of the finer threads had been wound around a stick. 'This is fine, as far as it goes,' he said. 'You need a cross. Remember, there is no weaving without a cross.' He found two sticks and patiently wove the first through every other thread. The second stick picked up the opposite threads. Then Rees took his makeshift shuttle. With the two sticks separating the warp threads, he pushed his primitive shuttle between the sticks. He reversed the positions of his sticks and pushed the shuttle back to the other side.

'Your first two rows are done,' he said, offering Aunt Suke the yarn wrapped stick. 'Just keep doing that.'

She looked at the rows and then at Rees. 'How do you know that?'

'I'm a weaver by trade,' he said, sitting down beside her.

Biting her lower lip, she copied him. The weft threads straggled across the messy warp.

Rees used his hand to push the threads down to meet his rows. 'Your tension is off,' he muttered. This would be loosely woven cloth at best.

'So, why'd you come to the Great Dismal with Tobias?'

'He asked me to come. We're friends. And I've known Ruth since we were kids.'

Aunt Suke turned to look at him. 'Is everyone in the north like you?'

Rees thought of his father. He wouldn't allow Tobias on the farm and had beaten Rees within an inch of his life for inviting him. 'Not really,' he said. 'But some are.' This conversation was too awkward to continue so he changed the subject. 'We came for Ruth. I hoped Ruth would leave with Tobias by now.'

Aunt Suke was quiet for several seconds. 'She scared,' she said at last.

'Scared of what? Tobias?' Rees looked at Aunt Suke in confusion.

This time she was silent for so long Rees thought she would not reply. Finally she said softly, 'You white and you a man. There are some things you can't understand.' Rees felt as though cold water had been thrown over him. He wanted to argue, but she was right: he didn't understand Ruth's hesitation to go north – to freedom. It seemed like such a simple decision.

'Explain it to me then,' Rees said. Aunt Suke smiled.

'I know you mean well. If Ruth wants to tell you, she will.' Aunt Suke shook her head at him. 'Anyway, why you worryin' over Ruth? You have trouble of your own with your wife.'

Rees stared at her in surprise. 'How do you know?'

'I see her lookin' at you and you lookin' at her.'

Rees glanced away from Aunt Suke. 'I did something that hurt Lydia. Hurt her badly.'

He expected Aunt Suke to ask what he had done or scold him for it. She did neither. Instead she asked a question. 'Why did you do that?'

'The woman was young and beautiful. It was spring.' It sounded weak even to Rees himself. Aunt Suke nodded.

'And you wanted to be free.'

Rees's mouth dropped open. 'How do you know that?'

'You lean on Lydia, more'n you know. Or want to know. So you try to push her away. But you need her.' Aunt Suke regarded Rees with a grave expression. 'Decide what kind of man you will be, Will Rees. A partner with your wife, or free but alone?'

'What do you mean?'

She did not answer. She bent over her weaving, signaling an end to the conversation.

TWENTY-TWO

After a dinner of fried fish and sweet potatoes, Rees took up a position on the steps of Quaco's hut. Although not convinced that Neptune's fear was well-founded, Rees did not want to take any chances. Neptune knew something. Since he seemed to be the only one here who did, Rees wanted to protect him as much as he could.

Unfortunately, sitting alone on the hut's steps gave Rees too much time to think. Was Aunt Suke correct? Was he dependent on Lydia for his happiness? And embarrassed by it? It was a troubling suggestion. Rees was glad to see Lydia approaching as dusk crept through camp with the jug of salve in her hands.

'Join me,' he said, shifting over to make room on the step. She handed him the jug and sat down. Rees liberally applied the ointment to his exposed skin. Although Jackman assured him the insects were fewer than they had been during the summer, he did not believe it.

Lydia sat beside him for a few minutes. The silence between them was heavy with all that was still unspoken. Finally, eager to break the silence, Rees burst into speech. 'I wish I had spoken to Neptune earlier,' he said.

Lydia turned a thoughtful look upon him. 'I know you've approached all the men.'

'Neptune avoided me so assiduously I almost forgot he lived here,' Rees said in a guilty tone. Lydia regarded him thoughtfully.

'Do you think Neptune is the murderer?'

'Possibly. At best, he knows something. But fleeing the village certainly makes him look guilty.'

'Lydia,' Ruth called. She waited above the incline, a squirming and crying Abram in her arms.

'Ruth needs my help,' she said as she rose to her feet. 'Abram is a handful. I thought Sandy would have returned by now.'

Rees watched Lydia climb the slope. The borrowed dress she wore had been shortened too hastily and the hem was drooping. Lydia and Ruth continued into the center of the village and disappeared from Rees's sight.

Already bored, he turned and looked in on Neptune. His eyes were open. Jumping to his feet, Rees hurried into the cabin. 'Neptune,' he said.

'Jackman,' Neptune said, his gaze fixing upon Rees.

'Do you want to speak to Jackman?' Rees asked.

'No. Toney. Cinte.' Neptune seemed to have trouble forcing out the names.

'Do you want to speak to them?' Rees asked, bending over the recumbent figure. Neptune clutched at Rees's sleeve.

'Jackman. Help me . . . Cinte.'

Believing Neptune had mistaken him for Cinte, Rees said, 'I'm here. You're safe.' Neptune's eyes closed once again, leaving Rees to wonder if Neptune had just accused Jackman of Scipio's murder.

As darkness fell and the air cooled, Lydia brought out a ragged blanket and a bowl of coffee. 'Aunt Suke thought you might want something to warm you,' she said.

'That was thoughtful of her,' Rees said, taking the blanket and eagerly wrapping it around his shoulders. But it was the hot coffee he really looked forward to. It had been boiled over the fire until black as tar and so strong the first sip sent a tingle through his body. Aunt Suke had sweetened it too, adding so much sugar Rees felt the undissolved grains on his tongue.

Lydia looked at him and then, as though making up her mind, she said, 'We should talk now.' She sighed. 'There so rarely seems to be enough time, even here, away from the farm and our family.'

'Do you want me to give up on this investigation?' he asked, hearing the note of annoyance in his voice. She stared at him. He was being unfair, he knew it and that made him even more irritable.

'Of course not,' she said. 'This investigation is important to these people, for Ruth and Tobias. Besides, it's part of who you are.'

Rees yawned. The coffee, strong as it was, seemed to make him even more tired. 'So, it's about the rope dancer again. I said I was sorry.'

'She was a symptom, I think. Aren't you happy with me? With the family?'

Rees stared at her with his mouth open. Is that what she thought? That he didn't love her any more? He yawned again.

'Of course not,' he said, his eyes closing.

Realizing how exhausted he was, Lydia patted his wrist and rose to her feet. 'We'll talk again tomorrow,' she said. Rees abandoned himself to sleep.

But nightmares troubled his slumber. He dreamed his older brother Mathias still lived, a brother Rees scarcely remembered. Almost twelve years older, Mathias had been apprenticed to the town blacksmith. Although Rees did not know all the story, Mathias had died in the smithy. But in Rees's dream, Mathias was still alive and a hale and hearty nineteen-year-old. He came after Rees brandishing a smith's hammer, a hammer that was twice the size of a real one. Rees tried to run but couldn't. He was running in place and Mathias was coming closer and closer. The hammer whistled past Rees's head and he knew Mathias was going to kill him.

He awoke with a start, shivering with cold, and stared around in confusion. Leaping to his feet, he started walking around, flapping his arms. It was very early in the morning, just past dawn. He could smell wood smoke and guessed Aunt Suke was awake and stirring up the fire to make breakfast.

Neptune.

Rees jumped on to the first step and peered into the hut. Neptune appeared to be sleeping soundly. But as Rees turned to descend to the ground, he realized something was amiss. Neptune's labored breathing had quieted. In fact, Rees heard no sound at all. Spinning around, he vaulted over the top two steps and into the hut. He leaned down over Neptune but heard nothing.

'Aunt Suke,' Rees called. 'Aunt Suke!'

He put his hand on Neptune's chest but did not feel it rising or falling.

'Oh no,' Rees muttered, a horrible premonition filling his mind. He lifted Neptune's eyelid. Red dots speckled the whites of the eyes.

'What's the matter?' Aunt Suke asked, hurrying into the hut behind Rees. He stood aside and allowed her to look at the body. 'He dead,' she said. Looking up at Rees she added, 'You knew that might happen.'

Rees did not speak for a moment. Everyone would assume Neptune's death was the result of the snake bite. But Rees knew better. 'He didn't die from the snake bite,' he said. 'Look.' He peeled back Neptune's eyelid. Aunt Suke peered at it. Rees did not know if she would recognize those red dots and for several seconds he was sure she didn't. But she had worked as a healer for a long time.

'Blood in the eyes,' she said, looking up. 'Neptune was suffocated.'

'He was murdered.' While Rees was unconscious, someone had slipped into the hut and smothered Neptune. 'Let me fetch Lydia,' Rees added. Although he was almost certain Aunt Suke was innocent of the murder, he could not be completely positive. Lydia was the only person, other than himself, guaranteed innocent. She was the only one he could trust.

TWENTY-THREE

Lydia was not pleased when he woke her. 'What time is it?' she asked, sitting up and rubbing her eyes.

'Just past dawn.' Rees sat down beside her. She examined his expression.

'What's wrong?'

'Neptune is dead.'

'What?' Her eyes widened. 'How? The snake bite?'

'Someone wanted us to think that. But he was smothered.'

'You're sure?'

'Aunt Suke agrees. And it's my fault he's dead.' He rose to his feet and paced around the hut a few times before sitting down once again. 'I fell asleep, Lydia. I was there to protect him and I failed.'

'Surely not—' Lydia began.

But Rees cut her off. 'I was sleeping. Whoever murdered Neptune crept over me and went into the hut.' Rees jumped up again, unable to sit quietly. Lydia stared at him for a few seconds, her expression coming fully alert.

'Wait,' she said finally. 'You aren't a heavy sleeper.'

Rees thought back to his uncomfortable night. 'No. But how else?'

'You were drugged.' Lydia looked at him. 'I wondered what was wrong last night. You were so sleepy. But I thought you were just tired.'

'Drugged with what?' Rees asked.

'Laudanum. Aunt Suke's laudanum. She has a bottle in her hut.'

'Yes,' Rees said. He had seen Aunt Suke use it. Then he thought of the amount of sugar in his coffee; so much that some of it had not dissolved. Laudanum was bitter; covering the taste would require a great deal of sugar. And then the fatigue that had come down on him so heavily he couldn't resist it. Finally, there were those strange dreams. 'You're right.'

'That means someone wanted you out of the way.'

'Who?' He thought of Aunt Suke and her hut full of herbs, of Jackman and of all the young men. 'It could have been anyone,' he said, meeting Lydia's gaze. She nodded.

'I would hate to think it is Aunt Suke,' she murmured. Turning her eyes upon him, she continued. 'We know one thing for certain now. The murderer is here, in this camp.'

While Lydia dressed, Rees returned to Quaco's hut. Jackman had joined Aunt Suke and they were both inside the hut bending over Neptune's body. Although nobody else was there, Rees knew soon everyone would be awake. Then they would gather around the hut and the body. Before then, when they were trampling everything and jabbering so much he could not think, he wanted to examine the body, the hut and its surroundings.

He paused in front of the hut. The door into the shack was visible to most of the camp. And Rees had been asleep on the step. Entering this way would have been terribly risky.

The steps into the hut told him nothing; there were no footprints or anything that Rees could see. But, as he stared at them, he wondered how anyone could have climbed over him when he was sprawled across the door. He was tall and burly and even unconscious he surely would have been aware of someone stepping upon him. Then he thought of the laudanum. Maybe not.

But if the murderer had not gone into the hut through the door, how would he have gotten inside?

Rees walked around to the back of the hut. The replacement board put up by Toney and Cinte still covered the opening in the back, but when Rees pulled at it, the panel swung open in his hands.

The murderer had detached the hickory straps from the wall, so carefully that a casual glance would not detect anything wrong. Now Rees knew why he'd been drugged: so he would not hear the activity at the back of the hut.

'What?' Jackman asked from inside the hut. Aunt Suke said a few words in a soft voice.

As Lydia came around the corner, Rees held his finger to

his lips. She nodded and tiptoed to his side. They remained quiet as the conversation inside the hut continued. Rees distinctly heard the words 'burial' and 'tomorrow' and Jackman's grunt of acknowledgment. They heard his stick tap down the front steps, the sound fading as he left the hut.

A few seconds later Aunt Suke said, 'All right, you two. Why you standin' out there listenin'? Come inside.'

Rees threw an embarrassed glance at his wife before pulling away the board and peering inside. 'We weren't eavesdropping,' he said.

'Sure seemed that way to me,' Aunt Suke said.

'We were examining the board,' Lydia said.

Aunt Suke expelled an audible breath. 'Why?'

Rees jumped up to the floor of the hut and then held down a hand to assist Lydia. When they were both inside, he said, 'Because that is the way Neptune's murderer got in.' He expected Aunt Suke to scream in denial, but she did none of those things. Instead she regarded them both.

'You sure?'

'Why else would I have been drugged?' Rees asked.

'Drugged?' Aunt Suke repeated.

'With your laudanum, we think,' Lydia said.

'In the coffee you sent me,' Rees added.

'Not my laudanum,' Aunt Suke said, horrified.

'This board, that just got nailed on, can be pulled away so carefully it appears whole,' Rees went on. Aunt Suke stared at him a moment longer before speaking.

'I wondered about Neptune's death,' she admitted. 'He was improvin'. He shouldn't have died. Course, that does happen sometimes. But,' she added with a significant glance at Rees, 'his money gone.'

'I could have figured that would happen,' Rees said grimly.

'Did anyone else know about the money?' Lydia asked Aunt Suke.

'You mean, besides me and your husband? No. I didn't even tell Jackman. Didn't have the chance.'

'So,' Rees said, 'only the three of us knew.'

'Four. The murderer knew,' Lydia said. Rees turned to look at her.

'Of course he did,' he agreed. 'And now he has it back.'

Aunt Suke glanced from Rees to Lydia and back again. She raised an eyebrow. 'So, Neptune was murdered for the money?'

'No. Well, maybe partly,' Rees said. 'I suspected him of Scipio's murder. He had cause. Scipio won all of Neptune's money. But now—'

'He dead himself,' Aunt Suke said.

'Neptune identified the murderer,' Lydia said.

'And blackmailed him for the money to go north,' Rees agreed, glancing at Aunt Suke.

'If Neptune blackmailed the murderer,' Aunt Suke said sorrowfully, 'that's why, when y'all brought him back, he got murdered himself. That boy desperate to be free.'

For a moment all three were silent. Even the birds hushed.

'I don't want anyone to know Neptune was murdered,' Rees said at last. 'Let the killer think he got away with it.'

'But Jackman has to know,' Aunt Suke objected. 'He be the headman.'

'Could you wait a few days before telling him?' Rees asked. 'I hope that, if the murderer believes no one knows Neptune's death wasn't accidental, he'll make some excuse to leave the village. Then we'll know.'

'Jackman already know,' Aunt Suke said with a frown.

'We'll have to warn him, then,' Rees said.

'Anyway, the murderer will escape,' Lydia said.

'Not if we restrict anyone who tries to leave to camp,' Rees said. He sighed. 'I know this will be hard to pull off. Does anyone have a better idea?'

No one spoke. Chewing her lip, Aunt Suke looked at Rees and nodded slowly. 'A day. I'll wait until after Neptune's funeral. That's all. And that's if Jackman agree.' She turned her attention to the body lying on the bench. 'Go along now,' she said. 'I need to wash and prepare the body.' Rees took Lydia's elbow and they left the cabin, through the front door this time.

As they started up the incline, he considered Aunt Suke. Surely, she could not be the murderer. He hoped she wasn't. But the laudanum was hers and she'd made the coffee with so much sugar he had not noticed the drug's bitter taste. 'But where would she have found the money to bribe Neptune?' he asked himself.

He did not realize he had spoken aloud until Lydia said, 'She doesn't need the money. She doesn't plan to go north and leave her family; the family that is still enslaved. Besides, she's a woman.'

Rees did not argue, but he thought even a woman could shoot a gun or smother an injured and comatose man. He liked Aunt Suke and did not want her to be the guilty one, but what did he really know about her anyway?

TWENTY-FOUR

Rees glanced at Lydia. They were walking so close together he could reach out and take her hand. But he hesitated. The weight of everything between them – all that should be said and hadn't been – had kept them apart more completely than a solid wall. But he believed – he *hoped* – Lydia was warming toward him. He reached out and took her arm. When she looked at him in surprise, he said almost at random, 'I should speak to Quaco again.' They conversed easily about the murder.

'I'd forgotten Quaco.' She turned to look at him. 'He is almost not a member of the village.'

'But he is. He moves around, unseen, at all hours. He knows something. I am sure of it.'

'Quaco did not help you before. Why do you think he might now?' Lydia shook her head. 'As far as he knows, nothing has changed. Especially since you don't want anyone to know the truth about Neptune's death.'

Rees nodded unhappily. Lydia was right. And he wasn't sure what he should do about it. 'Jackman warned me Quaco might not help,' he said.

'And how are you going to find him? Quaco hides in the swamp. Even Jackman doesn't know exactly where.'

'Jackman has a system. I'll ask him again.'

As they approached the camp's center, Rees was surprised to see everyone there but Aunt Suke. Jackman waved them over.

'I was just tellin' everyone about Neptune. We'll send him off as soon as we can, in the evenin'.' Rees looked at Lydia in dismay. It was already too late to put his plan into effect.

'Do we need to dig another grave?' asked Toney, not very happily. Jackman shook his head.

'We'll use the one we dug for Scipio.'

'We shouldn't wait. Not even for two days,' Cinte said. 'I know it be gettin' colder, but still . . .' His words trailed off. Rees had wondered the same thing and was glad Cinte had brought it up.

'We almost out of food,' Jackman said. 'We need supplies. Especially if we goin' to send Neptune off the right way.'

'The right way? People comin'?' Toney asked.

'Yes. And they'll need time to get here, hmmm?'

Toney and Peros exchanged excited glances.

'Are we goin' on a raid?' asked Cinte, his eyes lighting up. Jackman nodded. 'Tomorrow mornin'. Early.'

'What raid?' Rees asked, his heart sinking. He was afraid he already knew the answer.

'On Sechrest plantation.' Jackman bobbed his head emphatically. 'We'll take some of the supplies that're rightfully ours. The food created by our sweat and the labor of our kin.'

'We shouldn't do that,' Rees said. Even more than his reservations about what appeared to be theft, he feared the murderer would take the opportunity to run.

'Why not?' Jackman asked, his tone combative. 'You eatin' this food too.'

'Won't a raid be dangerous? Attract attention?'

To Rees's surprise, everyone started laughing.

'The slave catchers come to the swamp all the time,' Toney said. 'Not as far in as the village, maybe.'

'But they always lookin' for us,' Peros said in agreement. 'Even if we don't take their food.'

'How far away is the plantation?' Rees asked.

'Pretty far. We be leavin' this afternoon and will stop at another camp,' Jackman said. 'Spend the night. Tomorrow mornin', early, we visit the plantation.' He paused and eyed Rees. 'You should come, hmmm?'

'Me? Why me?' Rees shook his head emphatically. 'No.'

''Cause we can use a big strong man like you.' Jackman flashed his white teeth at Rees.

'What if he walks up to the big house and tells 'em we're there?' Peros objected, darting an anxious glance at Rees.

'He won't.'

'How can you be sure?' That was Toney.

Rees found himself conflicted. On one hand, he did not want to go on the raid. Jackman and the others here might feel that they were taking only what they were due, but to Rees it looked uncomfortably like theft.

On the other hand, he felt somewhat insulted that they would think him so untrustworthy. But, as Peros stared at Rees, he realized the other man wasn't seeing *him*. He was looking at his white skin. It was like he was not himself at all, but a representative of the plantation owners. 'I would never do that,' he said hotly. 'If I give my word, I keep it.'

Jackman looked at Rees and they exchanged a long look. 'Excuse us,' he said.

Gesturing to the other men, Jackman led them down the slope toward Quaco's hut. Rees drew Lydia to the log and they sat down. 'This sounds dangerous,' she said.

'Nothing happened when I went to the canal,' he said.

'That was totally different,' she retorted. 'This really won't be safe. There will be men with guns. Maybe dogs.'

Since that was true, Rees did not argue the point.

'Besides,' she added, 'I worried the entire time you were gone that something would happen to you.'

Rees stared at her. In the silence between them, the sound of the argument at Quaco's hut was clearly audible. He looked at the cluster of men. Peros was waving his arms emphatically at every word. Rees turned his attention back to his wife. She was regarding him gravely. In the second-hand faded dress and with her hair braided and lying over her shoulder, she did not look old enough to be a mother. The mother of his daughter. Rees wanted to tell her how much he loved her and how sorry he was that he had allowed a momentary attraction to the rope dancer to make him forget that. Another burst of shouting distracted him and when he looked at his wife again the moment had passed.

'I want to go,' he said. 'This way I can keep an eye on everyone.' When she did not speak, he continued, 'It's either that or tell Jackman why we think this raid is a bad idea right now and take the chance the murderer will escape.'

Lydia remained silent for a few moments, but this time Rees did not jump into the silence. 'I see,' she said reluctantly. 'And Scipio's body still has not been found. His murderer could turn it in for the reward and go north. We would never find him then.'

'Yes,' Rees agreed.

'Then I want to go as well,' she said.

'No.' The word was out of Rees's mouth before he knew he planned to speak.

'I will wear my boy's clothing.'

'It is too dangerous.'

'But it is all right for you to go.' Lydia shook her head at him.

'I allowed you to come here with me,' he said. 'You will be as safe as you can be here at the village.'

'You did not *allow* me,' she said sharply. 'I accompanied you because I chose to. Besides, while you are thinking of my protection, who is keeping me safe when you take one of your weaving trips?' Rees's mouth dropped open. 'You have no trouble leaving me with the children and the farm then.'

'But that . . . that is our home,' he stammered.

'Yes. And from our home our daughter Jerusha was kidnapped last winter.' She stared at him with furiously glittering eyes. 'How safe was it then?'

'Um . . . um . . . um.' Rees tried to speak but managed only a few sounds. He had never realized how much his absences from home bothered her.

'I will wear my boy's clothing,' Lydia repeated.

'Can you whistle?' Jackman asked, overhearing her as he limped up the slope. Lydia laughed and whistled a long sharp note.

'Tell her she can't go with us,' Rees appealed to Jackman.

He stepped backward, his hands upraised and with palms facing Rees.

'I won't get into the business between a man and wife, hmmm?'

'She needs to stay here,' Rees said. 'Where it is safe.'

'Black women are never safe,' Aunt Suke said, coming up behind Jackman. She smiled at Lydia. 'You can do it.'

'So, I will be with you,' Lydia said, turning a fierce glance at her husband.

He still didn't like it. But, not only was he outnumbered, Rees realized Lydia would do as she wanted anyway, despite his wishes. He nodded at Lydia reluctantly and she went to the hut to change her clothes.

As Rees drank the last of the bitter but still warm coffee in the pot by the fire, Aunt Suke bundled together some food, mostly roasted green corn and sweet potatoes, to eat on the way. While she worked on that, Tobias and Toney collected the guns and checked the available ammunition. Toney also strapped his scythe to his back. Peros gathered the few frayed canvas sacks. They all looked hard used. He handed the worst of the lot, the bag with the holes, to Aunt Suke. By the time she finished packing the food into that, Lydia was re-dressed and waiting. She had wound her braid on the top of the head and covered it with a cap. Rees inspected her. He thought her face was too feminine for this disguise to be truly believable, but hoped no one would come close enough to notice. And, although it was too hot for the vest, she needed it to disguise her breasts. Otherwise, she made a very creditable boy.

She smiled at him tentatively and he held his arms open. She came in for a quick hug and then went to stand with Tobias, who was standing with an arm around his weeping wife. Lydia had assured Rees that Ruth still loved her husband and he wondered once again why she persisted in refusing to accompany her husband north.

They might have to leave Ruth behind, Rees thought now. He and Lydia had been here for just over a week: far longer than they'd expected to stay. Of course several murders had intervened. But he was beginning to wonder what was happening at his farm. He missed the children and although Lydia had said little, he knew she did as well. Besides, although winter weather was more than a month away for Virginia, that was not true of Maine. They could have snow before Thanksgiving – sometimes it came before All Hallows' Eve – and he did not want to be on the road then. He wished he had some idea who among these people in the swamp had murdered Scipio and Neptune.

Rees turned his gaze on Tobias. He would have to choose whether he would stay here with Ruth – in a slave state where he was constantly at danger – or go home to freedom.

'Ready?' Jackman asked, looking around at the group. Everyone nodded. Tobias hugged Ruth and fell into step behind Rees.

TWENTY-FIVE

Jackman, with his bad foot, could not manage a swift stride. Rees found the pace set by the head man easy, almost a stroll. And Rees was confident in Jackman's ability to find his way, so he did not feel the need to watch his footing. Instead, he looked around him. They had left the dry oasis on which the village sat and were now in the heart of the swamp. Although they were walking on relatively solid ground, muddy but solid, he could see water glittering in every direction. After a little more than a week here, Rees did not find the Great Dismal quite as alien or as threatening as he once had. In fact, the lushness of this climate, so different from the more austere pine forests of Maine, had grown on him. Even with autumn, and the changing color of the vegetation, the swamp remained a world of water, of bogs and of thickets.

What was it like here in winter? Did all this water freeze? Was the footing icy instead of wet?

So intent on his thoughts that he paid no attention to anything else, he walked into Lydia and almost knocked her over. Jackman had put his hand up and the line of people had halted. Now

Rees heard it too; a slapping nearby followed by a crashing in the underbrush. Everyone waited, silent and still but hyper alert.

Instead of people appearing through the trees, a family of deer stepped into a pool of sunlight. One of the adults paused and stared at the group of people for several seconds before bounding into the shallow black water. The rest of the herd followed and within seconds they were gone. The smacking sound halted and then started up again.

'Beavers,' Jackman said with a gust of relief.

With some muted embarrassed laughter, the party started on again.

Now Rees's thoughts turned to the murders. As his gaze roved over the men walking with him, he wondered which of them was the killer. Toney? The oldest but for Rees and Jackman, he was the quietest and was not a man prone to emotional outbursts. A sober, steady fellow. What would have aroused him to murder? Rees found it hard to imagine.

Then there was Peros. A short, slender man, he was lighter skinned than everyone but Cinte and Neptune. And Peros was argumentative too. But Rees had seen no ill will between Peros and either Scipio or Neptune.

Besides, Rees thought with a rueful smile, it was white people that Peros detested.

Jackman? Would his injured foot have prevented him from killing either Scipio or Neptune? No. Like Aunt Suke, who Rees had also considered, a limp would not prohibit Jackman from shooting Scipio or drugging Neptune and then smothering him. Since he was in and out of her hut regularly, he would know where the laudanum was placed and would have easy access to it.

Rees did not like Aunt Suke for the murders. Where was the motive – unless it came down to the reward for Scipio? She had claimed she didn't need the money. But what if she saw Scipio as a danger to the community? He could see her doing almost anything to keep the village safe.

With that realization in his head, Rees thought again of Jackman. The same could be said of him. What if Scipio defied Jackman and refused to leave the village? What if Scipio confronted Jackman? He too would do almost anything to protect the village and the hard-won freedom of its inhabitants.

Scipio would not have feared either one.

But Rees had not seen Neptune speaking privately to Jackman or Aunt Suke as he attempted to blackmail the killer. Besides, could they have strapped Scipio's body to a board and manhandled it into the swamp? Jackman was lame and Aunt Suke, although strong and capable, was a woman. Maybe they worked together? Rees rolled that possibility around in his mind for a few seconds.

Finally, there were the women: Ruth and Sandy. Could Ruth have committed the murders? Rees did not want to even consider her. She'd grown up in his hometown; she'd been part of the landscape since he could remember. But Rees knew better than to discount anyone. Had Scipio molested her? Rees shook his head. As far as he knew, Ruth did not know how to fire a gun. He would have to find the answer to that question. But, like Jackman, she was in and out of Aunt Suke's hut every day.

Sandy? She had not been in camp for either Scipio's or Neptune's deaths. Of everyone, she was the only one who had anything approaching an alibi. Rees could not imagine her, with her airs and graces, picking up a musket – and that was if she could find one.

But Cinte *had* been in camp. Rees's gaze moved on to the young man. He was grinning as he and Toney talked in low tones. Rees could imagine Cinte murdering a man out of jealousy. But Aunt Suke had insisted there was nothing to be jealous of. And, indeed, Rees had not seen Cinte display that kind of rage.

Who else? Rees was back to his friend Tobias.

Unwillingly, Rees recalled the argument between Scipio and Tobias. He had been jealous of Scipio's attention toward Ruth. Tobias was experienced with a gun; Rees had seen it. Did he know about the laudanum? And would he have been stirred to murder on Ruth's behalf? Did he suspect Scipio had made advances and the baby Ruth was carrying was his? That would certainly give Tobias a motive and might explain why she did not want to go home with Tobias. She was ashamed.

But Rees had not seen any strong emotion between Ruth and Scipio. Rather, she'd treated him with a kind of muted disdain, as though he were an overgrown boy, amusing but someone who hadn't yet grown up.

Rees's glance fell upon Lydia, striding along in front of him. She had shared some of what Ruth had told her these past few weeks and he wondered if she knew more than the little she'd confided. She was the only one he could discuss this with anyway, the only one he trusted. A sudden surge of affection swept over him and he reached out to touch her shoulder. She turned with a weary smile. He squeezed and dropped his hand. Recalling his attraction to the beautiful rope dancer the previous spring, he wondered now if he'd gone temporarily mad. What had Aunt Suke said? That he leaned on Lydia and didn't like it. He didn't want to believe that was true.

They walked until dusk. Mid-afternoon, hearing voices in the distance, Jackman stopped again. This time, although Rees could hear the shouts and calls of men, he did not hear either gunshots or dogs barking. He did not think the group in the distance were slave takers but the maroons around him froze with terror. Even after the voices faded away, Jackman did not move his people forward until shadows began to steal through the trees. Only then did he gesture them onward.

As the light disappeared, the vast expanses of water diminished. Although they were still in marshland, the muddy ground underfoot became somewhat more solid. And ahead Rees could see the straight edges of man-made structures through the leaves.

It was the ruin of a village. Although some of the huts still stood, most had been knocked to the ground. Even the cabins that were still intact were dilapidated and ready to fall. As they walked into the clearing, already disappearing under new growth, Rees could smell the faint smoky taint of an old fire.

'We stop here for the night,' Jackman said. Rees could barely see the man through the gloom, but he could hear the faint sounds of his movement. Jackman scraped something together and a few seconds later the ember he'd brought from the village burst into life in the bundle of dry tinder.

'Is that safe?' Rees asked, gesturing to the fire.

'The slave catchers come out mostly durin' the day,' Jackman replied.

'Mostly,' Toney said. 'But we need a fire.'

Rees looked around for some sticks, but Cinte had already put some hickory scraps near the small flame.

'Hickory and oak,' Jackman said. 'We don't want anyone to know we here.' He nodded at Toney who disappeared into the darkness. Peros took sweet potatoes out of his sack as Jackman took some ears of green corn from his. They were distributed just inside the stones that marked off the fire.

Rees sat down beside Lydia with a groan. How far had they walked today? Thirty miles maybe? 'What happened here?' he asked, gesturing around him at the destruction.

'This was our original village,' Jackman said.

'It was too close to Sechrest,' Tobias said. 'The slave catchers found it.'

'What happened?' Lydia asked in a whisper.

No one answered for several seconds and Rees began to think they would not. But the small fire flickering comfortingly in the darkness created an intimacy. After a moment Jackman leaned forward to throw another piece of wood on the fire. The orange light slid along his skin, highlighting his nose and glittering in his eyes.

'One of our own betrayed us,' he said at last. 'They caught 'im and he showed the slave takers the village to save himself.'

'Most of us,' Cinte gestured to himself, Tobias and the other men, 'were out huntin'.'

'And the man s'posed to be guarding the village fell asleep, hmmm?'

'When we returned, the village was destroyed,' Tobias said.

'They caught most everyone else.' Jackman paused and cleared his throat. Rees, who had heard the emotion in his voice, waited until he could continue. 'Most of the women and children.'

'Including his wife,' Tobias said. The firelight ran along his hand as he gestured to Jackman.

Rees, who had wondered about Jackman's wife, stared at him and tried to imagine how he would feel if Lydia was imprisoned on a plantation while he hid in the swamp. He gulped.

'Your children too?'

'Them too. But the older ones, they already been sold away.'

The cry of a bird pierced the silence like a sword and Lydia's hand crept into Rees's.

'Will they – the slave catchers – come after us here, tonight?' she asked anxiously.

Rees wished with all his heart she had not come with him. He'd read articles in the papers about the treatment of white abolitionists; if they were caught their white skin would not protect them. He swallowed and squeezed her hand.

'Probably not. We stay here only one night, at the most two,' Jackman said. 'And we only use this place once in a while so we safe for now.'

'What do we do tomorrow?' Rees asked. He wanted this raid over and done with as soon as possible and all of them back to the safety of the swamp and the village.

'We leave before light tomorrow mornin',' Jackman said. 'By dawn, if all goes well, we be on our way home.'

'What happens if we get separated?' Rees asked.

'You stay with Tobias or me,' Jackman said. 'Don't wander.'

'We all know the way home,' Cinte put in.

'And my wife?'

'She stay in the swamp,' Jackman said.

'At the edge,' Tobias explained. 'I'll show her. She'll be hidden but she'll see everything. If there's trouble—'

'Or the overseer comes,' Cinte explained.

'Or they loose the dogs,' Jackman added.

'She'll whistle and warn us to run,' Tobias said. 'Don't worry. We've done this before.'

Rees did not speak. His heart was already pounding in his chest with fear. He looked at the men seated around the fire. Although it was growing cold and the fire was very small for so many people, he did not dare ask for more wood. Not after the story they'd told.

Wait. There were fewer people around the fire than there should be. Leaning forward, he peered into the gloom. Toney and Peros were missing.

TWENTY-SIX

After a few seconds of horrified staring at the places where the men should have been sitting, Rees jumped to his feet. 'Toney and Peros are gone!'

He turned to look at Lydia. She looked up at him, her face white. 'Do you think they—?' She stopped short.

'It's fine,' Jackman said, chuckling.

'What do you mean?' Rees turned to Jackman and the others. They were smiling at him; he could see the flash of their teeth in the darkness. 'What? Why?' The fire in his veins made it hard for him to talk. Didn't they realize Toney and Peros could be the murderers? And that they could be escaping? He was ready to run off into the darkness in search of the missing men.

'They be back soon,' Jackman said comfortably.

'They went to the quarters,' Cinte said.

'They went to . . .?' Rees could hear his voice rising. Why was everyone so relaxed?

'The slave quarters at Sechrest plantation,' Jackman explained.

'For food,' Tobias added. 'They went for food.'

'Food?' Rees's alarm began to seep away. Realizing that Jackman did not know his plan to catch the murderer, and that his sudden agitation looked foolish, he began to calm down.

'Whatever our kin can spare,' Jackman said.

'Are you certain they will return?' Rees persisted.

'Of course,' Jackman said comfortably.

'Toney be friends with the Sechrest cook,' Tobias explained. His tone of voice indicated Toney and the cook were more than friends. 'He'll bring something good.'

As Rees sat down once again, he heard footsteps crackling over dry leaves and, a moment later, Toney's low chuckle. He did not believe they had been gone for all that long. How close were these ruins to the plantation?

Then Rees put aside his questions as the enticing aroma of hot food reached his nostrils.

Peros carried both cornbread and white bread as well as cooked greens. Toney brought roast pork, already cut, wrapped in a kitchen towel.

'And I got this.' He brandished a bottle in the air. 'For Aunt Suke.'

Rees wondered how he had gotten the laudanum. Maybe Toney's friend, the cook, had helped. And he guessed that the pork had come directly off the master's table, but he was too hungry to argue. All of them, including Lydia, ate with their hands. They left nothing behind but the bones and wiped their hands on the towel. Toney passed around a jug of water and then everyone but Jackman, who had disappeared into the bushes, made themselves as comfortable as possible by the fire. Rees, who had spent many nights like this, knew it would be a cold and uncomfortable night and he worried about Lydia. He wrapped his arms around her and put her head on his shoulder. She fell asleep almost immediately, but he lay awake for some time. This had been a singular experience. He had thought, because he was used to traveling, that joining Tobias in the Great Dismal would be similar to every other one of his journeys, but instead the swamp and the small threatened village inside had turned out to be unlike anything he had ever experienced. A foreign world.

Rees wasn't sure his curiosity and his skill at identifying murderers would serve him here, where everything was so different from what he was used to. He kept making mistakes.

Toney woke everyone before dawn. Rees, who was sure he had not slept at all, felt sluggish and dull. Sitting up, he rubbed his gritty eyes. Lydia pushed herself to her feet and walked around the smoldering fire, slapping her arms with her hands to warm herself. As Peros kicked dirt over the embers, Rees looked around at the others. 'Where's Jackman?'

'Left early,' Tobias said. 'His wife is at Sechrest. He is taking the opportunity to visit her.'

'And Cinte?' Rees was suspicious of any man who left this

group. He knew it would be easy just to keep going, out of Virginia, heading north.

'This be Sandy's home,' Peros said tersely, in explanation.

'Cinte went for Sandy,' Lydia said. Understanding Rees's fear, she put her hand on his arm. Peros nodded.

'Yes. He can't leave that girl alone.'

The people of the village seemed to visit the plantation, almost at will. Rees's plan to identify the murderer based on who left the group was doomed to failure. He found it very unsatisfactory and quite frustrating.

Toney sounded a faint whistle. Rees could just see him waving his arms peremptorily through the gloom. The sun hadn't risen yet, so the light was that peculiar bluish radiance of very early morning. 'Hurry,' Toney said. 'We want to finish by dawn.'

Peros stamped out the fire. Leaving the ruins of the village behind, they began walking quickly through the swamp. Although Rees couldn't see his footing, he was aware they were following something of a path. The ground was still marshy here, but the vegetation had been trodden down so often it had left a narrow track. Even in the faint light it was visible. No wonder the slave takers had found the first village.

They were very close to the plantation. Too close for safety, Rees thought. Within half an hour of walking he could hear the sounds of any farm: the shrill crowing of several roosters first and then the lowing of cattle.

The marshy ground solidified, and the deciduous trees of what Rees thought of as forest instead of swamp increased in number. The leaves here had already turned color and quite a few had already dropped. Rees saw fields outside the swamp.

Toney halted inside a copse of oak and maple. From here they were within sight of the backs of a long row of cabins. 'Miss Lydia.' Toney pointed at a dead tree, two ivory branches pointing at the sky. Lydia studied it for a few seconds. Then, as the maroons watched in surprise, she jumped up to a branch and hoisted herself into the crook between the two dead trunks. Rees hid a smile. He knew his wife and the practical nature that subsumed even the prim behavior drilled into most young women.

'Now what?' Rees asked.

Toney pointed with his chin. Peering through the gloom, Rees saw Jackman as he kissed a woman farewell and began limping across the yard. Rees and Toney joined Jackman in the yard as Peros sped across the ground to a more distant building.

'Smoke house,' Jackman said, pointing to a small structure set a little apart and catty corner to the kitchen. A heavy-set woman stepped out on the step. She saw Toney, smiled, and disappeared back inside.

Jackman went to a small door on one side and opened it. Air, thick with the smell of smoke, rushed out to greet them. Jackman handed Rees a bag and waved them inside. 'Hurry.'

He left the door propped open; even then it was almost too dark to see inside. Jackman put a large ham in Rees's bag as Toney picked up what looked like a thick slab of bacon. That went into the sack slung over one shoulder. Jackman himself took a small barrel.

Since that was all they could reasonably carry, Jackman rushed them from the smokehouse. He shut the door and they quickly crossed the yard toward the tree. Panting, Peros joined them, his arms stretched around a sack of dried corn. Nearby, dogs began barking. Rees broke into a run.

Lydia stood up in the elbow between the two trunks and pointed. But she didn't whistle so Rees was unsure what exactly she meant. After a moment, Lydia clambered down from the tree and ran toward the big plantation house in the distance.

'Where she goin'?' Jackman asked, his voice rising in alarm.

Without replying, Rees changed direction, veering in the same direction in which Lydia was headed. As dawn broke and the light brightened, he could see two figures approaching. At first they were too close together to identify, but as he neared them he realized it was Cinte, supporting Sandy in his arms. She was moving stiffly and very slowly. Although Rees increased his speed, Lydia was closer and she reached them first. She lifted Sandy's left arm and put it around her own shoulders. Together she and Cinte urged Sandy forward.

Now that Rees was almost beside them, he could see the rictus of pain on Sandy's face.

'Hurry,' Cinte panted. 'The dogs . . .' He threw an anguished glance over his shoulder.

Rees looked over Cinte's head and saw the white shirt of a man walking to the kennels.

Thrusting the sack of meat at Lydia, he lifted Sandy into his arms. Turning, he began to run back to the dead tree.

Jackman and the other three were already disappearing into the woods behind the plantation. The baying of the dogs was growing in volume and when Rees glanced behind him he saw the white shirt wrestling with the gate. The dogs would soon be free. Rees quickened his pace.

'Not that way,' Cinte panted. 'The dogs! Follow me.'

He entered the trees directly behind the cabins. The ground here was criss-crossed with paths. Although Cinte followed first one, and then another for a minute or two, he soon left the paths behind, striking out into the swamp. 'Step where I do,' he ordered, and strode into a tarn of black water.

The yapping of the hounds sounded nearer. Rees increased his pace as much as he could. Although Sandy was of slight build, she was beginning to grow heavy in his arms. The water was a drag on him as well as it rose, first above his ankles and then to his knees. He could hear Lydia splashing behind him. He tried not to think about snakes.

Then Rees heard whining and barking behind him. He turned slightly to glance over his shoulder. The hounds had reached the edge of the water. As he watched, he saw one of the mastiffs jump in and begin swimming after them.

TWENTY-SEVEN

Cinte had gotten several paces ahead. When he looked behind him and saw the dogs, his face went pale. He splashed back to meet Rees, hurrying him along. Turning sharply to the left, he pulled Rees through the last of the water and up on to a bank into vegetation. 'Rest,' he whispered as Lydia, her mouth set in a grimace of fear, panted into the thicket after them. She still carried the ham in her arms. Rees lay Sandy down on the ground and shook his arms. Now that Sandy's weight was gone, the blood rushed back into his muscles. The pain followed like ribbons of fire. Catching his breath, he began rubbing his arms. His damp sleeves clutched at his hands. Startled, he looked down. Blood streaked the cloth. Rees stared at Sandy's back in horror. Her pretty dress was ripped, the skin underneath like ground meat.

'Oh my God,' Lydia gasped.

But this was not the time to question her. Several of the dogs were swimming now, still barking and coughing as water got into their mouths. But they had lost the scent and swam aimlessly in circles. Several men panted up behind them. One, a burly fellow with a heavy black beard and black boots, tried to follow the dogs into the water. Now Rees saw why Cinte had been so insistent that they step where he stepped; the slave catcher took a few steps and went into deep water.

'Help! I can't swim.' His head disappeared under the murky waters. One of his companions splashed in a few steps and tried to catch black beard's hand.

'Let's go,' Cinte said, rising from a squat into a crouch. He took Sandy's hand and drew her after him. She moaned faintly and he frowned at her, his finger over his lips. But any sounds they made were lost in the sounds of black beard's screaming, his splashing in the black water, and the excited barking of the dogs.

Lydia sidled through the underbrush, moving ahead of Rees, and striking out after Cinte and Sandy. Rees bent over and crept through the thicket after them.

The sun had risen high in the sky by the time Cinte halted again. They had traveled through several more ponds – Cinte seemed to seek them out – all shallower than the first, but every bit as wet and uncomfortable. The baying of the hounds had faded and finally disappeared.

The ground in the sun-dappled clearing where Cinte halted was drier. Most of the trees were pines and the ground was orange with dropped needles. Rees collapsed on the soft and fragrant needles and inspected his shoes with dismay.

Repeated soaking and then partial drying had left the leather hard and deformed. They no longer fit properly.

Lydia handed the ham to Cinte and sat down beside Sandy. 'What happened?' she asked as she examined the girl's lacerated back. She tried to tease some of the tattered cloth from the wounds but gave up when Sandy began to whimper.

'Miss Charlotte,' Sandy said with a sob. 'She said I was uppity.'

'She had you whipped?' Lydia exchanged an appalled glance with Rees. Sandy uttered a hiccupping sob.

'No. She done this herself.'

'What did you do?' Rees asked, horrified.

'Nothing.'

'Miss Charlotte jealous,' Cinte said. 'Sandy more beautiful than she is.' Lydia nodded.

'I agree. This is a personal attack.'

'Where was the young man? Gregory, is it?' Rees asked.

'She sent him away. To Williamsburg, I think.'

'I wouldn't a gone,' Cinte muttered, touching her wrist lovingly.

'This looks terrible,' Lydia muttered. 'Very inflamed.'

'Sometimes they put salt on the wound.' Cinte's mouth tightened. 'Make it hurt worse. But Aunt Suke will fix you up,' he assured Sandy, squeezing her arm. She nodded, her eyes swollen with tears. Cinte cocked his head, listening, and for a few seconds everyone was silent. The only sounds they heard were birdsong and the wind through the branches. The baying of the hounds had disappeared with distance and the thick muffling vegetation.

'We should go,' Cinte said. 'The dogs lost our scent. For now. We don't want to stay any place too long.'

'What about Jackman and the others?' Rees asked anxiously. 'Jackman can't run.'

Cinte bit his lip and shook his head. 'I don't know. I hope . . .' As he stood up he looked into the distance. 'They know the swamp too. We can hope they made it back all right.'

Lydia took off her ragged vest, once worn by Rees's son David, and helped Sandy into it. It was too big for Lydia and it was even larger on Sandy, but it covered her wounded back and offered some protection from the insects that swarmed to the blood.

'It hurts,' Sandy moaned.

'We don't want your back to get infected,' Lydia said. She helped the girl to her feet. Cinte handed Rees the ham and hurried to Sandy's other side. They began walking once again.

Because Sandy could not hurry, their progress was slow. They paused around noon to eat something. Cinte lit a small fire and Rees cut slices from the ham with his dinner knife. With the aid of a stick they roasted the ham in the flames. It had been competently smoked and its salty smoky bite was full of flavor. Rees could not enjoy it, however. He jumped up several times to look around. If it were only him and Lydia, or only him and Cinte, they would be much closer to the village, but Sandy slowed them down. Although he knew she was injured, he began to feel quite impatient with her. Didn't she know she was putting them all at risk?

They walked through the afternoon. As mid-afternoon eased into early evening, Sandy began to demand rest more and more frequently. Each time they paused so she could sit, Cinte glanced nervously at the sky. 'I don't want to spend the night here,' he said when he caught Rees staring at him. 'But we might have to.'

'I know,' Rees said. 'The light won't last very much longer.' Biting his lip, Cinte nodded. And now, when he inspected the position of the sun, Rees did as well.

They walked until the shadows underneath the trees made the footing too dark to see. Cinte chose a small clearing, bounded by rotten dead falls and with a narrow stream nearby. While Cinte lit a fire, Sandy collapsed on a log. Rees cut slices of ham once again. Although he ate his share, he did not enjoy it at all. Besides his nervousness about spending a night in the swamp, he was beginning to fear Cinte did not know his way home and they were lost.

No one spoke. Except for the faint snapping of the fire, and the distant lapping of water against a bank, all was silent. Rees felt his eyes beginning to close. He had had several exciting days; this last one had begun early and then he'd walked a long way. Sandy was already sound asleep, leaning against Cinte's shoulder. He was smiling, his teeth catching the firelight. Rees glanced at Lydia, who was still awake. She shifted slightly and Rees saw the pucker in her forehead that meant she was worrying at something. Well, he didn't blame her. Everything about today's events bothered Rees, from the raid on the plantation to the whipping that had left Sandy bloody and seriously injured. Somehow, reading newspaper articles about slavery did not convey the true horror of seeing a young girl's back reduced to chopped meat by a whipping.

Rees put his arm around Lydia and pulled her close. She resisted a few seconds before finally relaxing against him. 'I wonder—' she began, but before she could continue, they heard a soft footfall followed by the whisper of moving branches. Something was moving through the underbrush. It did not sound like an animal but more like a person trying to move quietly. As Cinte quickly scuffed dirt over the fire, Rees stood up and moved around, preparing to leap at the intruder.

'Cinte,' said Toney, cautiously poking his head through the underbrush.

'Jesus!' Rees exploded. 'I almost hit you!'

'We thought you was slave takers,' Cinte gasped. Peros pushed his way into the clearing after Toney.

'We been looking for y'all,' Peros said angrily, as though they had lost themselves in the swamp on purpose.

'Come on,' Toney said. 'Let's go back to the village. Jackman been worried.' Then he smiled and added, 'Hmmm?'

Like the others, and although Toney's impression wasn't that funny, Rees found himself laughing in great bellowing gulps.

TWENTY-EIGHT

'What happened to you?' Toney asked. 'We been searchin' for hours.' Walking forward, he bent over and blew gently on the embers Cinte had tried to extinguish. He got a spark. Toney wrapped a rag – his shirt – around a stick and blew until the ember blossomed into a small flame.

'So we don't fall in the water and drown or step on a snake,' he explained as he shuffled dirt over the campfire. 'Let's go.'

'They released the dogs,' Cinte said, falling into step behind that small flame.

'We know,' Toney said. 'Some of 'em came for us.'

'We just barely got away ourselves,' Peros said. 'We thought they catched y'all for sure.'

'We came up the eastern side of the Great Dismal,' Cinte said. 'And Sandy . . . they whipped her, Toney.' He gulped. Toney turned to glance at the girl who was stumbling along in the protective circle of Cinte's arm.

'Oh no,' he said regretfully.

'We had to travel pretty slowly,' Rees said.

'But y'all never lost the ham.' Toney spoke lightly, inviting them to laugh and lighten the mood. But this time his effort fell flat.

Everyone was quiet as they navigated a tricky stretch through water and around a thicket. Despite Toney's small torch, it was difficult to see. Rees worried about snakes and he suspected everyone else did as well.

'How did y'all find us?' Cinte asked, finally breaking the silence.

'Smelled the smoke,' Peros said.

'But we didn't know – y'all coulda been slave catchers,' Toney said. 'So we be cautious.' Then he put his finger over his lips. 'Quiet now. We can talk at camp.'

Afterwards, Rees could never decide how long it took them to reach the village. It felt like the whole of the night, but in retrospect it was probably only a few hours. They traveled slowly, not just because of Sandy's injuries but also because of the darkness. Everything looked different and unfamiliar. It seemed as though they arrived at the village with no warning. Suddenly they were easing their way through the thicket to the cluster of houses and the welcoming campfire.

As Aunt Suke saw them coming into camp, she pulled a pan of cornbread from the ashes and stood up. Rees guessed Peros had arrived with his bag of dried corn intact and one of the women had ground it into flour.

Cinte went straight to Aunt Suke. 'It's Sandy,' he said,

drawing her to the front. 'They beat her, Aunt Suke.' His voice trembled at the last and she patted his shoulder before taking Sandy's arm.

'Oh, my dear,' Aunt Suke said. She looked at the vest and glanced quickly at Lydia.

'I thought it would protect her,' Lydia said. Aunt Suke nodded.

'Let's take a look.' Taking a burning brand from the fire, she led Sandy to her hut.

Rees went first to the water barrel and drank several cupfuls of water before returning to the fire. As he sat down, he thought he might never get up again. Jackman cut the corn pone and handed Rees a large piece. 'Coffee's perkin',' he said, gesturing to the campfire.

'Thank you. Thank you,' Rees said. He fell on the gritty bread like a starving man.

'How did you escape the dogs?' Lydia asked Jackman.

'They went for you first,' Jackman said. 'Y'all bought us enough time to escape.'

'We got into the swamp before they came for us,' Toney said.

'By then,' Jackman continued, 'they had trouble catching our scent.'

'I heard,' Cinte said, speaking to Jackman even though his eyes were fixed on Aunt Suke's hut, 'about some maroons escaped when alligators ate the dogs.'

'Not the people?' Rees asked. That story sounded made up to him.

'No. Alligators preferred the dogs.' Cinte grinned.

'We be lucky this time, hmmm?' Jackman said.

'Pretty lucky,' Rees agreed. Even Sandy, he thought. Not lucky to be whipped, maybe, but lucky that Cinte arrived to free her when he did.

'Don't worry,' Tobias said. 'Aunt Suke will fix her up.' He had joined Ruth and she sat close to him.

'I was so afraid,' she whispered. Tobias put his hand over hers.

'Will she have scars?' Lydia asked in a soft voice. 'That would be such a shame.'

Jackman glanced at her. 'Maybe. Maybe not. Can't tell.'

Rees knew with total certainty that Jackman lied, so as not to upset Lydia. But he said nothing. He didn't have enough energy to contradict the other man; these past few days had been exhausting. Besides, that was a lie told from kindness.

Jackman, throwing a quick glance at Rees, filled a wooden bowl with the coffee and handed it to him. Even with a chunk of sugar, it was strong and bitter but he drank it gratefully. He wanted to stay awake for at least a little longer to savor the feeling of safety and peace here at the camp.

A few minutes later Aunt Suke came out of her hut. As she joined them at the fire, Cinte jumped to his feet. 'How is she?'

'She be fine. I dressed her wounds and gave her some laudanum to help her sleep.' She threw a quick glance at Rees. 'Glad Toney brought more. Old bottle almost empty.' He nodded to show he understood; he had been drugged by her supply. 'Anyways, Sandy cuddled up next to Abram right now.' As Aunt Suke moved into the firelight and sat beside Lydia, she added, 'I think she'll go north with you now, Cinte.' Straightening up with a wide grin, he threw a glance at his workshop.

'I'll go to the canal tomorrow and sell the last of my banjoes.'

'Tomorrow night we burying Neptune,' she replied with a shake of her head.

'Day after then. Next day we leave.'

'If Sandy's up to it.' Aunt Suke counseled caution. But Cinte was too elated to listen.

'I want to get as far north as possible before the snow flies.' Excitement, colored with incredulity that his dream was finally being realized, lifted his voice almost to a shout. Despite the darkness, he hurried down to his workspace and the partially finished musical instruments.

'I guess he wants to leave b'fore Sandy changes her mind, hmmm?' Jackman said with a chuckle.

Rees did not laugh. He glanced at Lydia. She bit her lip and shook her head. They both knew how unwilling Sandy was to join Cinte.

Rees's glance went to Tobias and Ruth. Would she change her mind and accompany her husband if he left for the north? 'It's been nine or ten days since we arrived,' he murmured.

'Gabriel Prosser has probably been hanged by now,' Tobias said. 'Little easier to get home. Richmond won't be full of people.'

Rees nodded. Like Cinte, he wanted to leave as soon as possible. He'd hoped to be home by now. He'd leave tomorrow if it weren't for his promise to Aunt Suke. The trip to Maine was a long one and he feared snow had already fallen. The weather would only worsen as they went further into the fall.

And what would happen if they did go home? Although he and Lydia had talked about the murders, they had not resolved the trouble between them. Oh, they were easier with one another, but should they go home without resolving the trouble between them? On one hand, Rees did not want to talk. He dreaded that conversation. But he knew they had to have it, no matter how difficult it would be. They had to stitch up the wound he had caused between them.

Yawning, Lydia slumped against his shoulder. Her eyes were only half-open and she appeared to be struggling to prevent them from closing entirely. 'It's time for both of us to retire,' he said.

'Bath first.' She yawned again.

'We laundered y'all's clothing,' Aunt Suke said. Rising to her feet, she held out her hand to Lydia. 'The dress. And,' she added as her gaze moved to Rees, 'your shirt and breeches.'

Lydia disappeared in the direction of Aunt Suke's hut. Rees picked up a stick from the fire and used it to light his way around to the water barrel at the back of the hut. He'd just begun stripping off his sweat-soaked clothing when Tobias appeared with the clean clothes. Rees washed, hastily since the cool water made him shiver in the chilly night air, and changed. He felt much better for being clean. Leaving his dirty clothing on the ground, he went around the cabin and back into the firelight. Everyone was gone except Jackman, who was banking the fire. Rees nodded at him and went up the steps into the cabin. How strange to realize this small window-less shack now felt like home. He straightened the linen sheet over the bench and lay down underneath it. He pulled the ragged blanket up. But he could not quite go to sleep. Although he didn't intend to, he was waiting for Lydia. A few minutes later he heard her step as she came into the cabin. Smelling of soap and whatever herbs Aunt Suke had washed the body linen in, Lydia lay down beside Rees. He turned over and put his arms around her. Now he could sleep.

The sound of voices woke him later that night. Rees rolled off the bench and went to the door.

Cinte and Sandy were sitting by a small fire, a brilliant orange eye in the darkness. 'Ask her,' he whispered fiercely. 'I know Aunt Suke will agree.'

'But my baby,' Sandy said as tears rolled down her cheeks.

'He not be mine,' Cinte said, his voice rising. 'And I won't raise him.' Sandy uttered a sob. 'Look,' he said, his voice dropping once again to a whisper, 'slave children get sold away all the time. And we'll have our own children. I promise to give you a good life, Sandy.'

'But my baby, my son.'

'He be someone else's son,' Cinte said. Leaning forward, he put his hand on her arm. She shook it off. Jumping to her feet, Sandy ran sobbing to Aunt Suke's hut and disappeared inside. Cinte stood up and stared after her. When she didn't return, he gave up waiting for her. Banking the fire, he went down the incline to the men's hut.

Rees shook his head as he returned to his own bed. He would have thought that Cinte, who had desired Sandy for so many years, would be willing to take her son as part of the arrangement. Did he think Sandy was so desperate she would accept those terms? Rees crept under the blanket next to Lydia. He knew his wife would raise her child alone before agreeing to such a Devil's bargain.

TWENTY-NINE

Rees awoke to the smell of frying bacon. Easing himself away from his sleeping wife, he stood up and stretched. His legs were sore from the long walks the previous few days and stung from the bug bites and sunburn. Ruth was asleep on her bench. Rees glanced at her, wondering when she had come into the hut. Sandy must have taken her place in Aunt Suke's hut.

With a final glance at Lydia, he tiptoed from the hut into the early morning light outside. There was no one there but Aunt Suke, who was squatting by the fire, frying bacon in the pan over the flames. Another spider sat in the ashes. The lid covering it told Rees it might be cornbread. He stared at it. He was heartily sick of grits and corn pone. A large flat wooden circle with a smaller plate resting on it and a film of golden dust indicated Aunt Suke's previous occupation; she'd been grinding corn.

She smiled at him in welcome. 'Breakfas' be ready in a moment,' she said.

'Where is everybody?' Rees asked.

'Jackman and the other men butcherin' a cow.'

'A cow?' Rees said, thinking of the small dark animals in the pen. She nodded.

'For after Neptune's burial.' Using a corner of her apron to protect her hand from the hot handle, she pulled the spider away from the fire. She pulled the lid away and the sweet smell of cornbread filled the hollow.

Rees found a wooden plate and held it out. She cut a square and put the lid back on the bread. She pulled it away from the fire so it wouldn't continue cooking but would remain warm. Rees helped himself to the bacon sizzling in the pan.

Aunt Suke went back to her work. Throwing a handful of dried corn on the stone, she set to grinding it into meal. The sound of the two wooden circles scraping together filled the village center.

'Today,' she said as Rees busied himself setting up the coffee, 'we say goodbye to Neptune. As best as we can.'

Rees nodded cautiously. He wasn't sure what she meant. They were Christians here, weren't they?

'At home,' Aunt Suke continued, 'everyone get new white clothes. We paint the body's palms and the soles of the feet red.' She sighed. 'Here we make do and use white chalk.' Rees remembered Aunt Suke had done the same to Scipio's body before it was stolen. That reminded him of something.

What was it? He tried to grab hold of the memory but it slipped away before he could catch it. And Aunt Suke was still speaking. 'We will have a feast and then, tonight, we dance and sing.'

Rees nodded again and said, 'This funeral sounds much different from the somber services I know.' Dancing and singing? The minister at his church would be horrified.

He wasn't sure if he and Lydia should attend but, just as if she heard his question, Aunt Suke spoke.

'You and Lydia should come. You live here now.'

'We will,' Rees said, his mouth full of cornbread. Today he would confront Ruth and demand a final answer to his question: would she accompany them north to home? He wanted to leave soon. He and Lydia had been away long enough.

'How is Sandy?' Rees asked.

'She be fine. But she'll carry the scars her whole life,' Aunt Suke said, her attention turning to Rees's hut. He followed her gaze. Lydia hesitated on the top step and yawned. Like her husband, her cheeks were flushed with sunburn. Aunt Suke gestured to her and she came down the steps to join them. While he cut a piece of cornbread for her, she took a piece of bacon from his plate and bit into it.

'Do you think she'll marry Cinte now?' Lydia asked around the bacon. Rees thought of the conversation he'd heard the night before. He wasn't certain. And Aunt Suke shared his reservations.

'I hope so,' she said, her forehead furrowing. Then, hearing something with her sharp ears, she added, 'Shhh.' Moments later Sandy, holding Abram by the hand, came out of the hut. Moving stiffly with pain, she walked across the yard to sit by the fire. She was no longer wearing the ripped and stained gown in which she'd arrived, but had put on an old and faded dress. Her hair had been brushed until it shone and had been braided. But it was Sandy's expression Rees noticed. All her animation was gone. Although still beautiful, she no longer drew one's gaze.

Lydia turned an anxious look upon her husband.

'Good morning,' Rees said. Sandy acknowledged him with a nod but did not raise her eyes.

'Have some breakfast,' Aunt Suke told the girl.

'Not hungry.'

Aunt Suke cut another piece of cornbread and pressed it into Sandy's hands. Although she broke off a piece and nibbled at a corner, Rees noticed that she gave most of it to Abram.

'Where's Cinte?' she asked.

'He left early this mornin' to sell the last of the banjoes.'

Rees saw a flare of emotion cross Sandy's face. To him, it looked like relief.

Aunt Suke grasped Sandy's hand. 'I talked to him. He still wants you.' Sandy nodded. 'I think it best you go north with him. You'll have a good life.' Sandy shook her head and did not speak. After a long moment, in which Aunt Suke regarded the girl in concern, the healer returned to her grinding.

Under cover of the loud sound, Lydia leaned forward and grasped Sandy's wrist. 'You don't want to marry him?' Sandy hesitated and then she shook her head.

'Why not?' Rees asked. Although he tried to speak softly, his voice sounded loud and intrusive. When Sandy shrank into herself, Lydia frowned at her husband.

'I know you don't love Cinte,' she said in a low and soothing tone.

'No,' Sandy agreed.

'But he loves you.'

'Mama, Mama,' said Abram into the silence. Sandy gave him more bread.

'He loves me too much,' Sandy said in a low voice.

'Too much,' Rees repeated blankly. How was that even possible?

'He is jealous?' Lydia asked in understanding. Sandy nodded.

'Very. I've known Cinte all my life. He doesn't like it when anyone takes his things. And Abram . . .' Her gaze turned to her little boy. 'I fear he will always be a reminder Cinte was not my first.' Her voice broke as she hugged her little boy to her. Rees, who had adopted several orphaned children, glanced at Lydia in surprise.

'I've seen it before,' she said. With a sudden warm smile, she patted Rees's arm and added, 'Not every man is as willing to raise someone else's child as you are.'

'But Abram is just a baby,' Rees said. 'Young enough to accept Cinte as his father.'

'I thought, when I went with Gregory, Cinte would give up.' Sandy stopped and blew out her breath. 'But he seems more determined to win me now than ever.'

'That which you cannot have is always more desirable,' Lydia said dryly.

'Yes, and what happens when he has me?' Sandy asked. She turned to look at Lydia. 'Will he love me then?'

Before either Rees or Lydia could respond, Ruth came out of the hut and down the steps. She hurried to Sandy's side and hugged her carefully. Rees had seen examples of a closeness between them previously and had assumed their circumstances as a new and soon-to-be mother had bonded them. Now he wondered if there was more to it than that. Before he could follow that thought to its end, Ruth spoke.

'How is your back?'

'Hurts,' said Sandy. 'Miss Charlotte threw saltwater on it.'

'Oh, my dear,' Ruth said. She reached out and lightly touched Sandy's shoulder. 'What happened?'

'She said I was "uppity". When I went to Gregory for help, she sent him away and beat me.' Sandy sniffed.

Without speaking, Ruth continued to gently pat Sandy's shoulder. Rees and Lydia exchanged a glance. For the first time in many days, Rees felt like an outsider. No, not just an outsider. Like someone who might be an enemy. He was both white and male. He did not like the feeling, but if there was something he could say to make himself seem less of an outsider he could not think of it.

THIRTY

With a sudden startling silence, Aunt Suke paused in her grinding. Wiping an arm over her sweaty forehead, she stood and approached the fire. 'I wish we had stones,' she said. 'They be much better. But none here.'

Rees nodded. Tobias had told him there were no rocks in the swamp.

'Would y'all grind some corn into meal?' Aunt Suke said, looking at Ruth. 'At least for now. I may have more chores later.'

'Yes, ma'am. How many people do you think are coming?'

'Fifteen, maybe twenty. A' course, they all bringin' somethin'.'

Ruth squeezed Sandy's arm comfortingly and went to the wooden grinding disks.

'And Rees, will y'all help me with the loom?'

Glad to leave the uncomfortable emotions behind – they reminded him a bit too much of his own situation – Rees rose to his feet. Lydia was right behind him. When he looked at her, she smiled faintly. She did not seem as uncomfortable as he was but then she was better at interpreting other people's emotions. Wondering if his feelings were as visible to her as everyone else's seemed to be, Rees turned a worried glance upon her.

'Where are the men?' Lydia asked as they followed Aunt Suke away from the fire to the hut in which Neptune lay.

'At Drummond Lake fishin'. We need a lot of food.'

When they reached the hut Rees glanced inside. Aunt Suke had put a plate of salt and ashes underneath the body, he did not know why. Despite the sharp astringent scent of the herbs covering the body, the stink of corruption permeated the small area and the buzz of flies made a steady hum that was audible even outside. Aunt Suke climbed the two steps and shut the door.

When she came down again, she gestured to the makeshift loom. She had succeeded in weaving several yards of rough cloth, more akin to burlap than to fabric. Because it had been woven with leftover yarns, mostly tow linen, ends stuck up throughout the piece like miniature explosions. In some cases, Aunt Suke had knotted the pieces. Rees realized he had not shown her how to lay the threads over one another so that this did not happen.

She pointed to the bottom. 'I don't know how to cut it off.'

'You have to do that on both ends,' Rees said. 'And tie it. You'll have a fringe . . .' He paused, unsure whether she would approve of that. She nodded.

'I don't think Neptune will mind.' She exhaled a breath. 'My first weaving job and it be a winding sheet.'

Rees carefully tied off the strings at the bottom – not an easy job since they were all different lengths. Once that was accomplished, he carefully began unrolling the woven cloth. When he could see the end, he knotted five or six strands together, moving across the top until everything had been tied. He handed the finished cloth to Aunt Suke. She stared at it.

'Amazing,' she breathed. 'Thank you. There be one more job.'

'Yes?'

'Will you fetch the coffin?' When she looked at Rees her eyes glittered with tears. 'Too much death.'

'Of course. Where is it?'

'Probably behind the hut. The men's hut, you know.'

With a nod, Rees started up the slope. Behind him, he heard Aunt Suke say to Lydia, 'Will you help me with the body? He needs to be washed. And Rees, would y'all ask Ruth to come down and help me too?'

He turned and nodded in acknowledgment.

When he reached the top of the incline Ruth had already stopped grinding corn and stood up. 'I heard,' she said, moving past him.

He put his hand on her arm to hold her still. 'Lydia and I will be leaving soon,' he said. Ruth looked at him. Although she did not speak, her eyes welled with tears. 'We must reach Maine before the weather gets too bad. Even here it is getting colder.' He paused, but still she did not speak. 'I expect Tobias will want to accompany Lydia and me. I know he wants you to join us.'

'I can't,' she whispered.

'Why not?'

'I just can't.'

'Lydia told me – she said you still love Tobias. Is that true?'

'I do.' Ruth's tears began to fall, glistening on her cheeks.

'Then why won't you come with us?' Rees's voice rose with frustration. He looked around guiltily, but no one was within earshot. 'I don't understand. You love him. You would be safer, at least a little safer, in Maine. And your child would have a better life.'

She rested her hand on her swollen belly and began to shake her head, weeping as she did so. 'I can't. I can't. This baby – there was an overseer who . . .' Burying her face in her hands, she began sobbing.

An overseer? Not Scipio?

Rees felt like a cruel monster. Knowing that he was way out of his depth, he rose to his feet and hurried down to Quaco's hut. Lydia and Aunt Suke were just climbing the steps.

'Lydia, Lydia,' Rees said. 'I need your help.' Ignoring Aunt Suke's curious expression, Rees took his wife by the hand and pulled her after him. When they reached Ruth, Rees stepped back. Lydia threw her husband a puzzled glance before going to Ruth's side.

'What's the matter, Ruth?'

Ruth only cried harder.

'What did you do to her?' Lydia asked, turning to her husband and glaring at him accusingly.

'I was just asking some questions.' Rees lifted his shoulders in bewilderment. 'All I said was that she would have a better life in Maine if she went north with Tobias.'

Kneeling by Ruth, Lydia put her arms around her. 'Don't you want to go home with us?' she asked in a soft crooning voice.

'I do,' Ruth said. 'I really do. But I can't.'

'Why not?' Now Lydia sounded puzzled.

'Because, when I was a slave . . .' Ruth spoke so softly Rees could hardly hear her. 'When Tobias and I were slaves on the plantation . . . there was an overseer.' Ruth gulped. 'We all knew about him. Not to ever be alone with him. Don't catch his eye. Don't do anything to draw his notice.'

Rees had a sudden horrible premonition. He suspected he knew where the story was going. And Lydia did too. She put her hand over her mouth as though she feared she would be sick. She did not speak until she could control herself.

'Did he interfere with you?'

'He put me up against the barn wall and held me there. I tried to push him away but he was too strong.' Ruth sobbed against Lydia's shoulder. Rees was so upset on Ruth's behalf that he could hardly bear to look at her.

'Does Tobias know?' Lydia asked in a whisper.

'No.' Raising her head, Ruth said fiercely, 'But you see why I can't go him with him. I don't know who the father of this baby is. What if it isn't Tobias? He'd be raising another man's child. I can't do that to him. He's a good man.' The anguish in her voice tore at Rees.

Lydia crooned to Ruth and held her tight.

'You should tell him, Ruth,' Rees said. 'He deserves to know about the baby. To make his own decision.'

'I can't.' Lifting her head, Ruth said fiercely, 'I can't. He'll look at me with disgust, with hatred even. Better he should believe I don't love him than that.' Rees began to argue but Lydia shook her head at him. She held Ruth for a little while longer until her weeping subsided. As Ruth pulled away, she whispered, 'Please don't tell anyone. I couldn't bear it. I just couldn't.'

Lydia patted Ruth's arm but she made no promises. Rees certainly didn't. He thought Tobias should know. Shouldn't he? Certainly he would still love Ruth. Wouldn't he? Rees tried to imagine himself in a similar situation and felt alternately furious and sick to his stomach.

He suddenly wondered if this was how Lydia felt when she had witnessed his attraction to the rope dancer. Rees swallowed painfully and turned to his wife.

'I'll walk you down to the hut,' he said, taking Lydia's arm. The left shoulder of her dress was sodden with Ruth's tears.

'No need. Get the coffin, as you promised Aunt Suke.' Lydia took Ruth's arm but then turned back to her husband. 'She is ashamed,' she said. 'Please don't tell Tobias.'

'Why not?' Rees asked.

'She's right. We don't know how Tobias will react. It may just make the situation worse.'

'He should know,' Rees said stubbornly. He didn't see how the situation could be made worse. Tobias would spend the rest of his life believing his wife no longer loved him and had chosen a life in hiding over living with him.

'It is not up to you to tell her story. Besides, I don't want you to impulsively confide the whole without thinking it through first. Make a reasoned decision.'

'My decisions are always reasoned,' he said seriously.

Laughing, Lydia joined Ruth and linked arms with her. Rees watched the two women descend the slope. Lydia did not stop laughing until she reached Quaco's hut.

THIRTY-ONE

Rees peered into the men's hut as he went by. The four benches had been removed, but he could tell which space was Cinte's by the litter of wood-working tools scattered on the floor. Rees shook his head, wondering which plantation he had stolen them from. It was easy to see why the young man worked on his banjoes outside; the space inside was too small – even with the benches removed, too cluttered and too dark.

Rees went around the back to a flatter area where Cinte preferred to sit and work. As Aunt Suke had promised, the coffin was standing against the back of the cabin's wall. The wood was already beginning to discolor, but it was a beautiful piece of workmanship. Put together with pegs instead of nails, the coffin was made mostly of hickory and the contrast of dark and light grains was attractive. To Rees's eye, the cover looked like pine with a handle of hickory. Cinte had spent some time planing the wood to a smooth finish.

Rees tried to pick up the coffin. It was quite heavy, even empty, and he wondered if he needed the help of another man. The lid, in contrast, was not as weighty. Two trips then. Rees hoisted the coffin on to his shoulder and made his laborious way to the other side of camp. The women had already wrapped Neptune in his winding sheet.

'Put the coffin on the floor,' Aunt Suke directed.

So Rees carried it into the shadowed interior. As Lydia and Aunt Suke steadied it, one on each end, he carefully eased the coffin from his shoulder and then the three of them lowered it to the floor.

They needed his help putting Neptune's body into the coffin

as well. Rees pushed it to the bench and then, taking Neptune's shoulders, lowered the top half of the body into the coffin. For a few minutes, the body lay half in and half out of the box. Rees thought fleetingly of his friend, Shaker Sister Esther, who would not have hesitated to grab the corpse's feet and slip them into the body's final home.

But these two women stood back and waited for him to finish the job.

The smell of corruption was almost too intense to bear.

Rees quickly moved the rest of Neptune's body into the coffin and stood back. 'I'll get the lid now,' he said and fled into the fresh air. He almost ran through camp to fetch the coffin lid. Placing that over the body would lessen the odor significantly.

Mourners began arriving that afternoon. Carefully guided by Toney and Peros, they came mostly in groups of two or three. Rees watched these strangers arrive in the village with a mixture of surprise and discomfort. He now felt the same dislocation as he had when he visited the diggers' camp by the canal. Too many people! He had gotten used to living within a small community.

As for the new arrivals, they eyed Rees with wariness and fear. The expressions on the faces of some of the children told Rees they had never before seen a white man. How long had some of these families been hiding in the swamp? He saw children aged eight or nine, so it had been at least that long.

All of them brought a gift: baskets of eggs, of onions, of artichokes, dishes nestled up against the food. Most of the women carried cooked fare, whatever they could spare. Lots of cornbread, hominy or beans. Aunt Suke directed them to the fire, banked now. One man brought a fine ceramic bowl which he presented to Aunt Suke with a flourish. Another brought a small keg of rum. Jackman took possession of that, carrying it away and hiding it. And finally, one young man brought a drum so Rees knew there would be music.

No one spoke to him or to Lydia as they walked down to Quaco's hut to look at the body. Rees wondered how Cinte would feel, to see these people mourning Neptune. The theft of Scipio's body had robbed him of this comfort. And what had happened to it? It had never reappeared and Rees guessed it had been turned in for the reward.

When Jackman called everyone together in front of the cabin in which Neptune lay, Rees counted twenty-two people. The village felt full to bursting.

'Welcome,' Jackman said, trying to shout over the chatter. 'We gather here to say goodbye to our brother, Neptune.' By the time he finished speaking, the hum of conversation had drifted into silence. 'He be a valued member of this village. A good hunter. We will miss him.'

He stepped aside and a woman moved into his place. 'My son,' she began, her face wet with tears. 'He rescued me. Brought me here, to the . . . to the . . .' Breaking down completely, she allowed a young man to lead her away. Aunt Suke embraced the woman and held her as she sobbed.

Other young men came up to speak, some of them with accents so strong Rees could barely understand them. 'He kind. Loyal. Took a whippin' for me once.' They all spoke about Neptune's honesty and fair dealing. Rees began to wonder if he had really tried to blackmail the murderer. Had the lure of the money necessary to fund his freedom been too great? Or had something else been going on?

After everyone who wished to speak had done so, Toney and Peros, and four other young men, carried the coffin from inside the hut. As Jackman went to the front, the men hoisted the coffin to their shoulders. As the drummer tapped out a rhythm, the mourners clapped in time. Rees and Lydia glanced at one another in surprise. They had been warned this would not be a somber affair but it was still startling to see what appeared as a celebration.

Neptune's mother began to clap and sing, melodious syllables that Rees could not understand. Although the song she sang was not a dirge, the anguish in her voice prompted Rees to recall the losses he'd suffered: first among them, his first wife. He took Lydia's arm and held it tightly.

They slowly marched from the village center to the cemetery. It wasn't that far from the village, but at this slow, measured pace it took much longer than if Rees had walked on his own. When they reached the open grave, the bearers put the coffin on the side. Jackman bowed his head and began to pray. His voice resonated through the small yard, his words flowing fluidly from his lips.

'As we bid goodbye to our brother, I remind you of what the Good Book says: "Who shall separate us from the love of Christ?"'

'No one,' chorused the group.

'Shall trouble or hardship or persecution of famine or nakedness or danger or sword? As it is written: "For your sake we face death all day long; we are considered as sheep to be slaughtered."'

'Amen.'

'No. In all these things we are more than conquerors through Him who loved us.

'For I am convinced that neither death nor life, neither angels nor demons, neither the present nor the future, nor any powers, neither height nor depth, nor anything else in all creation, will be able to separate us from the love of God that is in Christ Jesus Our Lord.'

'Amen.'

Since he did not hold a Bible, Rees could only assume Jackman was quoting entirely from memory. When he paused the mourners responded so that instead of a minister preaching, the service was more of a dialogue between Jackman and the congregation. Rees found it odd but curiously moving.

The coffin was lowered into the grave. Neptune's fishing pole and line were put in the grave with him along with small portions of food: eggs and sweet potatoes, a plug of tobacco. Then Toney pushed the dirt over it. Although a wooden cross was erected over the grave, as it would be for any Christian burial, Rees knew that cross would soon be festooned with charms and other items like the others had been.

This was an odd form of Christianity, a mix of the faith Rees knew and something other. Something exotic. He wasn't sure how he felt about it.

While the women walked back into the village to fetch the food they'd brought, the men went another way, toward that flat space at the bottom of the hill and closer to the water. Now Rees knew what had occupied Jackman earlier this morning. He'd built a large fire and suspended a haunch of beef over it to roast. Although Rees wondered how the beef would taste – it had not been cured at all – the smell of cooking meat brought the water into his mouth.

The benches from several of the huts had been brought down and arranged to serve as both tables and chairs. Children from other camps chased each other around the adults and ran toward the water at the edge of the space. Rees saw Abram, shrieking with joy, trying desperately to keep up with the older children. While some of them were as noisy as any child, several were strangely quiet even though they were grinning and happy. Rees stared at them, trying to imagine his own kids so restrained.

'They've been taught to be quiet,' Tobias said, coming up beside Rees and interpreting his expression.

'Taught?' Rees said, his gaze following a silent brother and sister in the center of the pack.

'So the slave catchers don't get them,' Tobias said. He glanced at Rees and then at the children. 'Their families must live closer to the swamp's edge. Kids from deeper in the swamp, where the white men don't go, aren't so frightened.' He turned to Rees and added, half-joking, half-seriously, 'They're only scared of the white man.'

'Not of me?' Rees said, aghast, glancing around. There were other pale faces here, Sandy among them, who could easily pass as white and would occasion no comment in Maine. But he and Lydia were the whitest, especially combined with their red hair. Rees gulped. *He* was the white man. Tobias nodded.

'Afraid so.'

That was a strange feeling, to know he was a frightening figure based entirely on the color of his skin. And it kept reappearing, as shocking the third or fourth time as it had been the first.

But thinking of Sandy reminded Rees of Ruth and he pushed his feelings aside to be examined later. He turned to Tobias. Should he say something now? Should he ask how Tobias felt? 'I spoke to Ruth,' Rees began.

'Here she comes now,' Tobias said, plunging forward. Rees turned. The women were coming down the hill, arms laden with baskets, wooden bowls and cooking utensils. Aunt Suke even carried the iron spider with the last of the original corn-bread in it. Rees looked around for Lydia and spotted her finally, helping Aunt Suke lay out the food.

The food was arranged on tables. Rees peered at them; recognizing the furniture finally as the benches that had been taken from the huts. While Jackman wielded the carving knife and cut the beef, the women, including Lydia, began serving the roasted sweet potatoes, the onions fried in bacon grease, the green corn. There was no bread, other than the corn pone cooked in the spider. Rees longed for fresh baked bread, the crust chewy over the softer interior. As he thought about food, he realized he also missed the humble beet, a staple in Maine. Suddenly, with a sharp pang, he yearned for the forests of pine trees, the dark green spruce against the coating of white snow on the ground beneath them.

Abram shrieked and ran past, his face and dress dark with dirt. Rees watched the child run. Most of all he missed his children. He wanted to go home, but not before he fulfilled his promise to Aunt Suke.

He went to find Lydia.

THIRTY-TWO

Rees and Lydia found a place to eat, on the steps of Quaco's hut a distance away from the crowd. Despite spending almost two weeks in the swamp, Rees felt out of place here.

'It feels odd here, with so many people,' Lydia said.

'Yes,' Rees agreed, smiling at her. His discomfort was due to more than that. He knew it. He, and probably Lydia too, were the topic of at least a few of the low-voiced conversations. Jackman, Aunt Suke, Toney, even Peros, had grown accustomed to these white people in their midst. But now,

with Neptune's funeral, Rees and Lydia were the reviled
outsiders once again.

But they were not the only ones who felt strange. Tobias
and Ruth, separately, climbed the slope to join them. Rees
wondered why they had chosen to sit with him and his wife,
but he didn't quite have the courage to ask. Instead it was
Lydia who hinted at their surprising decision.

'Do you know the visitors?' she asked. 'Those people who
came from other villages?' Tobias shook his head.

'A few,' Ruth said. 'But we are different. We were born free
in Maine.' Tobias nodded.

'We think differently.'

'We can read,' Ruth put in. Rees nodded. He remembered
her from the small one-room schoolhouse; a little girl with
fat braids.

'Horrifying,' Lydia said critically. 'The Shakers teach
everyone to read.' She jumped to her feet to help Sandy up
the slope. She was still moving stiffly, and Rees noted with
disapproval that her wooden plate bore only a small piece
of sweet potato and a fragment of beef.

'Where's Abram?' Lydia asked.

'Running around with the children,' Sandy said. Smiling
faintly, she added, 'He is far too excited to eat.'

She had no sooner spoken than a loud wail cut through the
wall of conversation.

'I think that's Abram,' Ruth said.

'Oh dear,' Sandy said without moving.

Casting her an annoyed glance, Ruth pushed herself
awkwardly to her feet. Her pregnancy was beginning to affect
her balance. She started down the hill as Aunt Suke, carrying
the squirming toddler, trudged up to them. 'He started hittin''
and bitin',' she said. 'He be tired and hungry.'

Ruth took the little boy in her arms, crooning wordlessly
to soothe him. She sat down and offered him a piece of
cornbread. He screamed and pushed her hand away. She
pressed the cornbread into his mouth. He tried to spit it out
but he was hungry and he chewed instead. Since Sandy
had nothing on her plate but a bit of gristle, the others all

contributed something from their plates. Tobias ran up the slope for a dipperful of water from the barrel. By the time he returned, Abram's eyes were closing.

'It's past five,' Ruth said, darting a practiced glance at the sky. 'And he had no nap today.' Then, as Abram released a flood of urine, she cried, 'Oh no.' Standing up, she eyed the large wet stain on her skirt in dismay. Aunt Suke rose as well and together the two women, Ruth still carrying the child, climbed the incline to the healer's hut.

Sandy shuddered daintily. 'I just can't bear that,' she said. 'At the plantation, one of the grannies always took care of it.'

Both Rees and Lydia turned to stare at her. 'That is part of raising children,' he said disapprovingly.

'He'll grow out of it soon enough and won't be a baby any more,' Lydia said, 'and you'll miss these times.'

Looking incredulous, Sandy snapped out a response, but Rees, no longer paying attention, did not hear it. Over her head he saw Quaco, sliding in and around the other people by the food, helping himself without speaking to any of them. Rees put down his plate and rose to his feet.

'I've got to speak to him,' he said, stepping around Lydia. 'I'll be back.' He hurried down the slope.

But Quaco saw him coming. Quickly threading his way through the crowd, he slid out of the hollow and disappeared into the vegetation. Rees hurried after him, not stopping when Quaco ran into the swamp. Rees followed closely behind, trying to keep the other man in sight. He jogged around thickets and splashed through the shallow waters beneath the trees. Even the sounds of the village – the chatter, the lowing of the cattle, and the crowing of the rooster – faded. Rees didn't notice. He kept running. But, although the shrubs and deciduous trees had dropped most of their leaves, Quaco quickly disappeared.

Realizing he had lost his quarry, Rees stopped. Breathing hard, he looked around. He did not see anything he recognized. He glanced over his shoulder, but the tangle of trees and the glint of the water looked exactly the same as the terrain in front. He could not hear the delighted squeals of the children or the chatter of their parents. All sounds from the village had disappeared, absorbed by the vegetation and the water.

'Damn,' he said in dismay, realizing that he was lost.

Rees was tempted to spin around and run back the way he'd come, but he forced himself to stand quietly. He would lose himself for certain if he ran aimlessly in a panic. Closing his eyes, he tried to slow his pounding heart. A bird flew overhead, uttering a sharp cry that made him jump. Opening his eyes, he looked around more carefully. The sun had already dropped below the tree line and, if he didn't hurry, he would be struggling through the swamp in the dark. Possibly even sinking deep within the peat. He looked at the ground. He could see his footprints, pressed deeply into the moist soil. He began to follow them.

When the trail went through small pools, it was easy to follow. But the larger flooded areas proved to be a problem and Rees wasted valuable daylight searching the banks for his tracks. As the sun sank lower and lower, shadows stretched over the ground and the imprint of his steps became harder and harder to see. He tried to hurry when he could.

'I'll kill Quaco when I catch him,' Rees muttered, repeating the threat over and over as he struggled forward.

Dusk transitioned into evening and now Rees could barely see the ground beneath his feet. He let out a bellow of frustration. But wait, he heard something. So faint he was not sure, but it sounded like it might be his name. He shouted again as he tried to identify the location of the sound. He walked forward, in what he thought might be the direction. Step by step, shouting until he was hoarse, Rees made his way through the tangled undergrowth. He could not tell if he was heading in the right direction but the voice he followed was growing louder as it approached. 'Rees. Will Rees.'

And he was nearing the village. He could hear a drumbeat and voices raised in song.

'Rees.'

'I'm here. I'm here,' he said. His voice sounded rough and gravelly.

'Stay where you are.' That sounded like Tobias. 'I'm coming for you.'

Rees turned in the direction of the voice and took a few steps before he paused.

'I see you.' Feet splashed through water and a shape appeared from the darkness.

'Tobias?' Rees asked.

'Yes. I've been looking for you for over an hour. Your wife has been wild with worry.'

'I ran into the swamp after Quaco,' Rees said, realizing for the first time how tired he was.

'He knows this area like the back of his hand,' Tobias said. 'You would never catch him.' He reached out and took hold of Rees's arm. 'We aren't far away from the camp now.'

'I hear the drum.'

They walked for another few minutes and then Rees saw open sky, not quite dark but already flecked with stars, and he knew they were almost home.

Tobias wound through the last of the forest and they came out at the bottom of the fields. Rees could see the graveyard, illuminated by the glow of the large fire beyond. The beef had been removed and the flames fed with more wood so they reached high and yellow toward the heavens. People were dancing and singing. Aunt Suke danced in the center. She sang as she moved and it looked as though she was throwing something, salt maybe, into the fire. Rees looked at Tobias.

'Dancing and singing.' Although Tobias had warned Rees, he was still surprised.

'This is how the slaves say goodbye,' Tobias said.

'But why are they singing?'

'Neptune is going home. His life of servitude is over. Instead of grieving, we are supposed to be happy for him.'

Rees glanced at the people gyrating in the flickering orange light. He now understood why Jackman had chosen the Bible verse he had. When Rees turned back to his friend, Tobias shrugged. 'It is a different way. Those of us raised in the north don't fully understand.'

'I see,' Rees said untruthfully. 'Lydia?' he asked. Tobias pointed up the slope.

'She said she would wait at the hut.' He turned to cut across the bottom of the slope toward the crowd beyond.

Although eager to join Lydia, and sit down with a cup of water, Rees called out, 'Wait.' Tobias turned. 'I need to tell you something.'

Tobias took a few steps back to Rees. 'What?'

'I talked to Ruth.' Rees paused. How would he feel if a man had abused Lydia as Ruth had been abused? Enraged. He would hunger to kill the other man. But would he despise his wife? This problem was difficult.

'And?' Tobias prompted impatiently.

Rees took in a breath. It was too late for him to second guess himself. 'She loves you, you know,' he said. 'She loves you, but something happened at the plantation.' He stopped. He knew Tobias was listening by the marked stillness of his body. 'She is afraid – it is possible . . .' Rees hesitated again. Tobias said nothing. Inhaling another deep breath, Rees spoke very fast. 'The overseer forced himself upon her and she sees herself as damaged goods and feels you deserve better.'

'Better,' Tobias repeated.

'And she feels you won't want her if you know.'

Tobias sighed and glanced over his shoulder at the fire with its necklace of dancing figures. 'I heard something about that,' he said. After a tense moment of silence he added, 'but she never said anything.'

'She is afraid of what you might think,' Rees said.

'What I think? I think I couldn't protect her,' Tobias said, his head bowed and his voice thickening. 'I knew that bastard liked her. I could tell by the way he looked at her. If I'd known he was going after her I would have beaten him, whether they killed me or not.'

'That is why she didn't tell you,' Rees said. 'She wanted to protect you.'

Tobias looked over his shoulder again. In the firelight Rees saw the shine of a tear as it crept down the curve of Tobias's cheek.

'And the baby?' he asked. Rees struggled with his answer. He wanted to tell the truth, but didn't want to persuade Tobias to push away the child as Cinte had done with Sandy's Abram.

'Um. Likeliest, the child is yours,' Rees said at last. 'But there is a chance that . . .' He stopped talking when Tobias spun around and began running toward the fire.

Rees stared after him. What would Tobias decide now that he knew the truth?

THIRTY-THREE

Rees trudged through the fields to the top of the slope and Quaco's hut. Lydia jumped to her feet. 'Will! Where did you go?'

'I chased Quaco into the swamp and got lost,' Rees said. 'Tobias found me. I'm knackered.'

'Let me get you some food,' Lydia said. She started toward the tables, her body outlined by the orange light from the fire. Rees leaned his head back and rested it against the rough wall of the hut. His feet burned with blisters and the muscles in his legs ached from the running and then the long walk that followed.

'Are you asleep?' Lydia asked when she returned.

'No,' he said, although he had dozed off. He sat up and took the plate from her. In the fitful light, it was hard to see what was on it.

'Meat and sweet potato,' Lydia said, handing him a wooden spoon. It had all been cooked into a soft brownish mash. Rees took a bite. It tasted fine and he cleaned the plate. He felt even more tired after eating.

'I may have made a mistake,' he said as he handed Lydia the empty plate. 'I told Tobias.'

'Oh, Will, you didn't.'

'Don't worry,' he said quickly. 'I did think about it.' No point in confessing when he'd thought about it and his sudden reservations after telling Tobias. 'He needed to know Ruth isn't hesitating because she doesn't love him. And if he doesn't know, and she goes north with him, that secret will always lie between them.'

'How did he react?' Lydia asked after a few seconds.

Rees thought about Tobias and his reaction. 'He blames himself for not protecting her,' he said in some surprise.

'He couldn't have done anything,' Lydia said.

'I know. They would have killed him,' Rees agreed. And then, without even knowing he was going to speak, he added, 'I am so, so sorry I hurt you.' Lydia blinked. 'I was never unfaithful to you,' he added. 'I swear on the Bible.'

Lydia looked away from him and did not speak for several seconds. Rees watched her anxiously. 'That was more luck than planning,' she said at last. 'She would have drawn you into her bed and you would have gone; I know it.'

He wished he was a better man than that, but he knew she might be right. 'I had a lucky escape, I guess,' he said. 'I love you and the children.'

'Then why were you so susceptible to her charms?' Lydia asked.

Now it was his turn to remain quiet. Finally, as the silence stretched on and became uncomfortable, he said, 'I don't know.' He tried to recall his feelings from last spring. 'I just felt . . . trapped, I suppose, by the responsibilities of the farm.'

'Was it me?' Lydia gulped. 'Do you still love me?'

'Of course.' Rees leaned forward and pulled her into his arms. He paused. 'Why did you say that? Do you still love me?'

'Yes. That's why I . . .' She stopped and pulled away. 'How would you feel if it was me yearning for another man?'

Rees stared at her. The shock of realizing how devastated he would be washed over him. He would love Lydia and hate her at the same time. Was that how Lydia felt about him?

'Aunt Suke says I am afraid of leaning on you too much,' he said in a soft voice.

'That rope dancer was barely twenty,' Lydia said, her glance shifting to the side. Rees remembered how young and how charming she'd been.

'Too young for me,' he said. 'Why did *you* marry me? I am an old man.'

'Old man?' She pulled back and stared at him. 'You are just forty years old.'

'My father died at forty-six.'

'Your mother lived until nearly eighty,' she said tartly, pulling away. 'Besides, your father was a drunkard. He fell off a wagon. While he was convalescing, he contracted a fever. None of that suggests you will die at the same age.'

'My mother lived an unusually long time,' Rees said. Lydia did not respond to that argument but stared at him for several seconds.

'Now I understand what this is about,' she said. 'You're afraid of getting older and dying. Or me dying.'

'No, I'm not,' he contradicted. 'Well, maybe a little. But it was more than that.' With spring, and the melting of the snow, he'd suddenly hungered for something different. He'd felt as though he could not stay on the farm for one more minute. 'I just needed a change,' he said. 'Identifying the murderer should have been enough. But she . . .' His voice trailed away as he remembered how attentive Bambola had been. He'd imagined himself a young man again, a man who would be attractive to a young and pretty girl. And a young woman besides who would shortly leave town. There would be no long-term responsibility for him. And all the while she'd been bewitching him for her own purposes. He cringed inside to recall that now.

'I never meant to hurt you,' he said softly. 'At first it was all part of the attraction of the circus. It was all so outlandish, you know. So exotic.'

'I remember,' she said, with a faint smile. 'Those gold horses on the carriages and the colorful costumes. I couldn't compete.'

'But none of that was real,' Rees said. 'It was all illusion.' He hugged her tightly to him. He was so grateful he had not surrendered everything he really cared about for a phantasm.

'Let's go to the hut,' Lydia said. 'It has been a busy day and I'm tired.'

'I am too,' Rees said. He rose stiffly to his feet and took a few steps, wincing with every step.

'What's the matter?'

'Blisters.' Rees looked down at his wet shoes. 'I probably should have worn stockings but . . .' His voice trailed off.

'Take your shoes off and go barefoot,' Lydia said.

Rees did as she suggested. He tried to walk up the slope, wincing as his tender flesh stepped on sticks and acorns. As a child he had gone barefoot every summer and coped with the itching in the fall as the calluses wore off. But he hadn't gone barefoot for many years now. Lydia began laughing as he staggered up the slope. 'Don't be a baby,' she said. And Rees knew by her teasing that she had forgiven him. Finally. Relief and joy swept over him and he turned to put his arm around her. She hugged him quickly and then, without speaking, she pulled him into the hut.

Afterwards, snuggled together in the thin ragged blanket and the linen sheets that had fallen from the bar, Rees stared blissfully into the darkness. 'We were right to come here,' he said. 'Even if I could not identify the murderer.' He frowned. 'This is the first time I've failed.' He did not like failure.

'Don't think of that now,' Lydia said. 'You did your best.'

'Soon we will be going home,' he said. 'And all of this, the swamp and the people who live within it, will seem like a dream.'

'I have something to tell you,' she whispered.

Rees kissed her. 'What?'

'I am with child,' she said.

'What?' Rees turned to her, although he could see nothing in the darkness. She laughed.

'Yes. I think he will be born next spring, probably April.'

'He?' Rees grasped on the one thing he could understand from her news. She chuckled again.

'Aunt Suke is certain it will be a boy.' She paused and then added, 'Not bad for an old man.' Then she added with a grin, 'Hmmm?'

THIRTY-FOUR

The drumming and singing continued until almost light. Rees did not think he would be able to sleep, what with the noise and his excitement at Lydia's news, but he did. He was awakened way too early the following morning by voices outside. Sliding carefully from underneath the blanket, Rees wrapped a sheet around himself and tiptoed to the door. The sky was still dark but a pale light toward the east hinted at the sunrise to come.

Aunt Suke and Jackman were sitting by the fire. Rees hurriedly threw on his clothing and went outside as well.

'What are y'all doing awake?' Aunt Suke asked. She smelled of rum and wood smoke, despite the water dripping from her hair. 'I thought you went to bed.'

'We did,' Rees said.

'We kept them awake,' Jackman said to her. 'The drummin' and dancin'.'

'No,' Rees said.

'We woke them,' Aunt Suke said.

'We were up late with something to discuss.' Rees could not help the grin that crept across his face. Aunt Suke looked at him sharply and smiled a particularly all-knowing smile.

'Why are all of you up so early?' Lydia asked from the steps of the cabin. Aunt Suke glanced over.

'Ah, here comes the wife,' she said. And then, as Lydia approached the fire, she added more loudly, 'You told him.'

'Yes.' A long look passed between the two women.

'Good,' she said, glancing from Lydia to Rees and smiling. 'Good. You be fine now.'

'Why are you all wet?' Rees asked.

'We bathed,' Aunt Suke said. 'It be important to wash away the dust of the grave before enterin' the house.'

'Don't want the ghosts of the departed to follow,' Jackman agreed.

'Most everybody still down in the water,' Aunt Suke said.

'Men down there,' Jackman said, pointing over his shoulder with his thumb to the area at which Rees had bathed.

'And women down there,' Aunt Suke said, gesturing toward the area where the women washed clothes.

Rees suddenly yawned, a huge gape that cracked his jaw. When he looked up at the sky he saw the morning star. There were only a few hours remaining before daybreak.

'We should go back to bed,' Lydia said, taking her husband's arm.

'Might as well,' Jackman said.

'Everybody'll be sleepin' late,' Aunt Suke said with a smile.

Lydia took Rees's arm and urged him upright. He went willingly. When he glanced over his shoulder, he saw Jackman and Aunt Suke banking the fire. The village center was plunged into darkness.

When Rees awoke once again, sun was streaming through the door of the cabin. He could hear conversation outside, interspersed with bird calls. Lydia was already gone. He struggled out of the sheets, which had somehow become wound around him, and dressed. He tried to put on his shoes but couldn't. Several blisters had come out, large inflated swellings on his feet that were far too painful for shoes. He went down the steps barefoot. He smelled bacon and there was a mess of eggs in the pan. Lydia rose from her place by Ruth and fetched a wooden plate to fill for him. As she began to make coffee in the small pot, he sat down on the log next to her where she'd been sitting and began to eat. He hungered for real bread; another reason to go home.

He realized suddenly that Ruth was smiling at him from the other side of Lydia's spot. He offered her a tentative grin, wondering why she was so happy today. 'I'll be returning to Maine with you, after all,' she said. Rees felt his mouth drop open.

Closing it so he could swallow, he said, 'Why? How?'

'Tobias and I talked,' she said in a whisper. 'We talked about what happened.' She glanced from side to side. 'He said I have you to thank for that.'

'Where is Tobias?' Rees asked, glancing around.

'Helping Jackman clean up. They're making sure the fire is out.'

'Aunt Suke is there too, collecting all the plates,' Lydia put in.

'I'll go down after breakfast and help bring back the benches,' Rees said. 'If I can,' he added, looking at his feet in dismay.

'I'm sure Aunt Suke has some herbs that will help,' Lydia said. 'Then we'll bind them. At least,' she added teasingly, 'so you can walk.'

'Some of the benches are already here,' Ruth said, as Lydia sat between her and Rees.

'Several of the people who came to the funeral left at first light. Some of them brought up seats, plates, leftover food,' Lydia explained.

'They left already?' Rees asked in surprise. He'd seen no sign of it when he and Lydia had gotten up earlier.

'All that could, left as soon as it was dawn,' Ruth said with a chuckle. 'And some weren't feeling very well.' Rees nodded. A keg of liquor had been stolen from the Sechrest plantation and at least one of the mourners had brought another. In Rees's opinion, the funeral and the wake that followed had more resembled a revelry than a solemn ritual. It was one more among the surprising differences between life in the swamp and in Maine.

Yawning, Sandy came out of the hut with Abram in tow. She had washed her face and braided her hair and her child had been recently changed. Although that clean dress would not stay clean, Rees thought, if Abram insisted on digging his fingers into the dirt. He remembered being as fascinated with dirt when he was a little boy and guessed boys were the same everywhere.

Sandy herself looked happier. She held out her hand for the little boy and together they walked to the fire. Both Ruth and Lydia rose to their feet to dish out some breakfast. Sandy consented to eat some eggs, although they were cold. And she smiled at everyone there.

Rees breathed a sigh of relief; Sandy, he guessed, would recover.

'You look well,' Lydia said. 'Not tired.'

'I didn't stay for very long last night,' Sandy said. 'I barely knew Neptune.'

'We didn't stay either,' Lydia said with a smile. Rees could feel his smile stretching his cheeks.

'I can't eat.' A voice floated up the slope. Rees looked over Sandy's head. Aunt Suke, trailed by several other people, was approaching the group by the fire. Since Aunt Suke carried a large wooden bowl with leftover food in it, Rees guessed she had been trying to persuade the people behind her to take some with them. The group, two men, a woman and two children, stared at Rees and Lydia by the fire and did not pause. They melted into the thicket, disappearing instantly into the swamp.

'They be sorry they didn't eat,' Aunt Suke said.

Rees looked at her. She seemed tired, and her braids, which were usually tightly plaited, were messy with hair sticking out in tufts.

'Anyone of our callers left?' Lydia asked. Aunt Suke shook her head.

'No, they all gone.'

'Can you tape up my feet?' Rees asked, extending them for her examination. 'I'll go and help Jackman.'

'You got yourself some blisters there,' Aunt Suke muttered. 'Put on some of your wife's pennyroyal salve. That should help.'

So Rees allowed Lydia to rub the salve on his feet. Then she tore one of the sheets into strips and wound them around his feet until they looked like two large white bulky blobs. Rees stood up. They didn't feel great but he could walk. And the thick layer of linen protected his feet somewhat as he walked over the ground.

By the time he joined the other men at the bottom of the slope where the animal pens were located, they were almost finished cleaning up. The fire had been extinguished and the charred wood scattered. The ashes had been collected in a barrel for later use; soaking them would produce lye to make soap or soak dried corn so it could be eaten. Most of the benches had already been brought up the slope.

Rees looked around, noting the smooth packed dirt where, the previous night, the dancers had gathered.

And staring at him from the seclusion of the forest was Quaco. Rees said, very quietly and gently, 'I can't chase you into the forest. But now two men are dead. I think you saw something. Tell me what you saw.'

'Tell him, please,' Jackman said. He repeated it again in the foreign tongue. Quaco looked from side to side as though he would flee, but he didn't. Finally, with Jackman translating the flood of strange syllables, he replied.

'I saw nothing unusual. Just Cinte paying his respects to his friend. Nothing more.'

'I don't believe it,' Rees said. He wouldn't believe it. 'That can't be all.' Turning to Jackman, he asked him to insist. Jackman refused at first but as Rees became angrier and angrier, Jackman finally agreed. But, when Rees looked back to the screen of trees, he discovered Quaco was gone.

'Damn liar,' Rees muttered angrily. He picked up the keg of rum, noticeably lighter than it had been, and started up the slope. 'Wait,' Jackman said, limping behind him. 'Wait.' Rees, who realized his feet were stinging as he stamped angrily away, slowed down.

'What?' Rees knew he sounded annoyed but didn't care.

'Quaco doesn't lie, hmmm?' Jackman said. 'If he said that was what he saw, then that's what he saw.'

'He knows something important, I'm sure of it,' Rees retorted. 'He's protecting someone.'

'He answered you. He told you what he know. If he didn't want to say, he would have run away.'

Since Quaco had already done exactly that several times, Rees couldn't argue. But he was still certain that the wild man in the swamp knew something more. He just wished he knew what it was.

THIRTY-FIVE

When Rees reached the village center, he found Cinte sitting by Sandy. He was smiling, aglow with happiness. She, however, was staring at her feet in silence.

'I did not expect to see you back so soon,' Rees said, trying to sound gracious.

'Once I sold everythin' I carried with me, I walked through the night,' Cinte said. 'I hurried.' He reached out to take Sandy's hand but she involuntarily twitched away from him.

'Where's Abram?' Rees asked. Lydia pointed to Aunt Suke,

sitting a short distance away with the child in her lap. She was tickling his feet and making him giggle uncontrollably.

'Are you going with us, when we leave?' Lydia asked Cinte. He shook his head.

'I've a mind to settle in the Northwest Territory,' he said. 'Ohio. It'll be a state soon. And slavery been forbidden.' He threw a look at Sandy. 'If she'll have me, of course.' Rees guessed Cinte felt pretty confident of a positive reaction if he announced his intentions so publicly.

Sandy looked across the circle. 'I should stay here,' she said. 'With Abram.'

'Aunt Suke'll raise 'im. You be too delicate, too womanly, to remain in the swamp. Always in danger of capture. We'll go north to freedom, pass as white and buy a little farm. Our children, yours and mine, will be raised like rich white people. You'll want for nothing, Sandy. We'll have a good life.' He reached forward and took her hand. She grimaced.

'You've finished selling all your banjoes?' Rees asked. Cinte nodded.

'Most of them. And the wood. Couldn't take it with me. But I'll bring my tools. I can always work as a carpenter.' He nodded. 'We'll do well.' His gaze went to Sandy. 'I'll give her everything she wants.'

Except her baby. Rees tried to imagine Sandy walking to Ohio and failed. Now Aunt Suke could do it; she had the toughness.

'That is a long way,' Lydia said, her thoughts mirroring Rees's.

'My plan is to walk to Suffolk. I have a horse and a carriage waitin'.' He threw a grin at Sandy. She was no longer looking at him. 'We be ridin' out of Virginia in style.'

'You're not afraid of being caught?' Lydia asked. Cinte shook his head.

'Someone in Suffolk is helpin' me.'

'For a price.'

'For a price,' Cinte agreed, flapping his hand dismissively as though money was no object. 'In a carriage, dressed in fine clothes, we be drivin' out like we's white. Drive through the night so we's get far away where no one knows us.'

Rees nodded. They could do it. Both of them were fair,

Cinte's hair almost blond. And Sandy, gowned in silk and with her lady-of-the-manor airs, would not be questioned.

'We'll leave as soon as we can,' Cinte promised. When Sandy did not speak, he added, 'I'll give you a good life, Sandy.' He leaned forward to kiss her. She didn't pull away, but she didn't respond either. 'You won't be sorry, my love.'

'No. No, I won't,' she said. But she didn't sound as though she believed it.

Into the awkward silence, Rees said, 'I'm sorry I was not able to identify your brother's murderer.'

Cinte shrugged. 'Y'all did your best. It were a long shot anyway.'

'I want you to know I haven't given up,' Rees said, stung. Cinte had never trusted Rees to do what he'd promised. 'I believe Quaco knows something. I'll talk to him today. Maybe, just maybe, with his help, I'll be able to find the killer before we all leave.'

Cinte nodded, looking doubtful. But he didn't argue. 'Didn't sleep last night,' he said. 'I'm going down to the hut. But before I do . . .' He pulled a sheet of paper from his pocket and handed it to Rees.

'What's this?'

'Saw this posted in the store at the canal. The sheriff be lookin' for you.'

Sandy stood up and came to the fire to peer over Lydia's shoulder. 'How do you know it's about him?' Sandy asked.

'It says big, red-haired white man,' Cinte said.

'How do you know that? You can't read,' Sandy said with a sniff.

'I read well enough for that,' Cinte said, sounding insulted.

Rees smoothed out the paper. Two simple drawings depicted a man and a boy. 'Wanted,' he read. 'Tall, red-haired white man and young boy. Theft from Sechrest plantation. Reward.'

He handed the poster to Lydia. She read it quickly. 'Fortunately,' she said, 'I am not a boy.'

'You'll have to wear your dress,' Rees said. She nodded.

'I planned to anyway.'

Rees sighed. Even with Lydia in her dress, the trip would

now be much more difficult. He would be looking over his shoulder all the time.

'You better get some sleep,' Cinte said to Sandy. 'Tomorrow be a busy day.' She nodded but, as he strode down the slope, she burst into tears. Rising to her feet, she fled into Aunt Suke's hut.

'Poor chick,' Lydia said. 'She must feel she has no choice.'

'Does she?' Rees turned to look at his wife. 'Does she have a choice? Staying here in the swamp. Eaten alive by the insects, too hot, too cold, probably hungry a lot of the time. Or going to a life of freedom, with a man who can make a good living. Hardly a choice at all.'

THIRTY-SIX

Maybe Aunt Suke could help him dye his hair. With that flaming mop, Rees was too identifiable. Ruminating on possibilities, he left the fire and went down the hill to find Jackman.

The village chief was gathering up the bones of the cow and putting them in a basket. When Rees looked at Jackman in surprise – the charred bones had been stripped of meat – he said, 'Aunt Suke can boil these up. With some corn and some greens, it'll make a good stew.'

'Could you signal Quaco?' Rees asked. 'I want to speak with him again.'

Jackman put down the basket. Turning, he glared at Rees. 'No. He done told you all he knows.'

'I think he knows something else,' Rees argued.

'He don't.'

'He saw something. I know it.'

'He didn't. He say he didn't and he don't lie.' Jackman folded his arms across his chest, but he did not quite dare to glare his defiance at a white man and instead kept his eyes fixed on the ground. Rees suspected he could force the issue and intimidate Jackman with his size and white skin. For a moment, as he wavered, the possibility hung in the air but then he stepped back, surrendering the win. He would have to find another way.

Jackman stared at Rees in surprise when he surrendered and made his way up the slope. Rees did not know how he felt to realize Jackman had expected him to press the issue. Jackman's experience with white men led him to expect the worst.

If Jackman wouldn't help him, Rees was determined to search for Quaco himself.

Half an hour later, Lydia found him in the cabin trying to push his bandaged feet into his shoes. But the linen wrapping was so thick around his feet he couldn't squeeze them into the leather.

'What are you doing?' she demanded, putting her hands on her hips.

'I have to talk to Quaco,' he said, unwinding the grubby strips.

'Why?'

'I know he knows something.'

'Wait.' She put her hand on his wrist. 'Instead of using brute strength we need to use our intellect. Think this through.'

'We don't know enough,' he said in frustration.

'Maybe we should identify what we know and what we don't,' she said.

Rees eyed her. 'Come with me,' she coaxed, gesturing to a basket outside. 'I am washing our body linen and the boy's clothes,' she said. Ah. That explained why she was dressed in the faded dress given her by Aunt Suke. Rees nodded. He knew she planned to wear David's old clothes to walk out of the swamp. Once they reached Norfolk she would change into the dress she'd brought from Maine and once again appear as the affluent farmer's wife. 'Come with me while I do the laundry. Let's talk this through.' When he did not respond, she added, 'You got those blisters chasing Quaco through the swamp. What makes you think you can catch him now?'

'I have to try,' Rees said.

'You can try later, if you've a mind to,' she said. 'And get yourself lost again, no doubt.'

Rees said nothing. He wanted to yell at her. It didn't help that she was right. Sulky, he rose to his feet. While she gathered the sheets for washing, he went outside and stood by the basket. When she joined him, they walked together through camp, past Quaco's hut, and down the path to the shore where the women beat the clothing clean. Rees looked around for a bit of wood to plant himself upon. From the vantage of a rotted stump, he watched Lydia dampen the linens, and the ragged clothing that had once belonged to Rees's son, in the black water. David would not want these clothes back. Everything was dyed brown from the water. And, after this time in the swamp, the fabric itself was beginning to deteriorate, the threads so worn they involuntarily parted.

Lydia lathered the wet cloth with the harsh lye soap and took up a thick wooden stick to beat out the stains. 'What do you think Quaco saw?' she asked between the thuds of the paddle on the laundry.

'The murderer,' Rees replied, raising his voice a little.

'I don't think so,' she said. 'It was night, and dark. Could he have seen and identified the murderer?'

Recognizing the last as a rhetorical question, Rees ignored it. 'If he's innocent, why does he keep running away?' he asked, sounding as annoyed as he felt.

'I didn't say he was innocent. I agree with you; I think he saw something. But what?'

Rees remained silent as he pondered his wife's question. 'I think he saw the murderer. Maybe he couldn't see the face, but he might have seen enough to know who it was.'

'Maybe,' Lydia said. 'He may not know what he saw is important.'

'I have to find out what it was,' Rees said, adding, 'that confirms what I have thought all along; that the murderer is here, in this village.' Lydia glanced at him over her shoulder as she dipped the breeches in the water.

'Yes,' she agreed. 'We've known that. The other mystery, and the one I think is key, is the disappearance of Scipio's body. A corpse is not so easy to hide. Did Scipio's murderer take it? Where did he put it? And why?'

'I have the answer to the last,' Rees said. 'The reward. It is a lot of money.'

'Of course,' Lydia said in agreement. 'That explains every-thing. The killer would have taken the body as proof. But that leads to another question. Where was the body hidden all that time? And how was it transported out of the swamp? If it was.'

Rees stared at his wife for several seconds. 'Well, the killer didn't use a wagon,' he said.

'Or a horse,' Lydia agreed, lifting Rees's good breeches from the water and shaking them out.

Rees stared at them, his gaze drifting away from the wet soil to the water that ran between the trees. 'A boat,' he breathed, recalling the trip through the lake. 'The body could have been floated somewhere else. Maybe to a waiting wagon.'

'It could have been stored in the pirogue,' Lydia said. 'No one would know – unless they wanted to take a boat trip.' Rees stared at her for a long moment. Then he turned to look over his shoulder. Although the vegetation remained thick, the leaves were beginning to fall. A faint burst of sunlight marked the place where the men went fishing.

He looked to his left. The black water wound its way through the trees, heading north. He could see animal tracks, appearing and disappearing, at the edge of the water. 'This is a stream,' he muttered. 'I'm going to follow it.' Although he might not find Scipio's body, he would at least come to the place where the small pirogues were docked.

'Your feet,' Lydia protested. Rees looked down at his bandages.

'I'll manage. I'll have to.'

'Then I'm coming with you,' Lydia said, tossing his breeches over a shrub. He glanced at her skirts. Understanding his concern, she pulled them up and tied them around her waist. She was not wearing stockings so her pale bare shins were on full view.

'But . . .' He gestured toward her legs.

'I doubt there will be anyone around to see them,' she said shortly.

With a nod – he knew better than to say anything further – he turned and started walking.

The going was difficult and the bandages covering his feet were soon sodden and heavy with mud. This watery avenue was not a stream as Rees knew it, with well-defined banks and a definite course. Sometimes he and Lydia walked ankle-deep in the water, keeping a sharp eye out for snakes. Sometimes the ground rose slightly and they looked down upon the dark opaque water winding through the trees. Rees tried to follow the tracks as best he could, even when it was a struggle to make it through the thick vegetation. And the growths popping up from the ground made the going even more hazardous. He could not imagine how the murderer could have possibly maneuvered the body through it.

Lydia was flagging, moving more and more slowly, and Rees's feet felt as though they were on fire. Realizing that it would take an additional half hour or more to reach the inlet where the pirogues had been stored, he began to consider turning back. 'Just to the next inlet,' he said, turning back to his wife. She'd stopped entirely. Shading her eyes with her hand, she was staring through the trees at the water.

'Look,' she said, pointing. Rees followed the direction of her finger. And there, half submerged in the water, was a board.

'C'mon.' Rees clambered over a fallen tree and crossed the small muddy beach. Although he tried to tug the board from the water, it was stuck fast. But that really didn't matter. Rees was sure this was the board taken from the back of Quaco's hut. On the exposed half was a dark brown stain, much faded by sun and water, but still visible.

Lydia climbed over the splintered trunk more slowly and joined him at the water's edge. 'This is where the murderer brought Scipio's body,' she murmured.

'Yes,' Rees agreed. Stepping forward, he grasped the ragged remains of a piece of rope. The tan color of hemp faded into the background and was invisible from even a few feet away. He would not have seen it if he hadn't stepped on to the beach. 'The murderer brought the pirogue here and tied it up. Then he brought Scipio's body and put it in the boat.'

'That is a long way to drag something through the swamp,' Lydia said, glancing at the thick and tangled vegetation behind her.

'I think he followed a different path,' Rees said, recalling the one the men had taken when looking for Scipio. 'A much shorter path. And then he sailed the body out of the swamp with no one the wiser.'

'This took planning,' Lydia said.

'A lot of planning,' Rees said. 'As we thought, Scipio's death was not an impulsive act of anger.' He glanced around once more and then gestured back the way they'd come. 'Whoever killed him thought the murder through very carefully.'

'So . . .' Lydia slowly drew out the word as she followed him to the fallen tree. 'The money Neptune had in the bag around his neck was from the reward?'

'Maybe some of it,' Rees agreed. Holding out his hand, he helped Lydia over the downed trunk. 'Now we know how he did it, we just have to find out who *he* is.'

They returned the way they'd come, following the faint path they'd made on the journey out. Rees was limping but, fortunately, this trip seemed shorter than the previous one. He remained lost in thought the entire distance. Who had both the strength and the freedom of movement to rip a board from the hut and then drag Scipio to the pirogue? Answer: any of the young men. Sadly, that included Tobias. But did Tobias know the ways through the swamp well enough?

The appearance of the laundry flapping on the shrubbery came as a surprise. Back already? And Jackman was waiting for them. Lydia hastily released her skirts so they once more fell properly to her ankles.

Rees lifted his hand in greeting but his smile died when he saw the expression on the other man's face. 'What happened?' he asked in a resigned voice.

'Why'd you do it?' Jackman asked accusingly. 'Why did you attack Quaco?'

THIRTY-SEVEN

Rees stumbled in surprise and halted. 'Wait. What?'

'Quaco was attacked?' Lydia asked, panting up behind her husband.

'Yes. Almost killed. He still alive, just barely.' His gaze moved to Rees. 'Why did you do it?'

'I didn't,' Rees said. He shifted from stinging foot to stinging foot.

'He didn't,' Lydia concurred. 'He's been with me. We've—'

Rees put his hand on her wrist to stop her. 'She caught me trying to remove my bandages and persuaded me to join her here, where she could keep an eye on me.' He grinned, but Jackman did not smile.

'We've been talking about the murders,' Lydia said.

Jackman shook his head. He didn't want to believe it.

'What happened?' Rees asked. 'And how did you come to find Quaco?'

Jackman shuffled his feet a few times. 'Well, I thought about y'all's request,' he said. 'The long and short of it is I changed my mind. I went to put up the white flag. But it was already up.'

'What do you mean, it was already up?' Rees asked.

'Just what I said. Somebody put it up to signal Quaco.' He paused and stared at Rees.

'And Quaco came.' Rees noticed Jackman's accusing stare but was too focused on the fact that someone had tried to murder Quaco to care.

'Yes. He came. And got hit in the head, hmmm?' Jackman's expression had segued into puzzlement. 'You really don't know?'

'I don't.'

'But who even knew Rees wanted to talk to him?' Lydia asked.

'No one,' Jackman said with a frown. 'And y'all be so angry when I refused you. That's why I—'

'Someone must have known,' Rees interrupted. 'I did not speak to Quaco. And I certainly did not hit him in the head.'

'He was here with me,' Lydia repeated. 'I swear it, Jackman.'

The headman hesitated. In the silence a bird screamed, sharp and loud. Then Jackman relaxed. Although still suspicious, he was willing to listen.

'You better tell me where Quaco was found,' Rees said with a heavy sigh. Turning to Lydia, he added, 'I knew he knew something. And the murderer must have guessed.'

Lydia looked at the wet clothing, several pieces waving gently in the water. She still had work to do. So angry and frustrated she couldn't speak, she bit her lip.

'I will come back,' Rees said. 'After I see where his body was found.' She nodded and he heard her mutter something. He did not want to know what it was.

Rees followed Jackman back into camp.

'Quaco in his hut now,' Jackman said, pointing. 'With Aunt Suke.'

'Will he live?' Rees asked. Jackman lifted one shoulder in a shrug.

'He in God's hands now.'

Rees followed Jackman away from the hut, down past the cornfield and the crude pen enclosing the feral cattle. The ground moistened underfoot as they penetrated the swamp. Rees thought they were heading for the area where he'd first spoken to Quaco; he'd gotten better at reading the swamp around him.

They hadn't gone too far when he smelled blood, the metallic stink overlaying the ubiquitous scent of water and rotting vegetation.

Jackman pointed to broken stems and crushed leaves lying half in a muddy hollow. Drying blood stained the leaves, bright as berries. 'There. I found him there.'

Rees wished now he had stopped to see Quaco in the hut; he couldn't visualize the scene. 'Where was Quaco hit?' Rees asked. Jackman pointed to the ground. 'No. I mean, on his body.' Jackman touched the right side of his head.

'Here.'

Rees tried to picture it. 'Quaco had to be facing his attacker,' he said. Jackman looked blank. 'How did Quaco fall, face up or face down?'

'Face up.' Jackman shuddered involuntarily. 'At first I thought he wasn't breathin'.'

'He knew the person who tried to kill him,' Rees muttered. 'He wouldn't let someone he didn't know, someone he didn't trust, get so close.' Turning to Jackman, he added, 'So, you see now I didn't attack Quaco. I couldn't have. He didn't trust me enough to allow me this close.'

For a moment the two men stared at one another. Then Jackman lowered his eyes and nodded. 'All right.'

'How long had he been lying here?' Rees asked.

'Don't know. His head done stopped bleedin'.'

'So, not too long,' Rees said with a nod. 'He is very lucky you found him. The killer probably hoped Quaco would die before anyone even missed him.'

Jackman nodded gravely. 'But I changed my mind, hmmm?'

Both men were silent as they considered the likely outcome if he hadn't.

'But how did Quaco's attacker get here?' Rees wondered, speaking once again. 'Get to Quaco I mean. Wouldn't someone have seen him?'

'No one came through the village,' Jackman said. 'I be eating by the fire.'

'He had to go around the other way,' Rees muttered. He looked around, trying to peer through the tangle of trees and bushes. 'He left the village and circled through the marsh.'

He looked at Jackman. 'That means he would have to know the swamp and know it well. And be comfortable in it.'

'We all know it pretty well,' Jackman said. 'We have to.'

Although Rees nodded, he did not entirely agree. Even Jackman avoided traveling through the swamp whenever possible. There had to be someone in the village who knew the Great Dismal better than everyone else – knew it and was comfortable in it. Rees just wasn't sure who that was. And, try as he might, Rees couldn't see the path Quaco's attacker would have taken. The black water hid the footprints and although Rees saw several broken stems, they did not follow a discernible path. The swamp itself concealed all traces of the would-be killer.

'I'd like to see Quaco now,' Rees said.

Quaco lay on the bench so recently vacated by Neptune. The sheets Lydia had brought had once again been pressed into service as bandages. The grubby strip around his head was darkly stained with blood and he was panting. Rees backed out and looked at Aunt Suke. She knew what he was asking and shrugged.

'I don't know,' she said. 'It be a hard blow with force behind it.'

'What was he hit with?' Rees asked. 'There are no rocks in the swamp.'

'A stick, I guess. A hard stick.'

Rees nodded and looked at Quaco once again, wishing he had confided what he knew. If he had, the murderer would have had no to reason to try and silence him.

When Rees left the hut, he joined Aunt Suke as she walked up the slope to the center of camp. Almost everyone was there, eating bone soup – made heartier by the addition of vegetables and leftover rice – and stale cornbread. Rees glanced around the circle. Lydia was absent and he felt a momentary spasm of guilt as he realized she was still washing clothes. But almost all the other members of this little village were present: Tobias and Ruth, who were sitting so close together their thighs touched; Sandy and Abram; Toney and Peros. Jackman invited Rees with a wave but he shook his head.

'I'll wait for my wife,' he said. 'I'll fetch her now.' He took a few steps away from the fire but turned back. 'Where is Cinte?'

'Sleepin',' Peros answered.

'Like a baby,' Toney confirmed.

'He said he walked all night,' Jackman agreed.

'Did he?' Rees said. He was suspicious of everyone now. Turning around, he walked down the slope to the men's hut. When he peered inside, he saw Cinte lying on one of the benches, a half-carved banjo by his side, his snores reverberating throughout the small space. He lay with his arms spread wide, his legs akimbo, and despite the downy hair along his chin he looked about twelve.

Rees stepped inside and pulled the ragged blanket over Cinte before backing out of the hut. Cinte was so deeply asleep he didn't even stir.

THIRTY-EIGHT

L ydia heard Rees approaching through the forest, despite the marshy ground that deadened footfalls. She turned. 'What happened?' she asked as soon as he was in earshot. 'Is Quaco dead?' Her voice hushed on the final word.

'No,' he replied. 'But badly hurt and unconscious.'

'What does Aunt Suke say?'

'She's not sure what will happen to him,' Rees said, recalling the healer's evasive answer. He sighed and added, 'I really don't think he is going to wake up and identify the murderer. Not soon enough to help anyway.'

Lydia was silent for a moment. 'Is there anyone you suspect of murdering Scipio and Neptune more than any of the others?'

Rees thought of the people grouped around the fire. 'No,' he said at last. 'I suspected Quaco for a time. He moves around the camp and the swamp so freely. But I don't any longer; he didn't hit himself in the head.'

'Unless there are two murderers here,' Lydia suggested.

Rees nodded. He had seen that before. 'But who?' he wondered aloud. 'Toney and Peros? Of all the people here, they are the friendliest with one another.'

'Ruth and Tobias?' Lydia suggested reluctantly.

'But their accord is recent,' Rees objected. 'Jackman and Aunt Suke?'

'They are both so independent . . .' Lydia's voice trailed away.

'It was Aunt Suke's laudanum,' Rees pointed out.

'The laudanum that everyone knew about,' she replied. Rees acknowledged that with a sigh.

'Cinte and Sandy?' he asked. Lydia shook her head at him, and he chuckled. 'I cannot imagine Sandy dragging a body through the woods.'

'She wasn't even here when Scipio met his end,' Lydia said. 'Besides . . .' she paused. 'They aren't really a couple, are they? I mean, Cinte wants to be, but Sandy has been resistant from the very beginning.' She hesitated again. 'Ruth and Tobias had their ups and downs. But Ruth never denied that she loved Tobias. Whereas . . .' She broke off.

'Sandy made it plain she wants nothing to do with Cinte,' Rees finished. 'Why do you think that is?'

'She is in love with Gregory Sechrest,' Lydia said. 'He's her first love. Wealthy enough to buy her all sorts of trinkets and the father of her child.' She shook her head. 'If I was Cinte, I would give up the pursuit. He is always going to be in competition with Sechrest. Even if he is in Virginia and Sandy is in Ohio.'

Rees thought about Cinte, who had yearned for Sandy since childhood. 'That's true. Considering the circumstances, he might win the girl but lose any chance of happiness.'

'It happens that way sometimes,' she said, her gaze turning inward as though recalling something from long ago.

Rees wondered what she was pondering; there was so much about her girlhood in Boston that he knew nothing about.

Coming back to herself, she smiled at him. 'Is there anything for dinner?'

'Bone soup with swamp vegetables.'

'I'm hungry enough to eat it.' Turning, she began gathering up the still-damp clothing distributed across the bushes. 'Help me gather up the laundry,' she asked. 'I'm too hungry to wait until it dries. We can put it in the hut.'

Rees moved very slowly to help her, his thoughts returning to Quaco. 'What did he know?' he asked himself.

'He must have seen something, as you thought,' Lydia replied.

'But what? I wish he'd told me what it was.' Rees's voice rose in frustration.

'I'm sure he wishes he had too. Confiding in you might have saved him from being struck in the head.' She paused for a moment, staring at her husband. 'Why didn't he talk to you?'

'Because I'm white. Because he felt threatened. Because I'm not really a member of this village.' Rees shrugged. 'All of them? I don't know.'

Lydia shook her head. 'Perhaps that was true the first time you talked to him, but by this last time wouldn't he have known you were trustworthy? That you were sincerely interested in catching a murderer?'

'Maybe,' said Rees uncertainly. He thought Quaco might never trust a white man.

She hesitated. 'Do you know of anyone who was his special friend? That he might have wanted to protect?'

'Jackman,' Rees said. He turned a horrified look upon his wife. 'Jackman didn't want me to question Quaco. Remember?'

'Would Jackman lie for him?' Lydia asked, staring at her husband with wide eyes.

Rees thought about her question. 'Jackman is very loyal to the people in the village. Would he go to these lengths to protect Quaco? Or maybe . . . do you think Jackman is the murderer?'

'I don't know.' Lydia straightened up, wet laundry in her hands. 'I don't want to think so.' She piled an armful of damp clothing into Rees's arms. 'But I can't help but believe that Quaco kept silent because *he* was protecting someone.'

Rees nodded. That made sense. Although he didn't want to imagine Jackman had anything to do with the murders, now that the thought was in his head he couldn't shake it loose. When he and Lydia, arms full of clothing, climbed the slope into camp, passing the hut in which Quaco lay, Rees paused and glanced inside at the still form lying on the bench. There was no denying that, of all the members of this camp, the one Quaco would be the least suspicious of was Jackman.

When Rees and Lydia reached the village center, Sandy and Aunt Suke were sitting outside her cabin in the afternoon sun. Tears glittered on Sandy's cheeks and Rees could hear her pleading with Aunt Suke. 'Please let me stay here with you.'

'Stay here? Why do you want to stay here? It be far better you go north with Cinte. Far better.'

'But I don't love Cinte,' Sandy objected.

'Foolish girl. He'll give you a good life.'

'I won't like it,' Sandy said. 'I won't be happy.' Aunt Suke reached out and touched Sandy's arm.

'Dear child, it be too dangerous to stay here. And Cinte done loved you since you were children together.'

Rees and Lydia hurried past, trying to appear as though they weren't listening. But when they entered their sleeping quarters, Rees dumped the damp clothing on the bench and took up a position by the door so he could hear.

'You didn't go north,' Sandy pointed out.

'My family – my sons and daughters – live at Grove plantation. My gran'babies are here. Your mama's dead. What's holdin' you here?' When Sandy didn't speak, Aunt Suke went on. 'I know y'all believe you love Master Sechrest. But he gone too. And you know there be no future in it.'

Sandy bowed her head, staring down at her lap in sorrow.

'No, it best you leave with Cinte tomorrow.'

Abram wailed from inside the hut. 'Don't worry. I'll keep your baby safe.' Aunt Suke looked at the door and then, with one last pat on Sandy's shoulder, she rose to her feet and went inside.

Sandy began to weep.

'My heart breaks to see her like this,' Lydia said to Rees as she joined him on the steps.

'I know,' he agreed. He missed the vivacity and breezy self-confidence which had so defined her before.

'I can't imagine surrendering my child,' Lydia said, her hand resting on her belly.

'I know,' Rees said again, trying to conceive of remaining here for the rest of his life and never seeing his children – his baby Sharon or his adopted children – and his tears blinded him.

'I must be getting old,' he said as he wiped his eyes on his shirt tail. 'Old and soft.'

'That's why I love you,' Lydia said, smiling at him. She took his arm as they climbed the steps.

THIRTY-NINE

Rees awoke sometime in the early morning. He'd had a hard time falling asleep the previous evening, not because he was excited at the prospect of returning home, although he was, but because he felt that he had failed Scipio and Neptune. And of course Quaco, who was lying so still in the hut with his bandaged head. Rees felt guilty about Quaco, who would not have been attacked if only the murderer had been discovered earlier.

Why, he wondered now, couldn't he resolve this puzzle and identify the killer? He had but a handful of suspects – the people living in this village. One of them had to be guilty. Still, depending on the circumstances, they all seemed not only possible but probable. Of them all, he was sure of the innocence of only three: himself, Lydia and Sandy. She had not been in the village when Scipio had been murdered, otherwise he would suspect her as well.

Rees considered the others once again. He knew of no motive for Toney, other than his irritation with Scipio. That of course did not mean he had none. Peros had lost money to Scipio, as had Neptune. Tobias had demonstrated a passionate jealousy of Scipio's attentions to Ruth, but he and Neptune had been friendly.

Then there was Quaco. Outside of Jackman, a member of the Ibo tribe like himself, Quaco had demonstrated no partiality for any of the others. Could Jackman, despite his limp, undertake the physically demanding job of moving Scipio's body, hiking through the swamp and moving it in the pirogue? Rees had a hard time imagining it. But he had relied on Jackman to translate Quaco's speech. Maybe Jackman had lied and Quaco had said something entirely different. Maybe Quaco had told Jackman he knew who was guilty. Rees pondered that for a few seconds. It was a scenario that was unfortunately too believable.

That left Cinte and the women. But Cinte, besides being brother to Scipio, had shown only affection for his brother and sincere grief at his passing. What could possibly be his reason? The reward? But Cinte, of them all, was the only one with a guaranteed source of income.

Sandy did not appear physically strong, certainly not strong enough to press a pillow over Neptune's face, and Ruth was with child. Of the women, Rees could visualize just Aunt Suke as a possible murderer. Only she had the courage and the strength of will to execute such an emotionally and physically challenging crime. But he did not want to believe it of her. He liked and admired her. And she was, after all, a healer and a religieuse. Surely those qualities argued against the cold selfishness required by a murderer.

After a few minutes of tossing and turning, Rees slipped out of bed and went outside. He took a seat on the steps.

Although the fire had been banked, the night was not completely dark. The moon – the harvest moon – was waxing and so bright the faint shadows of the treetops patterned the ground.

Now that he and Lydia were serious about leaving, he felt the stirrings of nostalgia. He remembered the first time he had sat out here and heard the wild scream of the bobcat. The swamp made the wilds of Maine seem almost tame.

That night Neptune had come out of the men's cabin and gone around the back. Rees sighed. Now Scipio was dead, Neptune was dead and Quaco fought for his life. When he turned his head, he could see the flare of light from a candle; Aunt Suke checking on her patient in the cabin. She'd been abroad the night Scipio's body was stolen as well. Suddenly suspicious, Rees rose to his feet and stumbled through the darkness to the hut. When he went up the stairs and into the cabin, Aunt Suke turned to stare at him in surprise.

'What are you doin' here?'

'How is he?' Rees asked, gesturing to the still form on the bench. Aunt Suke looked at him.

'Still livin'.'

Rees turned to study her expression. She did not sound hopeful. He nodded to show he understood; she was worried about Quaco.

As he gazed at her, he noticed a pallet and rough blanket made into a bed in the corner. 'Are you sleeping here?' he asked.

'No one is smotherin' this man,' she said fiercely. 'Not while I have breath in my body.' Rees, feeling guilty for his suspicions, touched her shoulder lightly.

'They are fortunate to have you here, in this village,' he said.

'You best go back to your wife,' she told him. 'Get your rest. I'll watch over Quaco tonight.'

When Rees awoke the following morning, Lydia was already up and dressed. She was standing in the light by the door and going through Rees's satchel.

'I thought we'd better begin gathering our things,' she said. Rees glanced around at the various items of their small clothes festooning the hut.

'I suppose they are all dried now,' he said.

'What are these?'

Rees rose from the bench and joined her, staying well inside the shadows. He was clothed only in his nightshirt. Lydia held out her palm for him to see. On it lay two handmade dice.

'Scipio's loaded dice,' Rees said, suddenly transported to the night of his and Lydia's arrival. He recalled Scipio's booming laugh as he'd teased his brother, striving to get a rise from him and failing. He'd flirted with Ruth – and drawn such jealous fury from Tobias they'd ended up in a brutal and bloody fight. Rees remembered Neptune's tears when he lost every penny of his runaway money to Scipio.

Now both of them were gone. And while Scipio had not been the worthiest of men, he'd been fully alive. He hadn't deserved to die like that. Or for his murderer to go free.

Rees looked up and met Lydia's eyes. 'We can't leave,' he said. 'Not until I find the murderer.'

'Are you sure?' And when he nodded, she added despairingly, 'The children will forget us.'

'I can't let this go unfinished.' Leaning forward, he put his hand on her shoulder. 'Do you understand?'

Exhaling in frustration, she nodded. 'I wish I didn't, but I do. But how?'

'We'll have to draw the murderer out.'

'Do you have any ideas?'

'Not yet,' he admitted.

'You'd better hurry then. The group will be scattering tomorrow.'

'I'll think about it today.' He reached out and took the dice from her. 'I am as anxious to leave as you are. But we have this one final day. And then, if I don't identify the murderer, he will escape. Possibly to kill again.'

She sighed but nodded in agreement. 'I know.'

When Rees went to the fire for breakfast, only Jackman remained there, sitting on the log in his usual place. Rees eyed the other man, recalling his earlier thoughts. Rees had relied on Jackman to translate what Quaco had said; maybe he had lied. Maybe Quaco had accused someone. Maybe he had accused Jackman. Rees put his hand in his pocket and allowed the dice to slide through his fingers, thinking.

'Y'all gonna eat?' Jackman asked.

Rees took bacon and a sweet potato. Like corn pone and grits, he was heartily sick of sweet potatoes. 'Where is everyone else?' he asked.

'Workin'. Toney and Peros out huntin'. Tobias smokin' fish for y'all to take when you leave.'

Rees nodded and poured out the last of his coffee. The beans were almost gone; he wouldn't have coffee again until they reached a town. And what would he do once they arrived at Norfolk where he'd left Hannibal and the cart? He suddenly realized that Tobias and Ruth wouldn't fit, not with himself and Lydia. He hadn't thought about that when he'd planned this journey. He would have to sell the cart and try to buy a larger wagon. Did he even have enough money left?

'Aunt Suke sittin' with Quaco.' Jackman looked at Rees and added, 'She be afraid the murderer will attack him.'

'I know,' Rees said.

Jackman favored Rees with a condescending smile. 'If Quaco lives, he can identify the man who hit him, hmmm?'

Rees stared at the other man. Of course. Quaco couldn't be allowed to live. Why hadn't Rees thought of this before? He could use Quaco as bait, to draw out the killer. But he would need help.

FORTY

After his late breakfast, Rees wandered through camp thinking. He missed his loom with an almost physical pain, not because he wanted to weave, but because the process helped him think. He wanted to get everything straight in his mind before he asked someone – probably Aunt Suke – for help. Although it was likely she was not the murderer, Rees was not certain. After all, her stated desire to protect Quaco could be all pretense. She might simply be waiting for a good opportunity to complete the assassination without drawing suspicion to herself. Or waiting for Rees and Lydia to leave.

No, he didn't believe it, but decided he wanted to give this more thought before he involved her.

So Rees rambled around the village, rolling the dice around in his hand as he thought. They served as both a reminder of Scipio and also a monotonous activity that allowed his mind to drift.

Picking his way cautiously down the slope, he wandered past Quaco's hut. Aunt Suke had come outside the shack and was trying to re-warp the loom. Rees nodded at her as he peered into the hut at Quaco. At least he was still breathing. 'I be havin' trouble with this,' Aunt Suke said, straightening up and looking at Rees. 'Can y'all help me?'

He glanced at the yarns of varying thickness and color knotted together in long string that she had carefully wound into a ball. She was trying to warp the loom without a warp board; that alone made it much more difficult. 'I'll return,' he promised. He didn't want to be interrupted right now while he was trying to work out a plan.

He continued on, down the slope. He followed the path to the water. He knew one of the women was there; he could hear the characteristic thud-thud of someone beating the linen clean. Ruth, on her hands and knees in the mud, was bending over the water and pounding with all her might. She looked up at him. He nodded politely but didn't speak, his thoughts entirely engaged as he recalled his journey north, to the inlet where the pirogue had been tied.

Then he turned and looked over his shoulder. Although he could not see Tobias, he could smell smoke. He would have continued following the stream but there was no easy path so he returned to the village along the drier trail.

From this vantage, he could see Tobias, moving around a smoky fire as he tended the racks of blackened fish. Rees made his way toward Tobias.

'I went fishing,' he said. 'I thought we could bring some with us.'

Rees nodded, although he did not think the smoked fish looked at all edible. His gaze went to the white flag hanging in its spot in the trees. He guessed Jackman had re-hung it in its place, ready to put out for Quaco. An action of hope; Jackman wanted to believe his friend would live.

'Try one,' Tobias said, offering Rees a small black fragment the texture of leather. Rees took it and hesitantly put it in his mouth. It tasted fishy but required a lot of chewing. It was, Rees decided, a real workout for one's jaws. He wouldn't eat it by choice.

He moved on, circling around the cattle pens.

The sun was overhead before he felt confident in his plan. He cut across the fields, cautiously since the stubble hurt his sore feet, back to Aunt Suke.

She was still struggling to warp the crudely built loom.

'Too much trouble,' she said, almost hurling a tangled mass of threads at him. He began smoothing out the thick fibers.

'I need your help,' he said. Aunt Suke looked at him, her golden-eyed gaze level. He thought again how beautiful she was. She did not have the childish beauty of Sandy Sechrest, but the hardships she'd experienced had given her face strength and character. She was a far more interesting woman for all the laugh lines that touched the corners of her mouth and eyes.

'You know,' she breathed. 'You know the killer.'

'I think I know,' he said. 'But it's all guesswork. I have no proof, no evidence. Nothing but my reasoning.'

'That be good enough for me,' she said. Rees smiled but shook his head.

'I need you to help me draw the murderer out, make him show himself.'

'How am I s'posed to do that?'

'Announce to everyone in camp that Quaco has awakened from his coma. Say he's still groggy but starting to talk.' And if no one came, Rees would give Aunt Suke another look.

Aunt Suke eyed him for several seconds. 'You goin' bring the murderer right down on that poor man.'

'I hope so. I'm going to stand watch in the hut, behind the door.' Rees paused and turned to stare over his shoulder at the hut. 'I'm betting he comes at night, after dark. But I'll be there all day. Waiting.'

Aunt Suke hesitated. 'What if you don't be quick enough? Or strong enough? Or you asleep?'

'I hope Lydia will be nearby too. And you. Between the three of us we should capture the murderer.'

Aunt Suke stared at Rees for a long second, then she turned and looked at the cabin. 'Yes-s-s. I'll do it,' she said.

Rees sat by the fire and watched faces as Aunt Suke announced, with almost believable enthusiasm, that Quaco had regained consciousness and was beginning to speak.

'What he sayin'?' Toney asked. He was nervous, Rees thought.

Aunt Suke shrugged. 'I don't know. Just nonsense. He still be groggy.'

'And you don't speak Ibo,' Jackman pointed out.

'True,' Aunt Suke agreed.

'But she can understand the names,' Rees said, just in case no one appreciated the danger Quaco presented.

But, although Rees watched everyone's expressions carefully, no one turned pale and cried, 'Oh no!' To an individual, they expressed joy that Quaco would live.

Was he wrong? Rees wondered, looking around at the happy faces. Maybe he wasn't correct about the killer's identity after all. Maybe his deductions had led him to the wrong conclusion.

If that were true, he would know for sure in a few hours.

After everyone had eaten something and returned to their tasks, Rees slipped into the hut and took up a position behind the door. Quaco, despite the story they had told the others, had not regained consciousness. Blood was leaking through the bandage tied around his head. Every now and then his hands twitched and Rees wondered if that was involuntary or if Quaco was dreaming.

Towards evening Rees heard Lydia's voice outside but he didn't dare peek out the door. He knew she carried food; he could smell it. He was famished but, more than that, he was thirsty. But Lydia did not come in. It was still too light outside and the cabin door was in full view of anyone seated by the fire. Instead, she stood in front chatting with Aunt Suke, waiting until it was fully dark.

It was well after sundown when she finally hurried up the steps. The cracks around the ill-fitting board at the back of the hut let in a murky illumination supplied by the bright moon and the stars outside. The interior of this shack was so black that night outside appeared radiant in comparison. The air had grown cold as well. Rees felt around for Aunt Suke's blanket but she had taken it outside with her. He wished he had thought to bring his own.

Lydia closed the door behind her. Rees could see her as movement and a silhouette against the light seeping through the cracks in the back wall. Except for that, she was invisible. He could smell the food she carried.

'I have food and water,' she whispered. 'Where are you?'

'Here.' He reached out for her, finally locating her warm arm. She put the plate in his hands.

'What time is it?' he whispered as she handed him the jug of water. It was far too dim to see his watch and anyway he doubted it had survived its dunking in the water.

'I think it's gone eight,' she replied.

'Eight!' Rees's voice came out almost in a shout. He had thought it was closer to midnight.

'Shh. Shh.'

'Sorry.' He knew only too well the importance of quiet.

As he tipped the water into his mouth, Lydia continued in a low voice, 'I'll be in Aunt Suke's hut with her. Waiting.'

Rees wiped his mouth on his sleeve and carefully put the jug to one side. He had drunk almost half, and he had to make it last. He didn't know how long he would have to wait, but it would be at least a few hours. As he picked up his plate he asked, 'Is everyone gone to bed?'

'Jackman is still up. He is sitting in his usual place talking to Toney.'

'I wish they'd go to bed. The murderer won't act until everyone is asleep. Until he believes everyone is asleep anyway.' Rees shoveled fried fish and another sweet potato into his mouth. He was too hungry to complain.

'I know.' Lydia patted his arm. 'Be patient.'

He didn't dare scrape the plate although he felt like licking it clean. Lydia took it from his hands. He heard the rustle of her clothing as she rose to her feet. She opened the door very carefully and they both peered through the crack. All was dark; the campfire produced the only light, glowing like a small orange eye. Rees saw Jackman, a black shadow against the ruddy light, shift slightly.

There was no other movement. 'Go now,' Rees hissed. Lydia leapt out into the dusky area and began running. For a few seconds Rees saw her outlined against the sullen reddish fire – she was wearing her boy's clothing, and he could see her legs – and then she disappeared into Aunt Suke's hut.

Rees settled down to wait.

FORTY-ONE

Rees dozed off and was half asleep when he heard a faint scrabbling at the back of the hut. He came awake, silently accusing himself of stupidity. He had just assumed the murderer would come up the steps and through the front door. Instead, he had come to the back and was now quietly removing one of the boards. Rees held himself as still as he could. He had hoped that when the other person entered, he would be hidden by the door as it opened. Now that would not happen. He could only pray that he would be veiled by the darkness.

With a muted crack, the board came off and Rees was staring into the somewhat lighter outside. A human shape, darker than the swamp behind him, stood just outside. With a heave, he pulled himself over the lip and on to the hut's floor. He approached Quaco, lifting his arm over his head. Rees saw the glint of metal. A knife.

'Stop!' he cried, lunging forward. As the form turned, Rees's weight took him backwards. He slammed into the bench holding Quaco and grunted. Rees tried to grab the arm with the knife but failed. The blade cut a long slash through his right arm. It felt as though fire was racing up his forearm and blood began dripping on the floor with a pattering sound like rain.

Rees let out a bellow.

But he was bigger and heavier than his assailant. Using his weight to bring down the other man to the floor, Rees grabbed the assailant's wrist and held it steady. Despite the pain and the blood, the wound was superficial and he had the strength to hold the man's hand to the floor. Reaching across with his left arm, he wrenched the knife away and hurled it across the floor. Then he clouted his opponent across his face.

He could hear shouts outside and running feet on the steps. The door burst open and torchlight flooded the interior. Rees hauled the other man to his feet. 'Hello, Cinte,' he said. He was not as surprised as he thought he should be.

'Cinte!' Aunt Suke stared at the young man in horror. 'Scipio was your brother.'

'I wasn't doin' anything,' Cinte said sullenly. 'Just checkin' on Quaco.'

'By taking a board off the back wall and sneaking in?' Rees asked grimly. 'By bringing a knife? I saw you. If I hadn't been here, you would have stabbed Quaco dead.'

'Why're you protectin' a black man anyway?' Cinte asked Rees in a nasty tone of voice.

'What is goin' on?' Jackman limped down the slope.

'Why are you awake?' Rees asked him.

'I knew you were up to somethin'. Sneakin' around camp, looking everythin' over. Whisperin' with Aunt Suke. I knew.' He looked straight at Rees. 'You don't trust me.'

Rees, who could see that Jackman was hurt by that, took refuge in bluster. 'I didn't know who I could trust.'

'So, we set a trap,' Aunt Suke said.

'Quaco not really be awake?' Cinte said. Rees shook his head.

'It didn't matter. He already told me what he'd seen.'

'When was that?' Jackman demanded. 'When? You don't speak Ibo.'

'No,' Rees agreed. 'But the names sound the same. And Quaco told me he saw Cinte visiting Neptune. I was too stupid to realize then to ask what time it was. I only realized today that Quaco was hinting.' Rees shook his head at Cinte. 'He tried to protect you. That's why he didn't want to answer my questions. And why, when he finally did, he was vague and evasive.'

'I don't understand why,' Jackman said. 'Why did Cinte kill his brother?'

'For this,' Rees said, grabbing the cord around Cinte's neck. The young man reached up to try to protect the bag hanging under his shirt, but Jackman seized one arm while Rees held the other. Rees pulled the bag over Cinte's head and handed it to Lydia. She opened it and spilled the coins into her hand. Several silver dollars rolled into her palm.

'It's the reward.' She held the money out to Jackman.

'But he earns money with his banjoes,' he protested.

'That's right,' Cinte said.

'I think, if you search his belongings, you'll find a lot more,' Rees said.

Jackman hesitated. 'Bring him to the fire,' he said at last. Moving quite rapidly despite his limp, he climbed the incline and disappeared down the other side.

Rees nudged Cinte forward. 'Move.' Cinte tried to pull away but couldn't; Rees had too tight a grip on his arm.

'Let go.'

'Not a chance,' Rees said.

When Rees and the two women arrived at the fire, Aunt Suke stirred it up into a respectable blaze. Lydia ground the last of the coffee beans and set about filling the little pot with water and putting it over the flames.

'You are a saint among women,' Rees told her. He pressed Cinte into a seated position. 'You gave yourself away several times,' he said conversationally. 'You had the most freedom of anyone here, wandering through the swamp at will. And you knew the swamp. I saw that when you guided me to the ditch. Also, I saw chalk dust on your pants from Scipio's hands and feet. I just didn't realize what it meant then.'

'None of that mean anythin',' Cinte said even as Aunt Suke shook her head at him sorrowfully.

'Jackman will find the rest of the money in your possessions,' Rees said. 'That will tell the tale.'

The coffee had not finished perking when Jackman, flanked by Toney and Peros, walked to the village center. In one hand

Jackman carried a satchel, in the other a wad of cloth. As they found places, Sandy came out of Aunt Suke's hut. Rubbing her eyes, she asked, 'What's going on? Why're y'all awake at this time of night?'

'What're you doing with Cinte?' Peros asked aggressively.

'He murdered his brother and Neptune and he tried to murder Quaco,' Rees replied.

'How do you know that?' Now the anger was directed at Rees. Toney put his hand on Peros's shoulder.

'Hear 'im out,' Toney said.

Jackman threw the leather bag to the ground. The jangle of coins crashing together rang loudly through the village center. 'Open it, please,' Rees said to Lydia. She untied the drawstring and a flood of money, mostly silver dollars, spilled out on to the ground. The ruddy firelight glinted off the metal.

Like blood, Rees thought with a shudder.

'I found it, right where you said it would be,' Jackman said, disillusionment warring with grief.

'Someone else put it there,' Cinte said.

'No,' Jackman contradicted him. 'You lie. I found it hidden in this.' He held out the bundle of pink silk; a lady's gown with lace on the bodice.

'You killed your brother for the reward?' Toney asked in disbelief.

'I suspect it was more than that,' Rees said, looking at Cinte. 'Resentment and anger because of the way Scipio treated you certainly had a part.'

'He be disrespectful,' Cinte muttered. 'And I was his brother. But I didn't kill him.'

'I believe, however,' Rees continued as though Cinte had not spoken, 'it was mostly about the money.'

'Is this true?' Toney stared at Cinte. 'Did you murder your brother for money?'

'A' course not,' Cinte said. 'He,' and he glanced at Rees, 'wants a black man to be guilty.'

The eyes of both Toney and Peros swiveled toward Rees and Peros shifted on his haunches. The threat of violence hung in the air like smoke.

'It was easy for you to murder your brother,' Rees said.

'You were with him, in the swamp, and he had a gun. You took it from him.'

'He taller and at least twenty pounds heavier,' Cinte said.

'I would guess you employed some trick; asked him to show you how to load the gun and shoot it probably, and then you turned on him and shot him in the back.' Several people gasped. 'I think you expected to return to the body, drag it to the boats, and hide it. But we found it first and brought it back to camp for burial.'

Cinte manufactured a slight smile.

'I wondered why you looked so shocked to hear we'd found him. I put it up to grief. But of course, that wasn't it at all. Was it?' When Cinte did not answer, Rees added, 'Jump in if I get something wrong. Please.'

'I think you be possessed by evil spirits and telling lies,' Cinte said.

'If you were going to win the reward,' Rees continued, 'you needed to turn Scipio's body in. So you removed a board from the back of the hut and slid it down to the pirogues. Then you returned to camp and pretended you had been here all along.'

'But Neptune, hmmm?' Jackman asked.

'Neptune saw something, didn't he? Enough to know you had murdered your own brother. His mistake? He tried to blackmail you. Since Scipio had none of the money he'd won while playing dice – I assume you stole it – Neptune just wanted what Scipio had cheated him of so he could go north. I thought he fled the village because he was guilty. But in truth he ran because he was afraid. What happened, Cinte? Did you threaten him? Or did he realize his life was in danger?' Rees paused but Cinte said nothing.

'Defend yourself,' Toney cried. 'Tell him it not be true.'

'A' course it not true,' Cinte said.

'So Neptune ran into the dark. And he was bitten by a snake. We found him and brought him back for treatment. He might have survived, but you made sure he didn't. Only this time, you were seen climbing into the hut. Quaco saw you. But when he spoke to me he spoke in riddles I was too stupid to interpret. As far as you knew, you'd gotten away with the two murders.'

'But why did he stay?' Peros asked.

'Because of Sandy,' Aunt Suke said. 'Don't that be right, Cinte?'

'Cinte has been in love with Sandy for years,' Rees said. 'He didn't want to go north without her. So, he stayed in the swamp, in the village, trying to persuade her to marry him.'

'You're a murderer,' Sandy said, staring at Cinte in revulsion.

'Sandy, Sandy; I did it for us,' Cinte said. Leaning forward, he stretched out his hands pleadingly. 'I wanted a good life for you, not scraping by. We could buy a carriage, ride north in style. Buy a farm. I could buy all the dresses you wanted.'

'What are gowns compared to a man's life?' Sandy said. She stared hard at him for a few seconds and then, shaking her head she turned away.

'Oh, Cinte,' Aunt Suke said sorrowfully. 'How could you? Your own brother.'

'For money. Like Judas,' Jackman said in disgust.

'Not just for money!' Cinte cried. 'For freedom; I got my manumission papers too. What was Scipio? A cheating, whoring drunkard. He be no loss. I won my freedom. This was for you, Sandy.'

'You betrayed all of us,' Jackman said.

'Rees,' Aunt Suke said into the heavy silence, 'when you go home, north to Maine, will you take Sandy and Abram? They look white. Maybe there they can still have a good life.'

'Take the money too,' Jackman said. 'As your fee.'

'No, no,' Rees protested. 'You'll need it.'

'Huh. I come into any store with a fistful of silver dollars and they arrest me on the spot,' Jackman said. 'No, you keep it. You might need it to get home. Especially with a few more mouths to feed, hmmm?'

'Take it,' Aunt Suke said to Rees. 'You earned it. You found the viper in our village.'

Rees ducked his head in acknowledgement. 'I'll leave you some—'

'Take it all. None of us want it,' Jackman said emphatically. 'That money be earned in betrayal and death.'

'And what about Cinte?' Rees asked.

'He ours to deal with,' Jackman said. Rees looked at the other man's grim expression and decided he would not want to be in Cinte's place. Rees did not want to know what Cinte's fate would be and doubted Jackman would tell him anyway.

It was time for Rees and Lydia to go home.

EPILOGUE

Rees did not take a full breath until they crossed the New Jersey line. It was still possible they would be stopped, but he thought – hoped – it would be less likely. Especially since they had been halted a few times.

The trip through the swamp with Sandy and her baby and the pregnant Ruth had been harrowing. Fortunately, since Tobias had already run away once, he acted as guide. They slept during the day and traveled at night. It took them several days to reach the Quaker Meeting House in Norfolk.

Once the Quakers had secured new clothes for Rees, he took Tobias and went into Norfolk. Just an affluent farmer with his slave. Although both Rees and Tobias were scared the entire time, no one gave them a second glance. Rees traded in the cart and bought a second-hand carriage and another horse. With Tobias as coachman, and the rest of the party partially hidden inside, they started for Maine.

The men that stopped the group in Virginia and again in Maryland saw, not a big red-headed man and a boy, or escaped slaves, but a family. They all performed their parts, presenting the appearance of a well-off family. Rees, in his new clothes, acted as paterfamilias and Lydia in her blue silk was his wife. No one would believe the prim and proper Mrs Rees would have worn boy's clothing in a raid on a plantation. Sandy played daughter in her pink silk and Abram as their young son. Ruth acted as nanny. They seemed to be of the affluent yeoman class, not wealthy but rich enough for a carriage and a few slaves. They were released and sent on their way.

They had spoken little these past few days, driving from early morning to as long after dark as they could. Tobias had pushed the horses as hard as he dared, stopping for the night only when they must. They'd spent more than a few nights camped by the side of the road.

But once they passed into New Jersey, everyone relaxed. Rees thought the rest of the journey would be much easier. He would not worry that someone would pick up the differences in speech between Sandy and her putative parents, or that he was far friendlier with Tobias than master and slave would be.

They would all enjoy the luxury of stopping at an inn for the night and eating a hot meal.

'Why didn't you love Cinte?' Lydia asked, leaning forward and putting one gloved hand on Sandy's. 'What did you know? He always seemed so loving, so kind.'

Sandy stared through the window for a moment. 'I didn't know anythin',' she said at last. 'But he was too . . . too domineering. And . . .' She hesitated again. 'I thought he could be cruel. Never to me. Not openly anyway. I had a little dog, given to me by Miss Minerva when I was a child. How I loved that dog. But it nipped Cinte and he wrung its neck right in front of me.' She shuddered.

'Oh dear,' Lydia said, her voice quivering.

'Scipio made friends with the dogs on the plantation. That way, he always said, they wouldn't chase him. But Cinte tormented them. When no one was lookin'. Because he could.' She paused again and then burst out, 'That's why, when Master Greg smiled at me, I was glad. A white man – I thought Cinte would have to leave me alone then. Then Miss Minerva died and Miss Charlotte came.'

'You're safe now,' Lydia said.

'What will happen to me?'

'We have time to figure it out,' Rees said comfortingly.

'Why, she and Abram can live with Tobias and me,' Ruth said. 'At least for the time being.'

Rees eyed the two women. 'Perhaps,' he said.

'Who would think love would become something so twisted,' Lydia murmured.

'I'd wager that more murders have been committed in the name of love than for any other reason,' Rees said. 'Love can be dangerous.'

'Not always,' Lydia said, directing a stern look at Rees from under her lashes. 'Not when it's proper.'

Rees took it as a warning and nodded. 'I know.' And then, 'I can scarcely wait to see the children.'

Lydia nodded and put her hand on his sleeve. Rees smiled down at her, so glad to be going home.

AUTHOR'S NOTE

The Great Dismal Swamp

When George Washington first rode into the Great Dismal Swamp, it measured over one million acres. The development of the swamp began soon after. Ditches were dug to drain the swamp – which is impossible since this is a peat bog. In 1793 the digging of the Great Dismal Swamp Canal was begun to connect the waters of Chesapeake Bay in Virginia and Albemarle Sound in North Carolina for the transport of goods. It was dug entirely by slave labor with pick and shovel as described in this book. This canal was not completed until 1805. The canal still exists and is still in use but during the intervening years has been both widened and deepened.

Many slaves escaped to the swamp. They were called maroons, from the French *marronage*, meaning 'flee'. Despite the difficulties of surviving, estimates of people living in the Great Dismal range from 50,000 to 100,000. They lived on the drier 'islands' in the swamp and it is believed that some of these people maintained villages and worked small plots. The maroons did indeed help make the quotas for the shingles, mainly in exchange for food and other items.

When a slave ship crashed and the people escaped, they made their way to the swamp. In my fictional world, Quaco is one of these men.

For more information on the Maroons of the Great Dismal

Diouf, Sylviane A. *Slavery's Exiles: The Story of the American Maroons*. New York University Press, 2014.

Price, Richard. *Maroon Societies: Rebel Slave Communities in the Americas*. Johns Hopkins University Press, 1996.

Sayers, Daniel O. *A Desolate Place for a Defiant People: The Archaeology of Maroons, Indigenous Americans, and Enslaved Laborers in the Great Dismal Swamp*. The University Press of Florida, 2014.

Cypress knees

The extrusions from the ground to which Rees refers as bumps are called cypress knees. There are hundreds of them all over the swamp. No one knows what they are for although the theory is that they help bring oxygen to the roots of the bald cypress.

Swamp cotton

Also called swamp grass or bog cotton, the flowers do look like cotton bolls. The local Native American tribes used swamp cotton medicinally and taught the uses to the maroons living in the swamp. Although used for wound care, the fibers, as Rees sees, are too brittle to be useful for textile production.

The dialect

In the primary sources I read, the dialect attributed to the slaves is almost unreadable and we don't even know if it is accurate. I have not attempted to duplicate that speech and instead I have chosen to minimize the use of the dialect and instead suggest that slow southern drawl. I apologize in advance if it is not entirely correct.

Gabriel Prosser

Slaves were frequently 'hired out' to generate an income for their owners, a common practice in Virginia where the soil had been depleted by tobacco farming. Gabriel was a skilled blacksmith and, uncommonly, could read and write. He arranged a slave revolt in Richmond that was supposed to take place on August 30. Heavy rain delayed the revolt and Gabriel and his brothers were betrayed by a member of the revolt for the reward (which was not fully paid).

Gabriel, his brothers and several other leaders were executed on October 10. Laws governing hiring out and teaching slaves to read and write were tightened up. Free blacks were instructed to leave the state or risk being enslaved.

Flora and fauna of the Great Dismal Swamp

I have tried to be as accurate as possible, with one exception: alligators. It was universally believed at that time that alligators lived in the swamp. This is now commonly accepted as a myth. Temperatures in Virginia fall below freezing during the winter, and the first frost generally hits mid-November – so it would be far too cold for alligators.

ACKNOWLEDGMENTS

Thank you to Katie Kelley who first told me about the Great Dismal Swamp. A special thank you to Park Ranger Penny Lazauskas who toured us around the Swamp and also graciously gave me her email address so I could send additional questions about the Swamp to her.